Praise for
the Magical Cat Mysteries

Sleight of Paw

"This series is a winner." ——— Gumshoe

"If you are a ——— ed to be reading this se———

——— Reviews

"Kelly's appeal ——— relatable characters set in an ——— location. The author continues to build on the promise of her debut novel, carefully developing her characters and their relationships."
—*Romantic Times*

Curiosity Thrilled the Cat

"A great cozy that will quickly have you anxiously waiting for the next release so you can spend more time with the people of Mayville Heights."
—Mysteries and My Musings Blog

"If you love mystery and magic, this is the book for you!"
—Debbie's Book Bag

"This start of a new series offers an engaging cast of human characters and two appealing, magically inclined felines. Kathleen is a likable, believable heroine and the magical cats are amusing." —*Romantic Times*

Also by Sofie Kelly

Curiosity Thrilled the Cat
Sleight of Paw

COPYCAT KILLING

A MAGICAL CATS MYSTERY

SOFIE KELLY

AN OBSIDIAN MYSTERY

OBSIDIAN
Published by New American Library, a division of
Penguin Group (USA) Inc., 375 Hudson Street,
New York, New York 10014, USA
Penguin Group (Canada), 90 Eglinton Avenue East, Suite 700, Toronto,
Ontario M4P 2Y3, Canada (a division of Pearson Penguin Canada Inc.)
Penguin Books Ltd., 80 Strand, London WC2R 0RL, England
Penguin Ireland, 25 St. Stephen's Green, Dublin 2,
Ireland (a division of Penguin Books Ltd.)
Penguin Group (Australia), 250 Camberwell Road, Camberwell, Victoria 3124,
Australia (a division of Pearson Australia Group Pty. Ltd.)
Penguin Books India Pvt. Ltd., 11 Community Centre, Panchsheel Park,
New Delhi - 110 017, India
Penguin Group (NZ), 67 Apollo Drive, Rosedale, Auckland 0632,
New Zealand (a division of Pearson New Zealand Ltd.)
Penguin Books (South Africa) (Pty.) Ltd., 24 Sturdee Avenue,
Rosebank, Johannesburg 2196, South Africa

Penguin Books Ltd., Registered Offices:
80 Strand, London WC2R 0RL, England

First published by Obsidian, an imprint of New American Library,
a division of Penguin Group (USA) Inc.

First Printing, May 2012
10 9 8 7 6 5 4 3 2

Copyright © Penguin Group (USA) Inc., 2012

PUBLISHER'S NOTE
This is a work of fiction. Names, characters, places, and incidents either are the
product of the author's imagination or are used fictitiously, and any resemblance
to actual persons, living or dead, business establishments, events, or locales is
entirely coincidental.
    The publisher does not have any control over and does not assume any respon-
sibility for author or third-party Web sites or their content.

ALWAYS LEARNING   **PEARSON**

ACKNOWLEDGMENTS

There are many people who have helped take this story from idea to the finished book you're holding in your hands. Thank you to everyone at my publisher, Penguin, particularly my talented editor, Jessica Wade, and her always helpful assistant, Jesse Feldman. Thank you as well to the staff at BookEnds literary agency, especially my agent, Kim Lionetti, for her patience and guidance.

Lynn Viehl is one of the hardest-working writers in this business, but she's never too busy to share her wisdom and expertise. Thank you, Lynn. To fellow writers Laura Alden and Krista Davis, I'm grateful for your support, your encouragement and for always making me laugh.

Once again, I am indebted to Police Chief Tim Sletten, of the Red Wing, Minnesota, Police Department, for sharing his expertise and being gracious when I play with the facts to suit the story. Any errors in police procedure are because reality didn't quite fit the fictional world.

Thank you to all the readers who have embraced Kathleen, Owen and Hercules.

And lastly, but certainly not least, thank you to Patrick and Lauren, who fill my life with magic.

COPYCAT
KILLING

1

I'd never heard a cat laugh before—I didn't think they could—but that's what Owen was clearly doing. He was behind the big chair in the living room, laughing. It sounded a little like hacking up a fur ball if you could somehow add merriment to the sound.

I leaned over the back of the chair. "Okay, cut it out," I said. "You're being mean."

He looked up at me and it seemed as though the expression in his golden eyes was a mix of faux-innocence and mirth. "It's not funny," I hissed.

Okay, so it was kind of funny. Owen's brother, Hercules, was sitting in the middle of the kitchen floor, wearing boots. Specifically, black-and-white boots to match his black-and-white fur, in a kitty paw print design with a fleece lining and antislip sole. They were a gift from my friend, Maggie.

"Stick a paw in it," I said to Owen. "You're not helping."

I went back into the kitchen. Hercules gave me a look that was part acute embarrassment and part annoyance.

"They are kind of cute," I said. "You have to admit it was a very nice gesture on Maggie's part." That got me a glare that was all venom.

"I'll take them off." I crouched down in front of him. He held up one booted paw and I undid the strap. "You're just not a clothes person," I told him. "You're more of an au naturel cat."

I heard a noise behind me in the doorway. "And Owen is very sorry he laughed at you. Aren't you, Owen?" I added a little extra emphasis to the last words. After a moment's silence there was a soft "meow" from the other side of the room.

I took the second boot off and Hercules shook one paw and then the other. I stroked the fur on the top of his head. "Maggie was just trying to help," I said. "She knows you don't like getting your feet wet."

Hercules was a total wuss about wet feet. He didn't like going out in the rain. He didn't like going out in the snow. He didn't like walking across the grass in heavy dew. Maggie had seen the cat boots online and ordered them. I didn't know how I was going to explain to her that boots just weren't his thing.

I stood up, went over to the cupboard to get a handful of kitty crackers and made a little pile on the floor in front of Herc. "Here," I said. "These'll help." Then I scooped up Owen. I could tell from the way his tail was twitching that he'd been thinking of swiping a cracker.

"Leave your brother alone," I warned, carrying him upstairs with me. "Or I'll put those boots on you and I'll tell Maggie you like them."

He made grumbly noises in his throat. I set him on the

floor and he disappeared into my closet to sulk. I pulled on an extra pair of heavy socks, brushed my hair back into a low ponytail and stuffed my wallet in my pocket.

Hercules had eaten the crackers and was carefully grooming his front paws. "I'm going to meet Maggie," I told him, pulling my sweatshirt over my head. "I'll figure out something to tell her."

I locked the kitchen door behind me and walked around the side of the house to the truck. My truck. Sometimes I still got the urge to clap my hands and squeal when I saw it. It had started out as a loaner from Harry Taylor, Senior, and when I'd managed to retrieve some papers about Harry's daughter's adoption, he'd insisted on giving me the truck.

I'd moved to Mayville Heights about a year ago to become head librarian and to oversee the renovations to the library building. Now we were just a few months away from celebrating the library's centennial. When I moved, I'd sold my car. I'd sold just about everything. Coming to the town was a new beginning for me, a chance to take a break from my flamboyant family, and to regroup because Andrew—handsome, charming Andrew— the man I was supposed to spend the rest of my life with, had gotten drunk after we'd had a fight and ended up married to a waitress from a fifties diner.

Mayville was small enough that I could walk everywhere I wanted to go. But it was nice not to have to carry two bags of groceries up the hill. And with all the rain we'd had in the past week, and all the flooding, I never would have been able to get to the library—or a lot of other places—without the old truck.

The morning sky was dull, and the air was damp. We'd had a week of off and on rain—mostly on—and the downtown was at serious risk of major flooding. The retaining wall between Old Main Street and the river was strong, but it had been reinforced with sandbags just in case. We'd spent hours two nights ago moving those bags into place along a human chain of volunteers.

This was the second day the library was closed. The building was on higher ground, a rise where the street turned, and the pump Oren Kenyon had installed in the basement was handling what little water had come in, but both the parking lot and the street were flooded.

Maggie was waiting for me on the sidewalk in front of the artists' co-op building. The old stone basement had several feet of water in it, and we'd spent most of the previous day moving things from the first floor store into the second floor tai chi studio, in case the water got any higher. There were still a couple of her large collage panels that needed to be carried upstairs.

"Hi," I said. "How late did you stay here last night?" There were dark circles under her green eyes.

"Not that late," she said, as she unlocked the front door.

I followed her inside. Mags and I had met at her tai chi class and bonded over our love of the cheesy reality show, *Gotta Dance*. She had the tall, lean build of a runner or a dancer, but she was an artist, a tai chi instructor, and she ran the co-op store.

"Why do you have two paper clips in your hair?" I asked.

Maggie put a hand up to her head. "That's what I did with them," she said, pulling the two clips out of her short, blond curls. "I was doing some paperwork over at the studio."

The two collage panels were up on a table, carefully

wrapped and padded. We carried them up the steps without any problems.

I was about to suggest we walk over to Eric's Place for coffee and one of his blueberry muffins when we heard someone banging on the front door.

"Kathleen, please tell me that isn't who I think it is," Maggie said. Before I could ask whom she meant, she was on her way downstairs.

Jaeger Merrill was outside, his back to the door. Maggie let out a soft sigh and went to unlock it. He turned at the sound.

"Good morning," she said.

Jaeger stepped inside. "The window in my studio is leaking," he said. "The side of the cabinet where I keep my tools was damp. Some of those things can't be replaced easily, Maggie." There were two deep frown lines between his eyebrows.

Jaeger was a mask-maker. He could turn what other people saw as junk into art. I'd seen him at the re-purpose store out by the highway, and a few days ago he'd been scrounging in a dumpster that was in the front yard of a house being renovated halfway down the hill from my little house. Jaeger sold both his masks and some of the elaborate preliminary sketches he made for them in the store.

"Ruby told me," Maggie said. "Someone's coming to take a look at it this morning."

"I wanted to get some work done and instead I had to waste a lot of time sticking my stuff in boxes. Again." He dragged his fingers back through his blond hair. A couple of weeks ago he'd cut off a good six inches. It made him look more serious, less bohemian. "The building needs a manager."

"River Arts does have a manager," I said. "The town owns the building."

"Too much bureaucracy and too little money," Jaeger said derisively. "The center should have a corporate sponsor. So should the store."

Maggie placed a loosely closed fist against her breastbone and took a slow, deep breath. I knew that was her way of staying calm and in control. "The artists own and run the store," she said. "So they can make the decisions."

He gave his head a slight shake. "Like I said before, what the hell does the average artist know about running a business?"

Maggie was the current president of the co-op board. I thought about how hard she'd worked to promote the artwork and the artists at the shop in just the year I'd known her.

"I'm sorry about the leak," she said. "There isn't anything anyone can do about all the rain. Everyone is frustrated and tired, Jaeger."

He crossed his arms over his chest. "This is a ridiculous way to run a business," he started.

"The weather and how we run the co-op are two different things," Maggie said. Her tone hadn't changed at all but there was something just a little intimidating about the way she stood there so perfectly straight and still. "If you have problems with River Arts, go to the town office, call public works, call the mayor. Save everything else for the meeting."

She tipped her head to the side and looked at him. If it had been an old Western, this would have been the point where the audience did a collective "Ohhh." Maggie could outstare anyone, even my Owen and Hercules, who were masters of the unblinking glare.

Jaeger's mouth opened and closed. He shook his head. "This is stupid," he muttered. He pushed past us and headed upstairs.

"What was that?" I asked once he was out of sight.

Maggie gave me a wry smile. "Mostly Jaeger being Jaeger. You know he's been pushing for the co-op to find a patron almost since he first got here?"

I nodded.

"With the flooding and having to move everything in the store, he's just gotten worse. There are days I regret welcoming him into the co-op and helping him get that part-time job at Eric's." She let out a breath, put one hand on the back of her head and stretched. Then she looked at me. "I should check the basement."

"Okay," I said. I followed her through the empty store to the back storage room. She flipped the light switch and unlocked the door. Three steps from the top of the basement stairs she stopped, sucking in a sharp breath.

"What is it?" I asked.

"Is he dead?" Maggie asked in a tight voice.

I leaned around her to get a better look at the body. "Yeah, he's dead."

"Are you sure?"

I moved past her on the steps so I could see better. The corpse of a large, gray rodent was floating on its back, near the stair railing, in the four feet of muddy, smelly water that filled the basement at the moment. "He's not doing the backstroke, Maggie," I said. "He's dead."

She shivered and pulled a hand back over her hair. "I'm not touching him."

"I'll get it," I said. It wouldn't be the oddest thing I'd ever done in the name of friendship. I grabbed the yellow plastic snow shovel that was hanging on a nail to the right of the cellar door and went down a couple more steps so I could scoop up the dead rat. Behind me I heard Maggie make a faint squeaky noise in her throat, probably afraid that it had just been floating, eyes closed in the filthy water, like some rodent spa-goer, and was now going to roll over and run up the steps.

It didn't.

I tightened up on the shovel handle and turned, swinging it in front of me. "I'm coming up," I warned. Maggie took a step backward. I grabbed the railing and something sliced into my thumb. "Ow!" I yelled, yanking my hand back. There was blood welling from a gash on the fleshy pad of my thumb.

The end of the shovel dipped like a teeter-totter, the plastic blade banging hard on the wooden step. The rat corpse somersaulted into the air like a high diver coming off a tower. I swiped my bleeding hand on the leg of my jeans and lunged with the shovel, but the rat had gotten a surprising amount of height and distance. It arced through the air and landed with a soggy splat on Maggie's foot.

She shrieked and jerked backward, banging into the door frame.

I scrambled up the stairs. "I got it. I got it," I said. "It's okay." I scooped up the dead rodent and squeezed past Mags, keeping the shovel low to the ground.

Out in the hallway I looked around. Okay, so what was I going to do? I couldn't exactly drop the rat in the metal garbage can in the corner.

Holding the shovel out in front of me, I cut through the empty store, opened the street door, and tossed the body of the rat out toward the street. It didn't do any elegant somersaults this time. It hit the sidewalk with the same wet splat as when it had landed on Maggie's foot. Except this time the rat rolled over, shook itself and scurried away. I said a word well-mannered librarians didn't normally use, and then realized that Ruby Blackthorne was standing by the streetlight. The rat had gone whizzing right by her head.

Crap on toast! "Ruby, I'm sorry," I said, holding the door for her as she came across the sidewalk.

She looked at me, still hanging on to the shovel. "Inventing a new sport?" she asked. "Because I don't think it's going to replace discus in the Olympics. And I'm pretty sure you just violated at least a couple of cruelty to animal laws."

"It was floating in the basement." I gestured behind me.

"And that was your version of rat CPR?"

I wasn't sure if she was joking or serious. Then I noticed just a hint of a smile pulling at the corners of her mouth. She was growing her usually spiked short hair and it stuck out from the sides of her head in two tiny pigtails, one pink and one turquoise, above her multipierced ears.

"I really thought it was dead," I said. "It was on its back in the water. It didn't move." I went to swipe my hand across my sweatshirt, which is when I realized my thumb was still bleeding.

"Hey, are you okay?" Ruby asked. "It didn't bite you, did it?"

I shook my head and felt in the pocket of my hoodie for a Kleenex. "No. I did that on the railing."

Maggie came out through the store then, holding a length of old pipe like a club, scanning the space as though the rat might come walking by. It didn't seem like a good plan to tell her it was possible it could.

"It's okay, Mags," I said. "It's gone." That much was true. "I put it outside." Also true.

She looked around again, and then tucked the piece of pipe between her knees.

I shot Ruby a warning look, hoping she remembered how Maggie felt about small, furry things.

"Is Jaeger still here?" Maggie asked, glancing at the stairs.

"I don't know," I said.

"I just saw him putting boxes in his car," Ruby offered. She rolled her eyes at Maggie. "So what was it this time? The we-need-a-corporate-sponsor speech? Or the we-need-to-expand-our-horizons rant?"

"The first one," Maggie said. "Plus he's upset because of that leaking window. He said the cabinet where he keeps his tools got wet."

"That's funny," Ruby said, "because that cabinet where he keeps his fancy Swedish power tools is across the room from the windows, by the door."

Maggie pulled one hand back over her neck and grabbed the pipe again with the other. Then she noticed my thumb. "Did you do that on the railing?" She caught my wrist. "I think that needs stitches."

"I don't need stitches," I said. "It isn't even bleeding anymore. All I need is a Band-Aid."

Maggie shook her head and mock-glared at me. "C'mon upstairs. I'll fix it."

Ruby and I followed her up the steps. Maggie knew I hated all things medical, especially hospitals. It went back to when I was a kid. Blame it on a weak stomach, a dark examining room, an artificial leg and way too many cheese curls.

"What exactly is this corporate sponsor idea Jaeger has?" I asked Ruby, while Maggie cleaned my cut.

Ruby made a face. "He thinks we should find some big business to subsidize the co-op, kind of like a patron of the arts." Ruby painted huge abstracts and also taught art. She looked at Maggie. "We still have the co-op meeting tomorrow, don't we?"

Maggie nodded. "Uh huh. And I have a meeting at city hall this afternoon."

Ruby rolled her eyes. "Maybe Jaeger will forget."

"If you did have a sponsor, what's in it for the business?" I asked. "I'm guessing something more than just goodwill."

"The use of our artwork for commercial purposes, among other things," Maggie said, fastening a big bandage around my thumb. "I'm not against that, necessarily. But I'm not about to give up the right to choose how my art is used. Jaeger thinks I'm wrong." She looked at me. "How's that?"

I wiggled my thumb and opened and closed my fingers a few times. "Perfect," I said. "Thank you."

"He's an asshat," Ruby said.

"A what?" I asked.

"Asshat," she repeated. "You know, someone whose head is so far up his . . . you know . . . he's wearing it for a hat."

"Sounds uncomfortable," Maggie said.

"Does Jaeger look familiar to either of you?" Ruby asked.

I shook my head. "No."

"Uh uh," Maggie said. "Why?"

"I can't shake the feeling I've seen him somewhere before, especially since he cut his hair."

"Maybe a workshop or an exhibit," I said.

"No, I don't think that's it." Ruby shook her head and

all the little hoops in her left ear danced. "Anyway, it doesn't matter. I just came to see if you guys wanted to go get something to eat at Eric's."

I glanced at my watch.

"Is this a cat morning?" Maggie asked.

"Uh huh." I was one of several volunteers who helped take care of a feral cat colony out at Wisteria Hill, the old, abandoned Henderson estate just outside town.

"Going by yourself?" She was all innocent sweetness.

"Maybe," I said. I knew where the conversation was headed.

For months, Maggie had been trying to play matchmaker between Marcus Gordon and me. Marcus was a police detective and we'd gotten off on the wrong foot the previous summer when he thought it was possible that I had killed conductor Gregor Easton, or at the very least been involved in some intimate hanky-panky with the man who was twice my age and a . . . well . . . pretentious creep.

But last winter Marcus had rescued me when I was left dazed, wandering through the woods in the bitter cold after an explosion. And we'd gotten closer since then; though not close enough to suit Maggie. She was indirectly responsible for our friend Roma's relationship with hockey player Eddie Sweeney and it had just made her worse where Marcus and I were concerned. Maggie believed in happily ever after and she had no problem in giving it a nudge, or even a big shove.

"Meeting anyone out there?" she continued.

"Don't start," I warned.

"Start what?"

Ruby grinned. She'd heard us do this before.

"Start on Marcus and I getting together. We're friends. That's all. He's not my type. He doesn't—"

"—even have a library card," Maggie finished. "Is that the only thing you can find wrong with him?"

Okay, so I had probably used that excuse too much. I thought about Marcus for a moment. He was tall, with dark wavy hair, blue eyes and a gorgeous smile that he didn't use nearly often enough. He was kind to animals, children and old people.

I caught myself and shook my head. I was supposed to be thinking of what was wrong with the man, not what was right. Maggie was smirking at me like she could read my mind. I stuck out my tongue at her.

"So how about breakfast?" Ruby said.

Maggie nodded. "Sounds good to me."

"I have to get out to Wisteria Hill," I said. "But I'll drive you two over and get a cup of coffee to go."

Maggie picked up the length of pipe again.

"Are you taking that with you?" I asked.

"Would it look stupid?"

"Well, not exactly stupid," I said. "More like you're about to start looting and pillaging."

"You know, I really do believe every creature has a right to exist. It's just"—she blew out a breath—"I don't want some of them for roommates." She set the piece of piping on the floor against the wall at the bottom of the stairs.

Maggie locked the building, and then we piled in the truck and headed for Eric's Place farther up Old Main Street. Even though I knew the town pretty well now, I still found the whole Main Street versus Old Main Street thing kind of confusing.

"Is it ever going to stop raining?" Ruby asked, looking skyward as we got closer to the café.

"There's more rain in the forecast," I said.

"It could be wrong."

"It could." I rubbed my left wrist. It had been aching for days and not just from slinging sandbags. I'd broken it the previous summer and now it was pretty good at predicting bad weather. Maybe the fact that it didn't hurt so much today meant the forecast was wrong.

The restaurant was warm and dry and smelled like coffee instead of wet feet. Eric's wife, Susan, worked for me at the library and I knew he had a heavy-duty sump pump in the basement.

I crossed to the counter. "Hi Kathleen," Eric said with a smile. "What can I get you?"

"Just a large coffee to go, thanks," I said.

He reached for a take-out cup, poured the coffee and added just the right amount of cream and sugar. He noticed Maggie's overly large bandage on my left thumb as he passed over the cup. "That doesn't look good," he said. "How did you do that?"

"She was scooping up dead things with a shovel and throwing them at me," Maggie said, behind me.

"New hobby?" Eric asked dryly.

"More like side job," Ruby said with a grin. "Rodent wrangler."

Eric nodded. "Yeah, the rain's driving them out of their hiding places."

Maggie put her hands over her ears and started humming off-key.

"Maggie has a hear no rodents, see no rodents, speak of no rodents policy," I said.

"We tried that with the twins when they went through their streaker stage," Eric said.

I handed him the money for my coffee.

"How'd that work?" Ruby asked.

"About as well as you'd expect. They may be four, but they have the tactical skills of Hannibal getting those elephants across the Alps. They always managed to be stark naked at the most embarrassing moment."

He handed me my change. "Thanks, Eric," I said.

Maggie dropped her hands. "Have fun with . . . the cats," she said. Her lips were twitching as she tried not to smirk at me.

"Nothing's going to happen out there," I hissed at her. "Nothing."

Of course I was wrong.

2

I made it out to Wisteria Hill before Marcus did. I drank the last of my coffee, got out of the truck and stretched, bracing my hands against the left front fender.

I had felt kind of strange about accepting the truck from Old Harry just for saving a few papers. Then a couple of weeks ago his son, Harry Junior, aka Young Harry, had come into the library to tell me they'd found the old man's daughter. I think I'd been almost as happy as he was.

I heard Marcus before I saw his SUV. The runoff from all the rain had left the driveway looking more like two trenches in the gravel and mud, and he eased his way slowly around the last curve. I patted the side of the old, brown Ford, grateful for its big, thick-treaded tires and good springs.

Marcus had brought two jugs of clean water and I had the food for the cats. "Hi," he said with a smile as he got out of the car. "Can I really see a tiny bit of blue sky or is that just an optical illusion?"

I smiled back at him. "I'm not sure about the blue sky, but my wrist feels pretty good so it's a possibility. I should tell you, though, the forecast I saw this morning was for more rain."

"I have more faith in your wrist's forecasting ability than I do in any weather report," he said. We started up the path to the old carriage house where Wisteria Hill's feral cat colony slept and ate. "Have you been downtown this morning?" he asked.

I nodded. "There's still a lot of water everywhere. We did get everything moved up out of the store into the tai chi studio, but there's at least four feet of water in the co-op basement, and I sort of threw a rat at Maggie."

"You were aiming at somebody else?" he asked, completely straight-faced.

"No," I said. "It was floating in the basement. I thought it was dead."

Marcus stopped and looked over his shoulder at me. "You thought it was dead? So you picked up a live rat and threw it at Maggie?"

"No . . . well . . . sort of." I could feel my face getting red. "It was more like I dropped it on her."

He was looking at me with what I thought of as his policeman look, basically no expression at all, barely even a blink. Then a lock of his dark, wavy hair fell into his eyes and broke his concentration.

"There was more to it than that."

He turned and started up the path again. "I'm listening."

I explained about scooping up the rat with the snow shovel, how it accidentally landed on Maggie's foot and then came to life when I flung it out onto the sidewalk. I left out the part about it whizzing by Ruby's head.

Marcus stopped in front of the side door to the old building. "That was littering," he said, pulling the wooden door open. The wood had swollen with all the rain and it would come open only about halfway.

"I wasn't going to leave it on the sidewalk," I said, starting to feel defensive. "I just wanted to get the thing out of the building. If it hadn't walked away, I would have done . . . something."

Then he laughed. "It's okay, Kathleen. I'm kidding," he said, reaching out to touch my shoulder.

How did I miss that? Maybe because I was tired. Maybe because he made me crazy.

I pictured a red balloon coming out of the top of my head—an acting exercise my mother liked to use. Then I imagined it getting bigger and bigger, inflating with all my frustration and exhaustion. Marcus squeezed through the doorway and I followed him, sliding a hand over the top of my head and sending that imaginary balloon up into the cloudy, gray sky. It was better than whacking him with a bag of cat food.

We set out the food and water and retreated back to the door again. The cats made their way out to eat, one by one, led by Lucy, the little calico cat who was the matriarch of the group. Both Marcus and I looked them over for any signs of illness or injury.

"They all look okay," Marcus said quietly by my ear. He was close behind me, warm and smelling like soap and coffee.

I tipped my head back, studying the weathered boards over my head. "I don't see any leaks anywhere in here," I said, "except for that one in the corner we already knew about." I pointed to the front left corner of the old building where the boards were watermarked.

"I'll take a look outside when we're done," he said. "If there's no more rain, we should be okay."

Big if.

When the cats had finished eating and moved away, we gathered the dishes and cleaned up the feeding station. Marcus refilled the water bowls and then took a look at the leak in the corner. There was no water coming in now and the wet areas on the floor and wall were actually starting to dry out.

Once we were outside he handed me the empty jugs. "I just want to walk around and see how the roof looks from the outside," he said. "Wait for me?"

"Sure," I said. He started around the back of the carriage house and I went to the truck and stowed everything on the floor on the passenger side.

I could hear the sound of rushing water. There was a stream back behind the carriage house, skirting a rise where the trees began. With all this rain it had to be swollen with water. If it overflowed, it could flood the carriage house, I realized.

I looked around for Marcus, but he still must have been on the other side of the building. I locked the truck again and started across the grass toward the trees. The ground was so soaked with water I left a small puddle with each step I took and I was glad I'd worn my rubber boots.

Climbing up the bank my feet slid, trying to get a grip on the wet ground. The water sounded even louder at the top of the bank. I eased my way through the dripping trees, trying not to skid on the leaves and mud under my boots.

The stream cut through a gully on the far side of the woods. The water was several feet higher than usual, maybe halfway up the side of the gully, splashing up onto the bank on either side. It looked cold and angry. The carriage house wasn't in any danger for now. But if we got more rain . . .

I headed back, sliding from one tree to the next. The mix of leaves, pine needles and mud underfoot was as slick as ice and I wasn't very good on ice. At the base of an old oak tree, near the edge of the embankment, I caught sight of a bit of purple, out of place in the old leaves and needles. I worked my way over, hooked one arm around the tree trunk and bent down to pick the thing up.

It looked like a tiny purple Afro wig, maybe an inch across, with a metal centerpiece. I exhaled in frustration. It wasn't the first time I'd found someone's trash thrown out here.

I could hear Marcus calling me. I stuffed the purple puff in the front pocket of my sweatshirt and took a step closer to the edge of the terraced hill. He was by the back of the carriage house.

I waved an arm. "I'm here," I yelled. At the same moment I felt something shift under my feet. It was as though a giant hand had grabbed the ground and was trying to pull it out from beneath me.

I put out a hand and then the entire slope dropped out from underneath me. One moment I was on the slick, grass-covered hill and the next there was nothing. I reached out, but all I caught was handfuls of air.

The momentum threw me forward. I went down, down, down, thrown forward and sideways at the same time so I couldn't get a sense of which way was up. There was a shower of earth and rocks around me and I folded my arms over my head on instinct.

My left foot twisted underneath me and caught on

something—a tree root maybe—and for a second it felt as though my whole leg would come out of its socket. Then whatever part of the ground that had grabbed me let go. I pitched forward, or maybe it was backward, I don't know, ending up finally against solid ground, on my right side in the wet earth, under the sheared side of the embankment.

I couldn't breathe. Gasping and wheezing, I struggled to sit up. I could see Marcus running toward me even as my vision began to go dark from the edges in.

I.

Couldn't.

Breathe.

My chest felt like an elephant was sitting on it. I pulled at the front of my sweatshirt, desperate to suck in air.

Marcus dropped to his knees beside me in the mud. His arm went around my shoulder, his hand against the side of my face as he pushed me forward, stopping me from getting up. "Easy, easy," he said over and over.

I slumped against him, eyes closed, concentrating only on not passing out. I caught a breath. And then another one. Then I started to cough. There was dirt in the back of my throat and in my mouth, gritty on my teeth and tongue. I hacked and wheezed, my chest burning.

Marcus moved his hand to my shoulder, keeping me tight against him, not that my shaking body could have moved if I'd tried. "It's okay, just breathe," he said, his face gray with concern. "I've got you."

I coughed until my throat was raw and finally I could breathe more or less okay. I leaned against Marcus, his arm still tight around my shoulders, and swiped the dirt away from my mouth with one hand.

"Don't move," he said, shifting sideways to reach for his cell phone.

"I'm all right," I rasped.

"No you're not."

I tried to shift myself upright and sucked in a sharp breath against the stab of pain in my left hand as it pushed against a large rock, half exposed in the dirt.

I held up my hand, rolling it over to see Maggie's bandage had come off.

My breath caught in my chest again. I could hear Marcus talking to me but his voice sounded very far away and I couldn't make sense of the words.

The cut on my thumb had opened up again. Blood was dripping off the tip . . . down onto the top of a dirt-streaked skull, lying on the ground.

3

"You're bleeding," Marcus said, grabbing my arm.

I tried to gesture with my hand. "There's a—"

"—I see it," he interrupted.

The skull was lying on what seemed to be a corner of an old piece of canvas. I could see what looked like a clavicle and shoulder bones as well.

I was shaking. I closed my eyes for a moment in a silent prayer that whomever the remains had belonged to, the person had died after a long, happy life and had been, as Maggie would say, welcomed by the light.

Marcus reached over and unwound the black scarf I was wearing around my neck under my hoodie, and wrapped it around my hand, pinning my bleeding thumb against my palm. "Can you stand up?" he asked. "We need to get out of the way just in case any more of that bank comes down."

Slowly, I got my legs untangled and got to my feet. For a moment the world whirled dizzyingly around me. I held on to Marcus, my fingers digging into his arm, and the feeling passed.

My left ankle was stiff and it hurt enough that I grit my teeth together so I wouldn't moan out loud. I put most of my weight on my other leg and leaned on Marcus as we made our way across the uneven ground toward the old house. I was covered with dirt and probably bruises as well, but nothing seemed to be broken and I hadn't hit my head. My jeans and sweatshirt were wet and caked with mud, but the only thing that seemed to be bleeding was my thumb.

When we got to the carriage house I looked back over my shoulder. The entire embankment at the edge of the trees had collapsed. For a moment my legs went watery. Marcus's arm tightened around my shoulders.

"You okay?" he asked, eyes narrowed with concern.

I nodded. "I am. Really." How had I managed to end up with just a few bumps and scrapes? Even my bleeding hand had been injured somewhere else.

I could see that there had been some kind of stone retaining wall holding up the rise and reinforcing the slope. Could there maybe have been an old burial ground up on the hill? Was that where the skull had come from? No one had ever talked about a Henderson family cemetery out here. Then again, people didn't really talk about Wisteria Hill much at all.

We made it to the main house and I sank onto the side stairs. Marcus took a couple of steps away from me and pulled out his cell phone, his entire demeanor shifting into police officer mode. I knew the authorities would have to figure out where the bones had come from.

I still had dirt and grit in my nose and mouth. I tried

to take a deep breath and started coughing again. I leaned forward, arms on my knees, breathing slowly.

Marcus turned, snapping his phone closed. "Ambulance will be here in a few minutes."

It took a second for me to realize he meant for me, not for the remains behind the carriage house. Hacking and wheezing I sucked in an uneven breath and then another. "I'm all right," I said, hoarsely, starting to get up and then flinching as I put my left hand down without thinking. Not only did the gash on my thumb hurt, it felt as though I'd done something to my wrist, too.

Marcus shook his head. "No, you're not all right." He gestured at the scarf-wrapped hand that I was hugging to my chest. "Your hand's bleeding. So is your forehead. You've probably got a sprained ankle and who knows how many other cuts and bruises. You fell a good ten feet, Kathleen. You need to be checked out."

My hand went to my face out of reflex and I squeaked at the pain. The entire right side of my head hurt and there was blood and dirt on my fingers when I pulled my hand away. "Okay," I said.

His eyes narrowed in surprise. "Okay? That's it?"

I nodded. He'd probably expected me to argue. It was what we usually did; squabble like six-year-olds.

For a minute we just looked at each other in silence. Then Marcus glanced back toward the collapsed hill.

"Do you think there's some kind of graveyard back there?" I asked, tipping my head to one side and trying to shake some of the dirt from my hair. For a moment the movement made the world spin again.

"I think there's a pretty good chance." He made a face and pointed at my hand. "Do you mind? Can I take a look at that?"

I held out my arm and he unwound one end of the scarf. Blood had soaked all the way through the material. "There was a smallpox epidemic in this area back in 1924," he said. "I know there've been a couple of other unmarked grave sites from that time found in this part of the state."

He inspected the cut, made a face and folded the fabric back around my hand. "It doesn't seem to be bleeding anymore." He squinted at my face and then reached over to brush dirt from my forehead.

I jerked back, involuntarily, and sucked in a sharp breath between my teeth.

He pulled his hand away. "Sorry. I'll let the paramedics take care of that."

"Could you pull my left boot off, please?" I asked. "It's full of mud." I'd been trying to toe off the heel with my other foot but it wasn't working.

I held up my leg and Marcus grabbed the bottom of the rubber boot and pulled. It came off with a loud sucking sound and clumps of wet earth fell onto the grass. There was more dirt stuck to my sock. I shook my foot and sent a spray of it into the air.

Even in the heavy woolen sock I was wearing, my ankle looked swollen. Marcus set the boot down and reached for my foot. "Does this hurt?" he asked, gently bending it forward and back.

I winced. "A little."

"How about this?" His fingers carefully probed my ankle. He had big, warm hands with strong fingers and a surprisingly gentle touch.

I was pretty sure I wasn't supposed to be liking this so much. "It's . . . um . . . it's all right." I pulled my foot back and reached for the discarded boot.

He handed it to me as the ambulance arrived, followed by the first police car. I recognized Ric, one of the two paramedics. He'd taken care of me the previous winter when I'd almost been blown to pieces in an explosion out on Hardwood Ridge. He remembered me as well.

"Ms. Paulson, what happened?" he asked, crouching down in front of me.

I explained about the hill collapsing, while his partner checked my pulse and looked into both my eyes. Once they decided I didn't have any life-threatening injuries or broken bones, they began bandaging the cut on my hand and cleaning the various abrasions on my face.

"How's your cat?" Ric asked as he carefully tweezered bits of gravel from my forehead. "Still sneaking into your truck to ride shotgun?"

I'd taken Owen with me the day of the explosion. Like me, he'd almost been caught in it. Everyone assumed he'd stowed away in the truck and I'd let the assumption stand.

Marcus knew the cat didn't like to be touched by pretty much anyone other than me, but one of the police officers on the scene hadn't taken his warning seriously. It was a wonder I hadn't regained consciousness to find Owen shackled in a set of kitty-sized handcuffs for assaulting a police officer.

"Sometimes," I said. "Mostly he's just terrorizing the birds in the backyard."

Ric grinned. "He hasn't gone head-to-head with any more police officers?"

"Thankfully, no. But he does have a stare-down going with a golden Lab that lives up the street."

I flinched as he pulled out a sliver of tree bark embedded in my skin.

"Sorry," he said softly.

I looked over his shoulder, focusing on watching Marcus work to distract myself while Ric continued to gently clean my forehead.

Marcus was a good police officer—meticulous and very observant. I thought he was too rigid sometimes, and he tended to come across as cold when he was working on a case, something I knew firsthand because I'd gotten tied up in two of his past investigations.

He'd thought I had no business being involved in either one of them. The fact that I hadn't wanted to be involved in a murder, or that he'd been investigating people I cared about—and the first time we met, me—didn't seem to be a good enough reason.

I wasn't a police officer. I wasn't even a lawyer. I was a librarian. I knew about books, grant proposals and the Dewey decimal system. The thing was, because of my parents' acting careers, I'd seen a lot of subterfuge and I was pretty good at spotting a liar. Plus I had Hercules and Owen who had the ability to stick their furry noses—literally—into places they probably had no business being. Of course, I couldn't share that with Marcus, or anyone else for that matter.

I tried to imagine his reaction if I told him that my cats' talents went beyond being able to hear a can of tuna being opened from a hundred feet away; that Hercules had the ability to walk through walls and Owen could disappear whenever it suited him, which was generally at the worst possible time for me. How could I explain it to anyone else when I didn't even understand it all myself? At best, I'd end up somewhere having my head examined, at worst the cats would.

Ric was just putting a gauze bandage on my forehead

when Officer Derek Craig came around the side of the carriage house. I'd met the young policeman for the first time the previous summer when I found conductor Gregor Easton's body at the Stratton Theater. He'd been at the library several times in the past couple of months, checking out books on the law and law school. I wondered if he was thinking about a career change.

"Is Ms. Paulson okay to go home?" he asked the paramedics.

Ric nodded. "We're done." He turned his attention to me. His partner was already packing their things.

"I know," I said, before he could start giving me his list of warnings. "I should see my family doctor. And if my head starts to hurt, or if I have problems with my vision or breathing, I should go to the emergency room right away."

"Or if you feel nauseated or start vomiting," he added. "In fact, you should make an appointment with your own doctor as soon as possible to get checked out. Just to be on the safe side."

"I will," I said. "Thank you." I leaned around Ric to thank the other paramedic as well. Then I turned to Derek. "I'm okay. And my truck's right there. I can get home."

He shifted uncomfortably from one foot to the other. "Ma'am, Detective Gordon told me to drive you home. He also said I should use handcuffs if I had to. Do I have to?"

I didn't want to leave my truck behind. On the other hand, Marcus wasn't above having those handcuffs put on me.

I shook my head. "No you don't have to. But do you have something to cover the seat?" There was mud on my boots, clumped on my clothes, even some still in my hair.

"Not a problem," he said with a smile. "A little dirt won't hurt anything. There's been worse in that car."

I got to my feet and brushed what dirt I could off my jeans and hooded sweatshirt. I looked around for Marcus. He was at the far end of the field, bent down, clearly studying the bones that had been unearthed by the hill collapse. He turned and straightened up then, almost as if he could feel my eyes on him. I lifted a hand to let him know I was all right and I was going—more or less willingly—with Derek. He raised a hand in return.

I limped my way slowly over to the police cruiser. My ankle felt a little better now that it was wrapped with a support bandage. Derek hovered beside me and I had the sense that he could and would toss me over his shoulder and carry me the rest of the way if I stumbled. I scraped what mud I could off my boots before I got in the car. He reached across me and fastened the seat belt. I wasn't sure if he thought I was too banged up to do it myself, or that I might bolt for my truck when his back was turned.

We crept down the rutted driveway, bouncing over every bump. I knew I had to have a lot of bruises I couldn't see and I felt every one of them with every lurch of the car.

At the bottom Derek turned to me. "Where are we headed?" he asked.

"Mountain Road," I said. "On the left-hand side, not that far from the top." I gave him the number.

He frowned. "Little white farmhouse?"

I nodded. "That's it."

We drove the rest of the way in silence. He pulled into the driveway and before I could tell him not to, he was out of the police car and around opening the passenger door for me.

"Thank you," I said, smiling up at him.

"You're welcome," he said with a dip of his head. I was at the back steps before I heard the car pull onto the street again. It was a safe bet that Marcus had told him to make sure I made it safely to the door.

I pulled off my muddy boots in the porch and unlocked the kitchen door. As if they had some kind of cat radar, Hercules and Owen both appeared in the living room doorway.

"It's not as bad as it looks," I said.

They exchanged glances, almost as though they were engaging in some kind of telepathic communication. Then Herc came across the floor to me. I pulled out a kitchen chair and dropped into it, biting off a groan when my right hip made contact with the seat. The little black-and-white cat sat in front of me, eyes narrowed, and looked me up and down.

"The bank behind the carriage house let go," I said, feeling a little foolish explaining myself to a cat. "I'm fine. Marcus called the paramedics, not that I needed them." I pulled my muddy sweatshirt over my head and dropped it on the floor.

Hercules recoiled and took a couple of steps backward. He sniffed the shirt, and then he sniffed at me, his face twisting in distaste at the odor.

"Yes, I know I don't smell very good," I said. "Kind of the same way someone did after they got into Rebecca's compost pile." I shot a quick glance at Owen.

Hercules came closer again. He stood on his back legs, put a paw on my knee and gently nudged my rebandaged hand. "It's just a little cut," I said, reaching down to stroke his fur with my other hand. "I actually did that down at the store with Maggie."

At the sound of Maggie's name, Owen bounded over to me. "Maggie's fine," I reassured him. He had a major kitty crush on her. "So am I, so you can stop worrying." Sarcasm was wasted on Owen—he was already poking my sweatshirt with a paw.

Hercules suddenly dropped back onto all four feet, looked at the refrigerator door—where I'd stuck the Wisteria Hill feeding schedule—then turned back to me, tipping his head to one side and meowing quizzically. He might have been asking if we had any sardines in the fridge. Or it was possible he was asking if Marcus was okay. Improbable, but not impossible, since Hercules and Owen weren't exactly ordinary house cats.

"Yes, Marcus is fine too, and in case you were asking about sardines and not everyone's favorite detective, no, there aren't any open."

The answer seemed to satisfy him. He turned to watch his brother still poking at my hoodie. I knew Herc had no intention of touching it. Not only did he dislike having wet paws, he didn't like having dirty ones either. Owen had found the little purple thingie I'd picked up out at Wisteria Hill. He gave it a swipe with one paw and it slid over the floor like a curling rock, ending up at my feet.

I bent to pick the thing up before Owen sent it underneath the refrigerator. I still had no idea what it was. A wig for some kind of tiny forest sprite, perhaps? It wasn't the oddest thing to be discarded out at the old estate. I knew that Harry Taylor and his younger brother, Larry, had found a full-sized, claw-foot bathtub out there in the woods. Being practical guys, they'd loaded it in the back of Larry's truck and it had eventually ended up in Larry's bathroom—with the approval of Everett Henderson, of course.

My entire right side ached and I guessed I was probably turning into a giant bruise all over that part of my body. I needed coffee and a shower and a couple of aspirin.

I looked at the cats. "I don't suppose you two know how to work the coffeemaker," I said. Owen's head immediately swung in my direction. He knew the word coffee generally meant I'd also be eating something he probably could wheedle a few bites of. "Yes, we'll have something to eat, too," I assured him.

I stood up, stretched and groaned a little, partly because everything hurt and partly for effect. Not only do cats not get sarcasm, they don't get shameless bids for sympathy either. I set the tiny purple puff on top of the refrigerator, washed my hands, started the coffee and headed upstairs for the shower.

"Maggie and I didn't talk about the boots," I said over my shoulder to Hercules as I got to the living room doorway. He was zealously cleaning the bottom of his left paw and didn't even look up. Even though I'd said Maggie's name, neither did Owen.

"I distracted her," I added.

Nothing, not even a tail twitch, or two.

I rubbed the back of my neck with one hand. "Yep, tossed a dead rat right at her. Of course, it turns out it wasn't exactly dead."

I would have sworn both cats did a double take. They bolted across the floor. Owen skidded to a stop just in front of me. Herc was a little more dignified. Throw the word rat into a sentence and suddenly they were interested.

They trailed me upstairs and sat just inside the bathroom door while I got cleaned up and told them what had happened at the co-op store and later at Wisteria Hill. I knew it was a little weird, okay, probably more than a little weird that I talked to the cats like they understood what I was saying, but I'd found it helped me to sort things out. There were times when it really did seem like they were following the conversation. And I told myself that talking to Owen and Hercules wasn't as bad as walking around talking to myself.

Owen gave me the cold shoulder while I got dressed. Clearly in his kitty mind I had wronged Maggie. But he came around once I started spreading peanut butter on toast for a peanut butter and banana sandwich. I gave each cat a small bite, glad Roma wasn't around to catch me. Then I pulled one of the other kitchen chairs closer so I could prop my left foot on it. I'd left the support bandage on in the shower, tying a plastic bag over it so it was only a bit wet on the top edge.

I poured a second cup of coffee and I closed my eyes for a moment, feeling the sensation of the earth dropping out from under me again. It was that same stomach-falling sensation as being on a roller coaster— without being belted in the seat—with the world flipping upside down at the same time and dirt flying everywhere.

I shook my head and opened my eyes. A furry black-and-white face and a furry tabby face were both studying me. "I'm okay, really," I told them, folding both hands around my coffee cup. "But I should call Roma."

At the sound of Roma's name both cats made little growly sounds in their throats. Hercules and Owen didn't exactly like her. They'd either been born out at Wisteria Hill, or abandoned out there as very young kittens. I'd found them when I was exploring the old estate, after I first moved to Mayville Heights. They'd followed me and I ended up adopting them. Sometimes I thought they'd adopted me. They didn't have the best people skills. A visit to Roma's vet clinic always involved a lot of yowling, hissing and a Kevlar glove.

Luckily Roma was between patients. I explained what had happened out at the old estate. "When the bank let go, Marcus thinks it disturbed some kind of grave site." I told her about the bones, picturing that dirt-encrusted skull again in my mind. I shook my head to chase away the image. "There's going to be a lot of uproar out there for the next few days and I'm worried about the estate cats," I said.

"And are *you* all right?" she immediately asked.

"I look worse than I feel," I said. "But I'm more concerned about the cats with all the people wandering around out there. They're not used to it."

Roma sighed. "I don't want to move them unless I absolutely have to. The change would be incredibly stressful."

"Maybe you don't need to," I said. "Marcus seemed to think the bones were from an unmarked burial site from a smallpox epidemic back in the 1920s. He said there have been other sites found in this area."

"He's right," she said. "A couple of rock hounds stumbled over one near here maybe a year and a half ago."

I pictured her, mouth pulled to one side as she thought about what to do. "I have time," she said. "I think I'll take a drive out there, talk to Marcus and see things for myself."

"Any chance you could swing by and pick me up?" I asked. "I'd love to get my truck."

"Are you safe to drive?"

"Marcus didn't think so, but I am," I said, shifting in the chair and wincing when more weight went on my bruised hip. "Bring your bag if you want to check me out first."

"Wouldn't be the first time," she retorted. "I'll be there in about fifteen minutes or so."

I pulled on a clean sweatshirt and put my wallet in the pocket. My rubber boots were still damp, but it didn't take long to dry them with the hair dryer—a trick I'd learned from Maggie. I was ready when Roma tapped on the back door.

She frowned and pressed her lips together when she saw my face. "Ow! Are you sure you feel all right?"

"Scout's honor," I said solemnly.

"And when were you a scout?" she asked, tucking her dark hair behind one ear and leaning in to get a better look at my scraped forehead.

"Okay, librarian's honor then," I said.

Roma shook her head but there was a hint of amusement in her brown eyes.

I stuck out my leg. "I twisted my ankle." I touched the side of my face. "I scraped a little skin off my face." I put one hand on my hip. "And I have some bruises that you're just going to have to take my word on. That's it."

"Your hand?" Roma asked, pointing.

"That doesn't count," I said. "I didn't do that out at Wisteria Hill." Like Maggie, the paramedic had put on a bandage that was a lot larger than I really needed. "I did that while I was helping Maggie."

"Kathleen, has it occurred to you that maybe you should have just stayed in bed today?"

"Hey, I've done worse," I said.

"I know," she said, dryly. "I've seen your worse." She crossed her arms over her chest and studied me. I had the feeling that any moment she was going to sprint back to her SUV and get her bag and I'd find myself being examined by some instrument that was usually used on the working end of a farm animal.

She gave me a stern glare. Or it would have seemed stern if there hadn't been the beginnings of a smile making her lips twitch. "Okay, let's go. But if you feel dizzy, or nauseated—"

"I'll say something, promise," I finished.

"And make sure you roll the window down," she said, letting the smile loose.

I locked the house and followed Roma out to her car. As we drove back out to Wisteria Hill I told her more about the hill collapsing. She shot me a quick, sideways glance. "You're really lucky you didn't break something, or worse."

I remembered the feeling of falling, out of control, as dirt rained around me. I blew out a breath. "I know," I said. "I was just trying to pick up that weird little purple piece of litter. You know what Harry Taylor would say? No good deed goes unpunished."

"I'm glad you're okay," she said, quietly, without taking her eyes from the road. She reached over and patted my leg.

There were more cars and police vehicles at the old estate. A lot had happened in the last hour and a half. The carriage house had been blocked off with plastic crime scene tape and Derek Craig was on "guard duty." Roma and I skirted the tape and circled the building so she could get a look at the collapsed slope.

"Good heavens," she said, softly.

My stomach did flip-flops, looking at how much of the hill had fallen away underneath my feet.

The entire field behind the carriage house was cordoned off as well. Marcus was at the far end, watching a woman who was sitting on her heels, examining something. It was a pretty safe bet she was looking at the bones that had been unearthed. There were two other people staking off a grid. Roma followed the yellow tape around the edge of the muddy, rocky ground and I limped behind her, working our way over to Marcus.

He turned as we got close, said something to the woman kneeling in the dirt, who nodded without looking up, and then came over to us.

"Hi," he said, peeling off a pair of mud-covered latex gloves. I couldn't miss the quick once-over he gave me before he turned his attention to Roma. "I was going to call you," he said to her.

"Thank you for sequestering the carriage house," she said, glancing back at the old building. "Are we going to have to move the cats?"

Marcus frowned. "For now, they're probably okay. Beyond that, we're waiting for Dr. Abbott to tell us more about the bones." He tipped his head in the direction of the woman hunkered down in the dirt. "She's an anthropologist."

"Do you think this is another of those unmarked graveyards from the smallpox epidemic?" Roma asked.

He shifted from one foot to the other, the wet ground pulling at his boots. "Probably."

She looked past him. "I don't know Marcus," she said, frowning. "That's Henderson land all the way back through the trees. Maybe you should talk to Everett."

"I plan to," he said. He turned his attention to me,

lowering his voice. "I didn't expect to see you back here. You okay?"

I nodded, a little surprised. I'd expected him to give me a hard time about coming back out to Wisteria Hill. Behind him the anthropologist, Dr. Abbott, got to her feet and started toward us.

"Detective Gordon," she called. She was holding something in her gloved hand.

As she came level with us I realized it was a heavy gold ring. From the size it looked as though it was a man's ring and the insignia on the front looked familiar.

"That's an old Mayville Heights High School graduation ring," Roma said, leaning past Marcus for a better look. "My father wore one," she added by way of explanation. "Those were his glory days. According to my mother, he never took it off."

"I thought it was a high school ring," Dr. Abbott said. She looked to be about forty, tall, with blond hair in a low ponytail.

"With the ring facing you, the date's on the left," Roma continued. "See the sixty-three right there?" She pointed, and then paused for a moment. "Funny. That's the same year my father graduated."

She looked up at Marcus. "It would have been a pretty small graduating class. It shouldn't be that hard to figure out who owned that ring." She shifted her attention back to the piece of jewelry. "In fact, some of the kids had their initials in raised lettering on the other side. I know my father did. T.A.K."

T, A, K? That didn't make any sense. Roma's dad's name was Neil Carver.

Dr. Abbott stiffened, still holding the ring between her gloved thumb and index finger. Beside me, Roma had gone rigid as well. It almost seemed as though she'd stopped breathing. "What are the initials on that ring?" she asked. The tightness in her body was in her voice too.

The anthropologist hesitated. Her eyes went to Marcus and back to Roma.

Marcus cleared his throat. "Thanks for the information about the ring," he said to Roma. "Dr. Abbott and I need to get back to work."

Roma ignored him, or maybe his words didn't register. "What are the initials on that ring?" she said again. "I can see a T. What are the other two letters?"

Her hand was at her side and her fingers were moving, bending, flexing, then closing into a fist again. I touched her arm. "Roma, we should go check on Lucy and the other cats," I said.

But her entire focus was on Dr. Abbott. "T.A.K.," she repeated, her voice low and insistent. "For Thomas Albert Karlsson."

It couldn't be her father's ring. Even if he'd changed his name—and it appeared that he had—how could his high school ring have ended up in the ground with the bones of someone who'd died in 1924?

Usually I'm not that slow.

"Those are the initials, aren't they?" Roma asked.

"Yes," Dr. Abbott said, in a voice so quiet I almost missed the word.

Roma swallowed and closed her eyes for a moment. When she opened them she looked out across the grass and dirt to where the skull and a few other bones were resting on a tarp. "That's my father," she whispered.

4

"What do you mean, that's your father?" Marcus asked, eyes narrowed in confusion.

I put my arm around Roma's shoulder. "We don't know who that is," I said. "We have to let Dr. Abbott get back to work so she can figure that out."

Roma turned her head to look at me. She opened her mouth to say something then closed it again. Her gaze went back across the field.

I gave her shoulder a squeeze so she'd look at me again. "Even if it is your father's class ring, it doesn't mean that's . . . him."

"It's his ring," she said in a low voice.

"Roma, are you sure?" Marcus asked, his voice surprisingly gentle. I knew he liked Roma, as a person, not just for all the work she did with the cat colony and pretty much every other stray animal in the area.

"I have a picture somewhere of him wearing it," she said. She couldn't take her eyes off those bones spread on a blue tarp. "I'll see if I can find it."

He nodded.

"He walked out on us," Roma continued, "when I was a little girl. At least that's what I thought. My mother always said he was just too young for the responsibility of a family."

"It's just a ring," Marcus said. "We don't know how it ended up out here. Let Dr. Abbott do her job. Let me do my job. I'll call you later."

"C'mon, Roma, let's go," I said. I had no idea who those remains belonged to, but I knew it wasn't good for her to be standing there, staring out at them. The pain I could see in her pale, still face made my chest hurt.

I looked at Marcus, and mouthed the words thank you. He nodded.

We made our way back along the edge of the field. I clenched my teeth, concentrating on not stumbling on the slippery, uneven ground. When we got level with the back of the carriage house Roma stopped and faced me. "Can we check on the cats and . . . and leave all of this until after? Please?"

I nodded. "Of course we can."

Derek let us duck under the yellow crime scene tape and I followed Roma into the old building, blinking as my eyes adjusted to the light. My ankle hurt every time I took a step and I tried to concentrate on the cats, on Roma, on anything else to distract myself. "What are we looking for?" I said.

Roma rubbed the top of her shoulder. "I don't really know," she said. "I'd feel better if I knew Lucy was here. The rest of the cats follow her lead."

Lucy wasn't the largest cat, but she was the undisputed leader of the feral cat colony. She may have been a tiny calico, but she had the heart and the spirit of a jungle cat.

There was no sign of Lucy anywhere. "Why don't we take a look at the shelters," Roma said.

The cat shelters were made from oversized plastic storage bins, well insulated to keep the cats warm during the freezing Minnesota winter. They sat in the far corner of the building in a space that had probably once been used to keep feed for the horses. Harry Taylor—the son, not the father—had made a raised platform for the shelters to sit on, and straw bales around the three walls added extra insulation and warmth.

I squinted in the dim light. There wasn't so much as a twitching whisker to be seen. Beside me Roma let out a slow breath.

"The cats could be asleep," I whispered. "They could be out prowling around. They're probably okay."

She pressed the heel of her hand against her forehead, between her eyes. "You're right," she said. "I just don't want them to get spooked and run."

I craned my neck, looking for some movement, some sign that some or any of the cats were around. Something caught my eye near the farthest stack of straw bales. I crossed my fingers it was a cat and not a field mouse.

"Lucy, c'mere puss," I called softly.

Roma looked at me like I was crazy. "That's not going to work," she said.

The cats were nobody's pets. They were skittish around people—even the volunteers they saw regularly. They didn't come when they were called. They were a lot more likely to bolt, but Lucy and I had a rapport that was impossible to explain.

I put a hand on Roma's arm. "Hang on a second," I said. I took a couple of steps closer to the shelter space and crouched down, biting my tongue so I didn't groan out loud.

"Lucy," I called again. I kept my eyes on the corner where I thought I'd seen that flash of movement and held my breath.

I saw the ears first. They poked up over the top of a straw bale, followed by the rest of a furry face. Lucy's furry face.

My shoulders sagged with relief. The small, calico cat tipped her head to one side and stared at me, almost as though she was wondering what the heck I wanted.

"She's fine," I said to Roma.

"As long as Lucy is here the other cats should stay around too," she said.

Lucy meowed and ducked back behind the straw. I had to put my good hand down on the rough wooden floor to push myself upright. My ankle objected and I almost fell over sideways.

Roma was looking distractedly around the space, checking for leaks, I guessed, but I knew the bones out in the field behind the carriage house were foremost in her mind.

I touched her shoulder. "Ready to go?"

She nodded. I followed her, waiting while she made sure the door was tightly closed. We ducked under the yellow tape again and I thanked Derek. I waited for Roma to say something, about the ring, about her father. But instead she busied herself brushing dirt that only she could seem to see off her jeans.

"Do you have time for coffee?" I said.

She gave me a blank look and then shook her head. "I'm sorry, what did you say?" she asked.

"Let's go back to the house and have coffee. Do you have time?"

Her eyes automatically went to the carriage house even though we couldn't see Marcus or Dr. Abbott from where we were standing. I could tell that she wanted to walk back out to see what was going on.

"I have cinnamon coffee cake," I said. Sitting down with a cup of coffee and a slice of coffee cake seemed like a pretty good idea to me. Even just sitting down would be good. I shifted my weight onto my "good" leg.

Roma noticed the movement. "Your leg hurts," she said. It wasn't a question.

"Just my ankle. It's a bit stiff," I said, tucking my hands in the front pocket of my sweatshirt.

Roma's gaze darted sideways again for a brief moment. Then she exhaled slowly and turned her full attention to me. "Let's go," she said. "You should get off that leg and I could use a cup of coffee."

We walked to our vehicles. Roma frowned as I pulled my keys out of my pocket. "Are you sure you're okay to drive?"

"Yes," I said. "I swear."

She gave me a half smile. "I know. Librarian's honor." She fished her own keys out of her pocket. "I'll follow you. If you feel sick, pull over."

"I will."

I climbed into the truck as Roma walked over to her SUV. I'd been hurt a couple of times last summer—accidents that turned out not to be so accidental after all. Roma had thought I wasn't taking those "accidents" seriously enough, and I'd thought she was taking them a bit too seriously. Right now she was fussing over me a little more than was typical for her. Maybe it was a way to distract herself from thinking about that old high school ring.

We lurched our way down the driveway and I turned onto the road, Roma close behind me. Except for my bruised hip and my slightly swollen ankle—that felt a little better now that I was sitting down—I really was okay. Seeing the sheared off bank had made me realize just how lucky I had been to walk away with just some aches and scrapes.

There was no sign of either Owen or Hercules when we got to the house—no surprise given that Roma was probably their least favorite person.

"I'll start the coffee," Roma said. "Why don't you sit?"

I was about to start my umpteenth recitation of the "I'm all right" speech when it occurred to me that maybe she needed to be busy, maybe she needed to keep her hands moving while she sorted out what had happened up at Wisteria Hill.

So I said, "Okay," and sank onto one of the kitchen chairs, propping my foot up on another. Roma started the coffee pot, found cream and sugar, cut the coffee cake and got plates for both of us. The entire time she talked about the Wisteria Hill cats, the kind of aimless chitchat I'd never heard Roma make before. She didn't sit down until the coffee was poured and we each had a mug. She looked at me across the table and all at once pressed her hand to her mouth.

I reached over and put my hand on her arm. She blinked hard and swallowed a couple of times before dropping her hand and wrapping her arm around her body.

"That's my father, Kathleen," she said. "Those pieces of bone that were ... lying ... on that tarp, they ... they're my father." She closed her eyes for a moment. I wasn't sure if she was picturing what we'd seen at Wisteria Hill, or trying to banish the image.

I gave her arm a squeeze and she opened her eyes again. "I didn't realize your dad—Neil—isn't your biological father."

Roma traced the inside loop of the cup handle with one finger, around and around and around. "No he's not. He married my mother when I was five. He's been my father in every way that matters, but he's not my birth father."

"Thomas Karlsson was."

She nodded.

I folded my hands around my own mug. "Roma, you said he left when you were little." I flashed to the skull in the dirt. "Where did you think he's been?"

She shrugged. "He was just ... gone. He and my mother were kids when they had me, right out of high school—kids when they got married, which I'm pretty sure was because they were having me, by the way."

I nodded but didn't say anything. My brother and sister—Ethan and Sara—had been guests at my parents' wedding—their second try at marriage.

Roma took a sip of her coffee and set the mug on the table again. "My mother always said he just got overwhelmed by the responsibility of having a family when he was really just a kid himself." She sighed. "She said he was probably ashamed that he had taken off, but the longer he stayed away from Mayville the harder it was to face people."

"And maybe that is what happened," I said. "Those ... remains, they may not be him at all."

She shook her head, the movement almost imperceptible. "That's his ring, Kathleen. It's the right year and the right initials."

"That doesn't mean he was wearing it. Maybe he lost it. Maybe he gave it to someone else to wear." I was trying to be the voice of reason.

"You heard me tell Marcus that I have a picture of my father—Thomas—wearing that ring?"

I nodded.

"It's a newspaper clipping. He played baseball. They were state champions his senior year in high school." Her mouth twisted into a wry smile. "I suspect that I was the result of the celebrations." She leaned back in her chair. "The seniors on the team got their class rings early. It was a big deal. They were big shots in school. Heck, they were big shots all over town."

"Glory days," I said softly.

"The photograph is Tom being presented with his ring. And there's another shot, a close-up of the ring itself."

She stumbled a bit over his name, I noticed. I took another drink of my coffee and waited while she collected her thoughts.

"And you're right, those were his glory days, his shining moment in the spotlight. Then it was gone. Like that." Roma snapped her fingers. "It was diapers and bottles and bills." There was an edge of hurt to her voice that sharpened her words.

I reached across the table and gave her arm a squeeze again.

"My mother told me once that he never took that ring off. He didn't wear a wedding ring but he always, always wore his class ring." Her eyes met mine and I could see the pain in them as well. "Those . . ." She cleared her throat. "It's him, Kathleen."

"I think you should call your mother and let her know

what's happened," I said. "Marcus is going to want to talk to her."

"You're right. I'd rather her hear about this first from me." She looked at her watch. "I need to get back to the clinic."

We both got to our feet. "Roma are you going to be all right?" I asked.

That got me a smile, albeit a small one. "I'm supposed to be asking you that," she said.

I smiled back at her. "I'm fine, just some scrapes and my dignity's a little banged up."

"Don't overdo it. Okay?" she said.

"I promise," I said. "You do the same. If you need anything, if you just want to talk, call me. Anytime. Please."

"Thanks," she said. "I'll probably be taking you up on that." She hesitated for a moment, and then wrapped her arms around me in a quick hug.

"Marcus will figure this out," I said.

She nodded. "It's funny. I'm always telling you what a great guy and a great police officer he is. I guess now I'm going to find out."

I walked her to the back door. She turned on the top step. "There were always two versions of my father—Tom—what my mother said about him and all the gossip whispered around town. I wanted to believe that he was a decent guy, that he was just young and scared and stupid. Now, I just want the truth, whatever it is."

I waited until I heard her SUV start in the driveway before I went back into the kitchen. Hercules and Owen were sitting in front of the refrigerator.

"You could have come out and said hello," I told them as I got myself a fresh cup of coffee. They stared at me, steady and unblinking.

I sat down again at the table. Owen's whiskers were twitching. He could smell the coffee cake. I broke off a bite and set it down on the floor for him. He scooted over and began sniffing it. "It's not hemlock, Socrates," I said. He ignored me.

I broke off another piece of cake for Hercules and held it out to him. Being a lot less finicky than his brother, he just ate the food from my fingers.

I took a long drink from my coffee and propped my leg on the chair again. "Marcus has an anthropologist out at Wisteria Hill, looking at the bones that were un-earthed when the hill collapsed," I said to the cats.

Owen had finally finished checking out his food. He didn't even look up at me. Hercules was sniffing around to see if there was any more, so all I got from him was an offhand glance.

I speared a piece of cake with my fork. That got both cats' attention. "This is mine," I said. They gave me their best pathetic kitty looks. They shouldn't have worked on me, but they usually did.

"That's enough," I said. "Roma is right, you know. I give you two way too much people food."

When I said Roma's name they exchanged glances. I took another sip from my mug.

Poor Roma. It really did look like the ring belonged to her biological father. And if it was his . . . it raised the question: what had happened to him and why had he ended up buried out at Wisteria Hill?

5

Later that afternoon I drove down to the library to check on things. The street and the parking lot were still flooded but the water barely came to the top of my boots—a good sign. Just a couple of days previously it had been knee-level. The building itself was still dry.

I spent the rest of the afternoon working at home, at the kitchen table with Owen and Hercules wandering in from time to time to see if I had anything good to mooch. The library board was planning a huge party to celebrate the building's one hundredth "birthday" in June. As part of that celebration I had a number of displays planned, showcasing some of the history of Mayville Heights, and the different groups that had used the library over the years. Everyone on staff was working on some kind of project. Maggie had volunteered her services, and several people had promised photos and other memorabilia. My neighbor, Rebecca, had offered to lend me some of her mother's old journals and drawings. Rebecca's mother, Ellen Montgomery, had been an expert on herbal remedies, and had taught more than one work-shop on the subject at the library.

I soaked for a long time in the bathtub after supper and went to bed before ten o'clock. I was stiff and sore when I woke up the next morning, so I was still drinking my first cup of coffee when the phone rang. I got to my feet and limped into the living room to answer it. It was Maggie.

"Hi," I said. "I thought you had an artists' meeting this morning."

"We're finished. It didn't take very long." she said. She blew out a breath. "I was going to go over to the studio and do some work, but we have orders from the store's Web site that I really need to get mailed. Plus there's one package that I need to get from Ruby plus another from Jaeger of all people and I have no idea where all the packing supplies are, and I just heard the forecast. It's going to rain again tonight."

I eased down onto the footstool. "What can I do?" I asked. She sounded frazzled so I decided not to tell her what had happened to me out at Wisteria Hill. At least not on the phone.

If she'd heard the details via the Mayville Heights grapevine, "What happened?" would have been the first question out of her mouth. I knew that the downtown business owners had had a meeting of their own and an-other with the town council. It had probably taken all of yesterday afternoon, which was probably why Maggie wasn't up on the latest scuttlebutt.

"Do you know any anti-rain dances? Or maybe where there might be a volcano that we could throw a sacrifice, say—I don't know—Jaeger Merrill into?"

"Sorry," I said. "But I do have a big roll of bubble wrap and lots of tape at the library."

"Does that mean the volcano thing is off the table?"

"I take it the meeting this morning didn't go well?"

"It's more that Jaeger's timing on this whole corporate sponsor thing just stinks," she said. "I'm tired. I need a shower. I've been moving boxes and shelving for days now. I've been slinging sandbags and bailing the basement and it's probably all been for nothing because it going to rain. Again." I could hear the frustration in her voice. "And all Jaeger wants to do is push his agenda to turn the co-op into the Acme Widget Artists' Co-op, like that's somehow going to make the rain and the four feet of water in the basement and his leaky window just disappear."

"So what happened?"

"We took a vote."

"And?"

"And I knew there were enough people who like things the way they are." She took a deep breath and slowly exhaled. I pictured her with her hand pressed against her chest, eyes closed. "But I don't think Jaeger's done. All I did was buy some time."

"Maybe a bit of time is all you need," I said. Owen wandered in and sat at my feet. "Once the rain stops, once things dry out a little, everyone's going to be in a better mood."

"I hope you're right," Maggie said. "With the store closed, Jaeger's guardian angel with a checkbook idea seems pretty good to at least a couple of people."

"It's what my dad calls selling smoke in a jar," I said, reaching down to lift Owen onto my lap. He rubbed the side of his face against the telephone receiver. "Owen sends his love."

"Give Fuzz Face a scratch for me," she said. Owen must have heard her voice because he started purring.

"Mags, why don't I bring the truck down? We can take whatever you need over to your studio and at least get those orders sent."

"Yeah, that's a good idea. If I can keep up with orders from the Web site, that's one less thing for Jaeger to complain about."

"I'll meet you at the shop in about fifteen minutes."

"Thanks," she said. I could hear the smile in her voice. "Hey, Kath, I forgot to ask you. Did you try the boots on Hercules? Did he like them?"

"He was . . . speechless . . . meowless," I said, cringing at how lame I sounded.

"I'm glad. I know he hates getting his feet wet."

"I'll see you shortly," I said.

I hung up. Owen looked at me, narrowing his golden eyes. "I didn't lie," I said. He continued to stare, not even a whisker twitching.

I bent my face close to his. "Remember what I said," I whispered. "We can always put those boots on you."

He blinked, gave his head a shake and jumped down to the floor. Then he disappeared.

Literally.

"I hate it when you do that," I muttered, heading back to the kitchen. I had no idea how he did it or why. It wasn't exactly the kind of thing I could ask Roma about when I took the cats for their shots. And Owen's little vanishing act had come in handy on occasion. Over time I'd just learned to accept it, kind of like Maggie's inexplicable love for the *Today* show's Matt Lauer. Some things defy rational explanation.

At least Hercules couldn't spontaneously become invisible. Nope. All he could do was walk through walls. Again, it sometimes had its uses.

I took a couple of aspirin. Then I pulled on my sweat-shirt and rubber boots and made my way out to the truck.

Maggie was waiting on the sidewalk in front of the co-op store. Her eyes widened when she saw me. "Good goddess, Kathleen, what happened?" she said.

I held up a hand. "I'm okay. It's not as bad as it looks." It probably would have been better if I hadn't held up the hand with the big bandage on it.

She shot a quick glance at the front of the truck. "Did you have an accident?"

"No." I shook my head. "The embankment behind the carriage house collapsed out from underneath me yesterday. The ground is completely saturated with water."

"Why didn't you call me?"

"Because I'm okay."

"You could have broken your neck."

"But I didn't," I said. "I've got some scrapes and some bruises and I twisted my ankle, but that's pretty much it. Marcus called the paramedics. Trust me, I wouldn't be walking around if he thought I wasn't okay. You know what he's like."

Maggie folded her arms across her chest. "I know what you're like too."

"Would it make you feel better to know Roma gave me the once over as well?"

"It would," she said. "If you were a horse, or a German shepherd."

"Roma has said I'm as stubborn as a mule," I said. "Does that count?"

Maggie didn't want to smile, but she couldn't help it.

"I swear I'm all right, Mags," I said. "But the thing is, when the hill collapsed there were some . . . remains that were unearthed."

"Remains?" she repeated. "You mean human remains?"

I nodded, shifting my weight more onto my right leg. If I stayed in one position too long the throbbing in my ankle got more insistent, as though it were doing the percussion intro to the *Hawaii Five-0* theme song.

Quickly, I filled in the rest of the story.

"This doesn't make any sense." Maggie shook her head. "How could a ring that belonged to Roma's father end up buried with some old bones out at Wisteria Hill?"

"They may not be old bones," I said.

"No." She made a dismissive gesture as though she were flicking away a bug. "You don't think that's Roma's biological father, do you?"

I shrugged. "I don't know. Maybe. Roma insists that he never took his ring off."

"Town gossip was always that Tom ran out on Roma and Pearl." Maggie gave me a wry smile. "I spent a lot of time with my grandmother when I was a kid. She knew everyone's secrets." She stuffed her hands in the front pocket of her hoodie. "How is Roma handling things?"

"She's in shock, I think," I said.

"The Wild are in the playoffs and Eddie's on the road."

Roma's relationship with Eddie Sweeney, star player for the Minnesota Wild hockey team, was only a couple of months old. I had no idea how much he knew about her family.

"I know," I said. "I'm going to call her later."

"I will, too," Maggie said.

"Okay, there's nothing we can do right now so let's get your stuff," I said, dipping my head in the direction of the building.

Maggie unlocked the front door and we headed up

the stairs. Halfway from the top she suddenly stopped. "Kath, if that is Roma's father, how did he end up buried out at Wisteria Hill?"

I slid my bandaged thumb along the wooden stair railing. "I don't know. Any of the explanations I can come up with aren't good."

Maggie unlocked the door at the top of the stairs. She looked around the tai chi studio space, piled with boxes and everything else from the store downstairs, and her shoulders sagged.

I reached over and gave her arm a squeeze. "The rain will stop, the basement will dry out, we'll stop growing penicillin in our boots and things will get back to normal."

"Isn't that what the neighbors said to Noah when he started working on the ark in his backyard?" she said.

I smiled at her and pointed to the far corner. "Look. There's the bubble wrap."

We threaded our way around stacks of boxes and disassembled shelving. Maggie eased past a metal cabinet and handed the long roll of green bubble wrap out to me.

"Maybe next time Jaeger starts up I'll just wrap him up in this stuff," she said with a sly grin. "Stifle his objections so to speak." It was good to see her sense of humor coming back.

We found the rest of the packing supplies and the boxes with the artwork that had to be mailed. For all that the space looked chaotic, I was sure that Maggie knew where everything was. Once we'd carried the boxes out to the truck, Maggie did a quick circuit of the empty store. There was no water coming in, no leaks from the ceiling or windows anywhere.

"Do you mind if I check the basement one more

time?" she asked. "I forgot to tell you: I talked to Larry Taylor. He may be able to get us a pump."

Larry Taylor was an electrician, son of Harrison Taylor, Senior, and younger brother to Harrison Taylor, Junior, or as Larry always explained it; Larry, Harry and Harry.

"Oh Mags, that would be great," I said as I followed her to the back storeroom. With all the rain, pumps were at a premium. Maggie had called anywhere she could think of within a fifty-mile radius of Mayville Heights and hadn't been able to find one.

"I know," she said. "Larry said it's an old gas-powered pump, but I don't care if it's the pump Noah used on the ark. The Taylors will be able to get it working and if we can just get the basement dried out, maybe—maybe I can get Jaeger out of my hair." She fished her keys from her pocket. "I know I shouldn't let him get to me."

"It's not you," I said. "Ruby doesn't like him either."

Maggie looked over her shoulder at me. "We were standing here this morning right after the meeting, because, of course, everyone had to see the basement for themselves, and there was a moment when he was on the stairs that I had the urge to push him in the water. I could actually hear the splash in my head." She turned the key, opened the door and felt for the light switch.

There was only one light fixture at the top of the stairs, but there was enough light to see Jaeger Merrill partly submerged, floating faceup in the water that half filled the basement.

He was dead.

6

Maggie made a strangled sound in the back of her throat and scrambled down the steps, her foot skidding on the fourth one from the top.

I grabbed the back of her sweatshirt. Momentum pulled us forward and for a moment I thought we were both going to end up in the cold, dirty water. I reached out blindly with my free hand for something to hold on to and found the top stair post, and Maggie somehow managed to keep her balance.

I sucked in a breath. "You okay?" I asked.

She sagged against the railing and nodded, her face pale. I let go of her shirt.

Jaeger's feet and the bottom half of his legs were on the stairs, the rest of his body was in the water. My left leg was trembling and I could feel my pulse thumping in the hollow just below my throat. I was pretty sure Jaeger was dead but somebody had to make sure. I sank onto the top step and eased my way down to the next one and then the next one.

"Careful," Maggie warned. Her voice was shaky. "It's wet." Her right hand hovered in the air, ready to grab me if I slipped.

Most of the top part of the body was underneath the water; just the eyes and nose were above the surface. Jaeger's head was turned slightly to the right, his eyes were half closed, and his mouth was partly open.

I reached forward, keeping most of my weight on my good leg and lifted his left arm, feeling for a pulse at the wrist. It was icy cold and his body already seemed to be stiffening. There was a cut on the fleshy part of his palm and the skin around it was puckered and wrinkled. Clearly he'd been in the water for a while.

There was no pulse.

"He's dead, isn't he?" Maggie asked.

I turned to look at her. "Yes," I said.

"Should we . . . pull him out of the water?"

I shook my head. "No. I think we've already touched more than we should have."

She held out her hand and I grabbed it, stood up, and climbed carefully back up the steps. Maggie glanced back over her shoulder at the body and then we went out into the storeroom. I wiped my hands on my jeans and pulled out my cell phone. She slumped against the wall.

"We should probably go wait by the front door," I said after I'd made the call.

Maggie nodded without saying anything and we made our way back to the front of the building. I leaned by the door, watching for the first police car. I was afraid if I sat down I wouldn't be able to get back up again. She dropped onto the steps, leaning her elbows on her knees.

"What was Jaeger doing in the basement?" she said after a minute.

"I don't know," I said. "Seeing how much water there was for some reason, maybe."

"That doesn't make any sense. We were just down there at the meeting a couple of hours ago."

"You said that you didn't think Jaeger was going to let this sponsor thing go. Maybe he was looking for—something, I don't know—something he could use to make his case."

Maggie shook her head. "In the basement? In four feet of water?"

A police cruiser came around the corner then, no siren, pulling in at an angle behind my truck. The paramedics were right behind them. I wasn't really surprised when Ric and his partner got out of the ambulance and grabbed their gear.

I'd seen the police officer that had responded around town and in the library a few times with his kids. He was tall, with dark hair cut close to his scalp and the kind of posture and assured bearing that suggested he was ex-military.

Heller? No. Keller. I couldn't remember his first name.

Maggie got to her feet and pulled out her keys. "I'll take them," she said as I opened the door. "You should sit down."

"Ms. Paulson?" the officer asked. I saw a flash of recognition in his eyes.

I nodded. "The uh . . . body's in the basement."

Maggie gestured toward the storage room. "This way."

Ric nodded hello, but didn't say anything.

"Please wait here, Ms. Paulson," Officer Keller said.

The three of them followed Maggie through the empty store to the back of the building.

Movement out on the street caught my eye. Another vehicle had pulled in at the curb. I realized it was Marcus's SUV just as he got out of the driver's side.

I met him on the sidewalk, trying hard not to limp. "Hi," I said. I was uncomfortably aware of the fact that this was the second body I'd found in as many days.

He gestured at the building. "Hi. What happened?"

"Maggie and I found one of the artists—Jaeger Merrill—in the . . . uh basement. It looks like he fell down the stairs and drowned."

He exhaled slowly. "That's two bodies in two days, Kathleen."

I shifted uneasily—and painfully—from one foot to the other. "I know," I said. "I'm sorry."

"I wasn't blaming you," he said, quietly.

I cleared my throat. "I thought you'd still be out at Wisteria Hill."

Marcus shook his head. "Dr. Abbott and her team are finishing setting up a grid to search the area where you found the remains. There isn't anything I can do out there right now." He gave me a quick, appraising once-over. "How are you?"

"Just a little stiff."

His eyes narrowed as though he didn't quite believe me but for once he didn't challenge what I'd said.

"Marcus, do you think those bones actually could be Roma's father's?" I asked.

His mouth moved and he pulled a hand back over his hair before answering. "This stays between you and me," he warned.

I nodded. I'd kind of expected to get his stay-out-of-my-case speech. Maybe we were finally moving beyond that.

"Dr. Abbott doesn't think it's a smallpox burial site. She doesn't believe the bones are that old."

I rubbed my fingers over my bandaged thumb, picking at a loose edge of adhesive tape with one nail. "So it's possible?"

He shrugged. "It's just way too soon to tell." He gestured toward the co-op building. "So why were you here?"

By now I was used to the way the conversation could abruptly change course with him. I looked back over my shoulder. "I brought the truck down to help Maggie take some things over to her studio at River Arts. She had some orders from the co-op Web site to pack."

"Okay."

"After we had the truck loaded, she wanted to check on the basement again. Larry Taylor may have a line on a pump, but there's more rain in the forecast and there's a lot of water down there already."

"Who found the body?"

I stuffed my hand in my pocket before I could pick off the tape that was holding the gauze in place on my thumb. "We both did. When I realized Jaeger was dead, Maggie and I went out into the storeroom and I called 911."

He nodded and looked around as though maybe there was something important here on the sidewalk. "The body was in the water?" he asked.

"Partly. His . . . feet were on the stairs. He . . . uh . . . was faceup, just the eyes and nose out of the water. There was water on the steps. They're old—just painted wood— without any safety treads so they get slippery."

He nodded again. Marcus never wrote anything down, that I'd ever seen, but he remembered everything. His blue eyes were focused on my face, but I could see that his mind was already working, shifting through my words. Just then Ric came out the door, stopping to pull off a pair of blue latex gloves. He looked at Marcus and gave a quick shake of his head.

"Do you want Maggie and me to stay around?" I asked.

Marcus patted his pocket. Looking for his phone, maybe? "No you can go. Where are you going to be?"

"At River Arts for a while," I said, pointing down the street. "Then the library. Then home."

"I suppose I'd be wasting my time to suggest you take it easy for the rest of the day?" he said, almost smiling at me.

"Pretty much," I agreed, and I did smile back at him.

Ric joined us. Like Marcus he looked me over quickly. "How's the ankle?" he asked.

"Better, thank you," I said.

"What about your thumb?"

I pulled my hand out of my pocket and held it up so he could see the bandage was still in place.

"Try to keep it dry," he said.

I nodded. Ric turned to Marcus and Marcus looked at me. I was about to be dismissed. "I'll talk to you both later," he said.

"All right," I said. Maggie was waiting by the door and I walked over to her.

"I thought you said Marcus was out at Wisteria Hill," she said.

"He was, but the anthropologist has more work to do

out there. It's going to be a while before they figure out . . ." I wasn't sure how to finish the sentence.

"Before they figure out if it's Roma's father."

I thought about what Marcus had said. "They need to be certain how old the remains are first." I was picking at the tape on my thumb again without realizing it. I jammed my hand back in my pocket.

Maggie looked past me at Marcus and Ric still talking on the sidewalk.

"Let's get out of here," I said.

"Is it okay?"

"Uh huh. Marcus said we could leave. He'll have some questions later."

"I should give him my keys," Maggie said, running a hand back over her short blond hair so she looked a little like a poodle that had just had its head scratched.

The men stopped talking as we came level with them. Maggie held out her key ring. "The silver-colored one is for the front door," she said. "The gold one is the basement lock. You might have to wiggle it a bit. It sticks sometimes."

Marcus took the keys from her. "Thanks," he said. "I'll talk to you both later." His eyes slid briefly over to my face. I wasn't sure whether I should say anything or not. Not getting the third degree from him felt a little strange. I settled for a slight nod and a tiny smile.

Maggie got in the passenger side of the truck. I checked the boxes we'd loaded into the back and then squeezed between the truck bumper and the side of the police car to get around to the driver's side.

Once I'd eased the truck out from between the police cruiser and Marcus's SUV and started down Main Street, I glanced over at Maggie. "Are you okay?" I asked.

She stared at me blankly for a moment. "What? Oh, yeah, I'm all right." I watched the road and waited for her to find the words she needed for what she wanted to say. "It just doesn't make sense," she said finally. "There was no reason for Jaeger to be down in the basement. None."

"It doesn't have to have been a reason that would make sense to anyone else," I said. "Just to him."

"How did he end up down there?"

"The stairs were wet. He didn't have boots on." I pictured Jaeger's feet on the steps. He'd been wearing leather shoes—black, with red laces and red stitching. Not gum rubbers or anything with a good tread.

She slumped back against the seat. "No, I don't mean how did he end up in the water. I mean how did he get into the basement in the first place. The door was locked. I remember locking it after the meeting, Ruby was standing beside me, and"—she gestured with one hand—"you saw me unlock it before we found ... before we found him."

"Does anyone else have keys to the building?" I asked, turning into the narrow alley that led to the art center's parking lot.

"Ruby. But I don't see her giving them to Jaeger."

Ruby's truck, the twin to mine, was parked in her assigned spot. "Neither do I," I said. "But she's here. We can ask her."

I backed up to the rear door of the building and got out to help Maggie unload, moving stiffly around the side of the truck. It showed how preoccupied Maggie was that she didn't notice.

We piled the boxes at the bottom of the stairs and I pulled the truck into Maggie's parking spot—she'd left her bug at home.

"I can carry this stuff up, Kath," Maggie said, setting the roll of green bubble wrap on top of the stack of boxes.

"I'm okay," I said. I was starting to sound like a broken record.

She frowned and looked pointedly at my left hand with the overbandaged thumb.

"I'll take the bubble wrap and the brown paper," I said. "Neither one of them is very heavy." I wanted to make sure Ruby actually was in her own studio. I didn't want to leave Maggie by herself to brood about Jaeger and I did need to get to the library at some point.

I grabbed the roll of paper and tucked it under one arm. After a moment Maggie surrendered the bubble wrap. She took the top two boxes from the stack and headed up the stairs.

Ruby must have heard us. As we came out of the stairwell she stepped out of her studio, holding a mug of what I guessed was herbal tea. It smelled like lemon and cranberries.

"Hi," she said. She was wearing a paint-spattered denim shirt with the sleeves cut off over her jeans and long-sleeved T-shirt. She looked from Maggie to me, and her smile faded. "Something's wrong," she said. "Don't tell me that there's more water coming in at the store?"

Maggie sighed and set down her boxes. "No, it's Jaeger," she said.

"Good dog!" Ruby said, shaking her head, which made her little pigtails bounce. "What did he do now?"

I held up a hand before she said something that in another minute she might be sorry had come out of her mouth. "Ruby. Jaeger's dead," I said quietly.

Her mouth fell open. "Dead? But . . . but how? We were all just at the meeting. Are you sure?"

"Yes," Maggie said.

I nodded.

For a moment Ruby didn't seem to know what to do with her free hand. Finally she wrapped her arm around her midsection, like she was hugging herself. "What . . . what happened?" she asked.

I glanced at Maggie. Her face was gray and there were tiny, pinched lines between her eyebrows.

"He, uh, fell down the basement stairs."

"You mean at the co-op?" Ruby shook her head slowly from side to side. "No. That's not possible. I saw him come up the steps and . . . and . . . I saw him leave." Her face had gone pale as well.

Maggie looked down at the floor for a moment. "He came back," she said, finally. "I don't know why. And I don't know what he was even doing down there." She bent and picked up the boxes again. "I'm going to put these in my studio." She moved past us, fished out her key to unlock the door and then went inside.

Ruby was still shell-shocked. She took a couple of steps toward me. "Kathleen, did Maggie find . . ." She didn't finish the sentence, but I knew what she was asking.

"We, uh, we both did."

Her face softened. "I'm sorry," she said. Then finally she noticed my scraped forehead. "What happened to you? Are you okay? You didn't fall down the stairs too, did you?"

I shook my head. "No. I slipped out at Wisteria Hill. I'm all right."

"Good." She looked over at Maggie's open studio door, and then shifted her attention back to me. "None of this makes any sense. What was Jaeger doing in the co-op basement? How did he get down there, anyway? I saw Maggie lock the door and put the keys in her pocket."

She had the same questions Maggie had been asking and I still didn't have any answers. I shrugged. "I don't know. The police are going to have to figure all of that out."

Ruby made a face, her mouth twisting to one side. "I wish I could remember where I know Jaeger from. I have the feeling it's important."

I couldn't see how Ruby figuring out where she may have seen Jaeger Merrill before was going to turn out to be important, especially now that he was dead.

"I need to put these in Maggie's studio," I said, picking up the brown paper and bubble wrap again.

Ruby had been staring off into space, but she looked at me when I spoke. "Yeah, okay," she said. "There's something I need to check out on the computer, anyway." She indicated her own open studio door. "Tell Maggie I'm here if she needs anything."

"I will," I said.

Mags had put the two boxes on her big worktable in the center of the room. She was just taking the last figure from a carved, wooden chess set out of the smaller of the two cartons.

I set the paper and bubble wrap on the end of the table.

"Thanks," she said. "I'll just go get the other couple of boxes."

While Maggie went downstairs I put some water in her kettle and plugged it in. I waffled for a moment between the box of peppermint tea bags and the canister of dark chocolate cocoa mix. The chocolate won.

"Are you making tea?" Maggie asked when she came back in with the last three cartons.

"I was going to make hot chocolate," I said. "But I can make tea if that's what you'd like."

She set the boxes on the table and rolled her head slowly from one side to the other. "No. I want chocolate," she said. "Lots and lots of chocolate." She stopped in mid-neck roll. "Look in there, on the bottom at the back." She pointed to the old pie safe where she kept the mugs and the tea and the electric kettle. "I think I have some marshmallows."

The marshmallows were in a little snap-top plastic container. I could smell vanilla when I popped the lid. "Hey, did you buy these at the market?" I asked.

She had one arm behind her head, stretching, pulling down gently with her other hand. Maggie was very flexible. "Dina made them," she said.

"Dina?" I said. The water was boiling. I filled both cups. "The Jam Lady?"

"Uh huh."

I'd been a little homesick and a lot heartsick when I'd arrived in Mayville Heights just over a year ago. I'd eaten a lot of toast smothered in The Jam Lady's strawberry rhubarb preserves in those first few lonely weeks. And a fair number of brownies too. If it weren't for all the walking I'd have ended up looking like the Pillsbury Doughboy. And I probably wouldn't have Hercules and Owen either.

Maggie emptied the boxes and when the water boiled

I made the hot chocolate and added marshmallows to both cups. I gave one to Maggie. She took a long sip and then smiled at me over the mug. "Ummm, that's good. Thank you."

I took a drink from my own cup. The mix of dark chocolate and vanilla tasted as good as it smelled.

Maggie pulled her hand over her hair again. "I can't believe Jaeger's dead," she said, her expression troubled.

"It's not your fault."

"I know," she said, but there was something in her voice that told me she wasn't completely convinced. I looked at her, without saying anything else, until she lifted her head and met my gaze.

"What?"

"Jaeger's not dead because he wanted to bring in a corporate sponsor for the co-op and you didn't. It's not your fault he was in the basement. It's not your fault the stairs were wet."

"I know. I do. I just keep thinking if we hadn't had the meeting today maybe he wouldn't have gone back down to the basement."

"Then you would have had it another day. And Jaeger could still have been down in the basement this morning. Or this afternoon, or next Tuesday."

I leaned against the worktable to take the weight off my ankle "It was an accident, Mags. An awful, stupid accident."

"Why are you always so sensible and logical?" she said, the beginnings of a smile pulling at her mouth.

I took another drink of my hot chocolate. "Probably because my mom and dad are masters of drama." I set the cup down. "Right before I came here my father broke his ankle. Can you guess what he was doing?"

"Probably not taking out the garbage."

I shook my head. "Uh uh. He was doing the balcony scene from Romeo and Juliet. My father. On the fire escape. In January." I sighed. "No wonder I'm sensible. It was the only form of teenage rebellion left."

Maggie laughed. She'd never met my family in person, but she'd heard a lot of my stories about them.

"Seriously Mags, I know you feel bad. But it's been raining for a week. You're tired. You're wet and if you're like me, there are probably some funky mold spores growing in your boots." I tucked a stray piece of hair behind my ear, wincing when I inadvertently touched the edge of my scraped forehead again.

"I'm sorry about Jaeger," I said. "I really am. But it's not your fault." I hugged her and I could feel some of the tension seep out of her body.

"I should get these parcels packed," Maggie said, breaking out of the hug.

"And I need to check on things at the library." I grabbed my cup and drained the last of the cocoa. "You're still coming for supper?"

"Absolutely. I wouldn't want to disappoint Owen."

"You'll be the highlight of his little kitty day," I said. "Call me if anything changes."

Maggie was already unrolling the bubble wrap. She waved over her shoulder in my direction.

I stopped in the hall to pull out my keys and glanced through the open door to Ruby's studio. She was on the floor, underneath one of the tall windows, her back to the door, chin propped on one hand, surrounded by books, engrossed in whatever she was reading.

It had seemed pretty obvious when Ruby told me she had something to check on her computer that what she was planning to do was stick Jaeger Merrill's name in a search engine. I was happy to see that she'd given up on trying to figure out where she'd first seen him. It didn't matter now, anyway.

Of course I was wrong.

On both counts.

7

I ended up having to park the truck on a side street near the library. Even though that whole block of Old Main Street was on higher ground than where the artists' co-op was located, because of the slope of the land and drainage problems, the section of street in front of the library was still covered with water, blocked off by three town sawhorses and a large yellow caution sign, but at least the level had dropped a couple more inches.

Inside the library, the pump Oren Kenyon had installed the previous fall seemed to be easily handling what little water had seeped into the basement. I went down the steps only as far as I needed to see that the cellar was staying dry. And I held on to the railing with both hands.

The main floor of the building was eerily quiet without Abigail leading story time and Susan shelving books, her dark hair up on her head with a couple of pencils or a crochet hook stuck in the topknot, steering readers to the latest science fiction as well as her favorite classics from Ray Bradbury and John Wyndham.

I emptied the book drop, checked in the returned books and reshelved everything. Then I called Lita, Everett Henderson's assistant.

Everett had funded the library renovations—his gift to Mayville Heights—and he was president of the library board. I knew Lita would be able to find out when the building could reopen a lot faster than I would. It seemed as though she knew every single person in Mayville Heights, plus she was related in one way or another to most of the town as well.

"It's going to be another day at least, Kathleen," Lita said. "Probably two. Right now it all depends on how much rain we get. I'll call you tomorrow and let you know."

I thanked her and hung up. Everything in Mayville depended on how much rain we got. I rubbed my left wrist. It was a bit sore from falling down the embankment, but it didn't have the bone-deep ache that usually meant rain.

I turned on the computer at the front desk and signed in to the system. I'd been keeping up with e-mail from my laptop at home so there wasn't much to deal with. Then, because I was curious, I pulled up the archives for the *Mayville Heights Chronicle* and read the article about the disappearance of Roma's father.

It wasn't much of a story. Thomas Karlsson's car had been found abandoned and out of gas. There was no sign of foul play. There were more lines in the brief article about his glory days playing high school baseball than there were about him going missing.

Since there wasn't really anything else I needed to do at the library, I decided to walk over to Eric's Place and get some coffee and something to eat. Breakfast had been a long time ago.

There was a black, extended cab pickup truck parked parallel to the yellow sawhorses out on the street when I came down the library steps. As I got closer to it the driver's window rolled down and Burtis Chapman stuck his head out.

"Morning," he said. "I'm lookin' for Harry Junior. Don't suppose he's at the library?"

I shook my head. "I'm sorry. I haven't seen him."

Burtis was a big block of a man—with wide shoulders and a barrel chest. I had no idea how old he was; his face was lined and weathered and the few tufts of hair sticking out from under his Minnesota Twins cap were snow white. He was whip smart and extremely well read I knew. But he wasn't above playing the hick from rural Minnesota if it suited his purposes.

"What happened to your head?" he asked, tipping his at mine.

Without thinking I put my hand up to my forehead and winced. When was I going to learn to not do that? "I was out at Wisteria Hill," I said. "The bank let go underneath me."

"Out behind the old carriage house, I'll bet."

I nodded. "How did you know?"

He gave a snort of laughter. "Spent some time in those woods in my younger days. Whole area's swampy. Never did drain well. You're lucky you didn't break your neck."

He reached over and started the truck. "Well, if you see Harry, tell him I'm lookin' for him."

"I will," I said.

"You be careful out at the old house," he said. "Real easy to get hurt in those woods." He put the truck in gear, backed up and pulled away. I headed for the café.

I wondered why Burtis was looking for Harry Junior. Burtis was the kind of person who was always looking to make a deal of some kind. I'd heard hints that at one time he'd worked for Idris Blackthorne, Ruby's grandfather who'd been the area bootlegger. He had at least half a dozen little businesses, everything from selling hardwood to renting commercial tents for weddings and parties. In another week or two Burtis would be selling fiddleheads out of the back of that truck of his.

Eric was in his usual spot behind the counter at the restaurant. The place was almost empty. Having half of the downtown blocked off couldn't be good for his business. He picked up the coffeepot when he saw me come in and reached for a cup. I slid onto a stool and he set the mug in front of me.

"You read my mind, Eric," I said. "Thank you." I added cream and sugar. The coffee was hot and strong, just the way I liked it.

Eric studied my scabby forehead. "Have you been doing more rodent tossing or have you moved on to some other sport?"

I gave him a wry smile. "I was out at Wisteria Hill yesterday and the slope up behind the carriage house let go. The ground's just so wet the water's not draining away."

"You're okay?"

I nodded. "I am, thanks. I'm probably going to be one giant bruise for a while, though."

"How about a brownie?" Eric asked. "Chocolate has medicinal qualities."

I leaned my elbows on the counter. "Tempting. But I was thinking about a breakfast sandwich." I looked at my watch. "Even though it's not exactly breakfast time."

He held up a finger. "Are you feeling adventurous?"

I smiled sweetly at him. "No."

He gave me a bemused look and headed for the kitchen.

"What if I don't like whatever you're thinking about making?" I teased. There wasn't much chance of that happening. Eric was an excellent cook.

"You will," he said as the door swung shut behind him.

And I did. By the time I'd finished the sandwich Eric had made for me—fried tomatoes and bacon on toasted homemade sourdough bread—and had another cup of coffee I felt better. I wasn't as damp, as sore, or as tired.

"That was good," I said, pushing my plate away.

"I'm thinking of adding it to the menu," Eric said. "Susan gave it a thumbs-up. Now you."

Eric liked to tinker with the menu at the café. His wife, Susan, was always his first tester, and because she worked at the library, sometimes the rest of us were as well.

"Would you tell Susan it looks like at least another day before we reopen?" I said.

He nodded. "I will. The boys aren't happy about the library being closed. So Abigail promised to come over and give them their own private story time."

That sounded like Abigail, and it reminded me that I needed to call the rest of the staff and let them know we were going to be closed a little longer.

I paid Eric for my sandwich and coffee, getting a cup to go for myself and after a moment's hesitation, one for Marcus.

I figured there would be an officer at the door to the co-op, but as I got closer I saw Marcus himself, on the sidewalk beside his vehicle.

I held up the coffee and he smiled. "This is getting to be a habit," he said, as I reached the SUV and handed him the paper cup.

When conductor Gregor Easton had been killed, Marcus and I had had more than one cup of coffee as he tried to figure out if I was involved in the conductor's death. And we'd shared a fair number of thermoses of coffee and hot chocolate out at Wisteria Hill while feeding the cats.

He took a long drink. "A good habit, by the way. Thank you."

"You're welcome," I said.

"You didn't come to check up on things, did you?" he asked, gesturing at the building.

"Me?" I said, giving him a look that was all wide-eyed innocence. I took a sip from my own coffee.

He let that pass with nothing more than slightly raised eyebrows. "Since you're here, you could answer a few questions for me," he said.

"All right." I shifted from one foot to the other.

Marcus's eyes flicked down to my ankle. "Did you call your doctor yet?" he asked.

"Not yet. I will," I said.

He exhaled a lot more loudly than he needed to. It sounded like a low growl in the back of his throat. Then he said, "Tell me about finding the body."

I didn't mind the change of subject. I closed my eyes for a moment and pulled out the image of the basement stairs and Jaeger's partly submerged body. "Maggie unlocked the door. She saw him first. She started down the steps. They were wet. She slipped partway down. I grabbed her."

"Then what?"

I explained about making my way down the stairs, feeling for a pulse, leaving the basement and calling 911.

"What time did you get down here?" Marcus asked.

I glanced at my watch and calculated backward in my head. "After ten thirty," I said. "Probably more like ten forty-five."

He nodded, sipping his coffee. Out of the corner of my eye I could see people moving around inside the co-op store. I couldn't tell what they were doing.

"When did you pick up Maggie?" he said.

I gave my head a little shake and focused all my attention on Marcus again. "I didn't. The co-op members had a meeting first thing this morning. She was already here."

"By herself."

He said the words so casually, looking at his cup instead of at me, but I saw the slight tightening of his jaw.

"I don't know," I said, keeping my own voice equally casual. "You should ask her."

"Did you see anyone when you got here?"

I took a long drink before I answered. I could feel a lump of annoyance pressing up in my chest and I couldn't seem to swallow it down. "No I didn't. The only person I saw was Maggie." I pointed to a spot on the sidewalk a few feet away. "She was standing right there."

"She wasn't inside?"

"No." Why did I feel that I'd said the wrong thing? I studied his face. There were no clues in his blue eyes to what he was thinking.

He drank the last of his coffee and set the empty takeout cup on the hood of the car, his hand over the top. "Okay. Maggie was waiting out here. You went inside. Then what?"

"Actually, we stood here talking for a minute," I said. "Maggie noticed my head." I lifted my hand toward my forehead, but didn't actually touch it this time. "She wanted to know what happened. I told her. Then we went inside."

I held up a finger before he had a chance to say anything. "We went upstairs. We loaded some boxes in my truck. Maggie wanted to check the basement. We found Jaeger. I called 911. That's it."

"Did she say why she wanted to check the basement?" Marcus asked, frowning.

"She just wanted to take one more look before we went down to River Arts." I couldn't keep the defensive tone out of my voice. It was as though Marcus and I were a couple of sumo wrestlers, circling, each waiting for the other to make a move. I reminded myself that he was just doing his job. He knew Maggie. He knew she wouldn't push Jaeger or anyone else down those basement steps.

Still, I felt I had to say it out loud. "Maggie didn't push Jaeger Merrill down the stairs." I put a hand to my mouth to stifle a yawn. I was tired. My head ached. My jeans were damp from being down in the co-op basement, and what I really needed was to go soak in the bathtub for a while.

"I didn't say she did. I didn't say anyone did. I just want to know what happened, Kathleen," he said. "That's all." He looked over at the building, then back at me.

Just the facts. It frustrated me that when he was working on a case, all Marcus seemed to be concerned about were the facts, not what he knew about the people involved. On the other hand, I knew it frustrated him that whatever was going on, I was going to filter the facts through what I knew about the people.

"Is there anything else you need to know?" I asked. I wanted to go home, spend some time with Hercules and Owen and soak up some kitty sympathy.

Marcus shook his head. "That's it for now." He studied my face for a moment. Then he reached over and very gently tucked a loose tendril of hair behind my ear.

All at once I didn't see the tall, intimidating police detective with the serious, almost stern expression standing in front of me. I saw the man in the waiting room at Roma's veterinary clinic just last week, sneaking little fish-shaped crackers to Desmond, the clinic cat, when he thought no one was looking.

The moment stretched between us just a shade too long.

He looked away first, taking a step backward. "You uh, should go home and get off your feet."

I nodded, and shifted my take-out cup from one hand to the other. "I am. Call me if . . . if there's anything else." I turned and started back up the street.

"Kathleen," Marcus called out as I reached the corner. I stopped and after a moment's hesitation, turned around.

He held up the empty take-out cup. "Thank you for the coffee," he said.

"You're welcome," I said. I turned and just as I was about to step off the curb to cross the street my cell phone rang. It was Ruby.

"Hey, Kathleen," she said. "Where are you?" She was talking faster than usual.

"I'm walking back to the library. Why?"

"Are you close enough to come down to River Arts?"

"Why?" I asked. "Is something wrong? Is Maggie okay?"

"Yeah. She's fine," Ruby said. "She went home to change. It's just" — she paused for a moment — "I figured out where I'd seen Jaeger." There was an edge of excitement to her voice. "I know who he is, Kathleen. Or I guess I should say, who he really was."

8

"What do you mean, who he really was?" I said.

"It's too complicated to explain over the phone," Ruby said. She exhaled slowly. "There's something I need you to see—I need somebody to see."

I looked back over my shoulder. Marcus must have gone inside the building.

I could turn around, find him and tell him Ruby had maybe found out something about Jaeger Merrill that might be useful.

Or might not.

Then he'd tell me to stay out of his case—even though it didn't look as though there even was a case, I'd get annoyed and go meet Ruby.

"I'll be there in a few minutes," I said. I was going to end up over at the studio building anyway. It just seemed like a good idea to eliminate a couple of steps.

I decided it made more sense to get the truck and drive over to River Arts so I could just go home afterward. Ruby was watching for me at the back door.

"You're not going to believe this," she said, as I followed her up to the top floor.

"Believe what?" I asked. Somehow the stairs had gotten steeper since the last time I'd climbed them a couple of hours ago.

She patted the top of her head with one hand. "You just have to see this. Trust me."

There was a hardcover book open on one of Ruby's worktables in her studio. She pointed to a black-and-white photograph of several men that took up half of the left page. "Recognize the guy in the middle?"

The hair was shorter and darker, the nose was a little longer, he was heavier, and he was several years younger, but it was Jaeger Merrill. I think I would have recognized him even if I hadn't been expecting to see the man. "That's Jaeger," I said.

Ruby gave me a knowing smile. "Not exactly," she said.

"You're not going to tell me he has an identical evil twin, are you?"

"Nope."

I looked at the caption underneath the picture. According to that, Christian Ellis was the man in the center of the photograph. "He changed his name," I said slowly, turning the book over so I could see the cover: *Divine Provenance: The Greatest Art Fraud in U.S. History*.

"He did more than that," Ruby said. "He changed the way he looked—different nose, different hair. I'm pretty sure different eye color. He lied about his age. He lied about his background. As far as I can tell, nothing about Jaeger Merrill was real."

I flipped the book so I could look at the picture again.

"So Jaeger—when he was still Christian Ellis—was involved in some kind of art fraud?"

She nodded. "Religious icons. Fakes. Good ones. I looked him up online. He created some elaborate forgeries that fooled some of the best art experts in the country. Heck, in the world. You could call him a con artist." She gestured at the book. "Funny thing is, I got that at the library book sale last summer. I'd looked through it, but I never had a chance to actually read the whole thing."

"I assume he got caught," I said.

"He spent eighteen months in jail."

"So he came here for a new start with a new name." I set the book back on the table.

Ruby slid the twisted cord bracelets she was wearing up and down her arm. "The thing is, I'm not sure that's what it was."

"I'm not following you," I said.

"I get that when someone has been in jail, they want a brand-new start," she said. "But becoming someone else?" She held out both hands. "It's so melodramatic."

I glanced at the photograph again. "Maybe he was embarrassed. Or ashamed."

She put her hands on her hips and cocked her head to one side. "Oh c'mon. Did Jaeger Merrill strike you as the kind of person who embarrassed easily? Or at all for that matter?"

"No," I said.

"So why did he go to so much trouble to create a new identity for himself, then?"

"You think he was up to something—another scam maybe."

Ruby stared out the tall windows for a moment, and

then her gaze came back to me. "I think it's possible." She gave a small shrug. "Maybe I've gotten more suspicious after everything that's happened over the past few months."

Ruby had been arrested back in February for the hit-and-run death of her junior high principal and mentor, Agatha Shepherd. If she was a little less trusting now, it was understandable, given everything she'd gone through before Agatha's real killer was found. That didn't mean her instincts weren't good.

My hair was coming loose from its ponytail. I pushed the strands back behind my ear. "But even if you're right, even if he was working on another scam, does it matter? He's dead."

She was silent for a moment, and then she nodded slowly. "I guess you're right. There's no scam without the scam artist." She looked down at the photo again. "There's one more thing, Kathleen, that I didn't tell you."

"What?"

"Jaeger," she shook her head, "I'm sorry, I just can't think of him as Christian Ellis—ended up being defended by a lawyer who was just starting out. You know the clichés. Just out of law school, fighting for truth and justice, la, la, la."

"The lawyer is someone you know," I said, slowly.

"Someone you know too. Peter Lundgren. Look at the picture on the next page."

She was right. It was a younger version of Peter Lundgren in an ugly, ill-fitting suit. I made a face. Peter was settling Agatha Shepherd's estate. He was helping Ruby with the money she'd been left in Agatha's will. "I guess that explains how Jaeger ended up here."

Ruby picked up the book and closed it, but I noticed

she kept a finger between the pages to mark where the photos were. "I don't get why Peter kept Jaeger's secret."

"Peter was his lawyer. And maybe there was no secret. Maybe Jaeger changed his name legally. Maybe he was a huge Rolling Stones fan. Maybe Mick Jagger was his idol. Maybe ... maybe he had plastic surgery on his nose because he snored too loud and kept waking himself up at night. And he dyed his hair because he wanted to see if blonds really do have more fun."

Ruby laughed.

I smiled back at her. "Or you could just ask Peter."

She nodded, still clutching the book with her finger between the pages. "I think I will."

She walked me down the stairs to the back door. Ray Nightingale, one of the other artists who had a studio in the building, was just coming in. He gave me a quick nod and turned to Ruby. "The police are at the co-op. Do you have any idea what's going on?"

Ruby pulled a hand over her neck. "There was ... there was an accident." She exhaled slowly. "Jaeger fell ... on the basement stairs."

"What the heck was he doing in the basement?" Ray asked. He was about average height, with a smooth shaven head and a fairly laid-back attitude from what I'd seen.

She shrugged and twisted her bracelets around her arm. "I don't know."

He shook his head, blew out a breath. "But he's okay, right?"

Ruby looked down at the floor. "No. He's dead," she said.

Ray stared at us, openmouthed. "What do you mean, he's dead? You said he fell on the stairs."

"He drowned," I said, quietly. "I think he might have hit his head."

Ray swore and looked away. "That's awful. I didn't really know him, but still." He swiped a hand over his mouth. "Does Maggie know?" he asked after a moment.

"Yes," I said. I wondered which side Ray had been on over the corporate sponsor issue. He did these large, intricate, acrylic ink drawings that to me seemed like a cross between an elaborate mosaic and *Where's Waldo*. In each one, somewhere, there was a tiny rubber duck, no more than an inch or so long, wearing a pair of sunglasses and a fedora. Half the fun of the artwork was looking for the duck, whose name was Bo.

Like the rest of the artists who were part of the co-op, Ray did other things to help pay the bills. He'd designed a poster for the jazz festival in Minneapolis and a postcard for the James Hotel. And he collected and sold vintage ink bottles. He even used some of the old ink in his art. I'd seen him completely engrossed by the contents of an old rolltop desk at an estate sale I'd gone to a couple of weeks previously with Abigail.

Along with working at the library, Abigail also wrote children's books and she'd wanted my opinion of several of the old picture books in the sale. She'd gotten interested in collecting books after she'd found a box of old, and it turned out valuable, books at the library the previous summer.

Ray slid a hand back and forth over his smooth scalp. "So that means the co-op is pretty much off limits, I'm guessing," he said. Then he made a face. "I'm sorry. That was insensitive."

I held up a hand. "It's okay. And you're right, the co-op is off limits for the moment."

"What about Jaeger's stuff?"

Ruby looked at me. "I don't know. Kathleen?"

"I can't see any reason why the police would need to go through his studio," I said. "I don't think this building is going to be off limits."

"That's good," Ray said. "All this rain has put me behind." He looked at Ruby. "If I can help with anything, let me know." He moved past us and went up the stairs.

"Same here, Ruby," I said. "If there's anything I can do, call me."

"I will," she said.

I cut through the parking lot, got in the truck and started up the hill.

So Jaeger Merrill was really Christian Ellis, a convicted forger. He'd gone to a lot of trouble to create a new life for himself. Was Ruby right? Had he been working on another scam?

9

Hercules was sitting by the back steps when I came around the corner of the house, one paw on a black feather, with an iridescent purple sheen to it. He looked up at me and if a cat could look self-satisfied—and this cat certainly seemed to be able to—he did.

"Score one for the cat," I said, bending down to pick him up. He nuzzled the side of my face and then looked down at the feather. Hercules was having a little war with, as far as I could tell, one lone grackle. Up until now the grackle had been winning.

"Have you thought about what you'd do with that bird if you actually caught it?" I asked as I unlocked the back door.

Herc tipped his head to one side and seemed to be considering my question. Then he licked his lips.

"Oh sure, you're going to eat it," I said, setting him down on the kitchen floor. "You? Mr. I-Don't-Eat-On-Sale-Cat-Food?"

That got me a snippy meow.

I folded my arms and looked down at him. "Do I have to remind you about the caterpillar?"

Hercules immediately turned away and hung his head. I got the feeling he would have blushed if he could have. He may not have understood all of what I'd said, but he knew the word, caterpillar.

Of the two cats, Owen was the hunter, not Hercules. It's hard to stalk anything when you don't like getting your paws wet. One day, early last summer, Owen had caught a fuzzy black-and-yellow caterpillar out in the backyard—mostly because it crawled over a cracker he was sniffing at the time.

Hercules, who had already finished his own food because he doesn't have to inspect every bite first, poked his head in to take a look at his brother's prey. First he just sniffed the caterpillar. Then he rolled it over with a swipe of his paw.

Owen tended to see himself like a lion prowling a dusty savannah on an African plain. Which meant the caterpillar was the equivalent of a downed wildebeest—not for sharing.

Paws were raised. Yowls were exchanged. Before I could step in, Hercules swallowed the caterpillar.

And promptly hacked it up again. Because, number one: it was like eating a piece of shag carpeting. Nothing that fuzzy is ever going to taste good. And number two: The caterpillar wasn't exactly dead.

"You think having caterpillar fluff stuck in your teeth is bad," I warned Herc, "try picking feathers out."

I headed upstairs, switched my damp jeans for a pair of yoga pants, and then carefully cut the grubby gauze off my thumb, replacing it with a couple of big adhesive bandages. Then I warmed up the last of the apple pudding cake. Between spoonfuls I told the cats about Maggie and me discovering Jaeger's body, and Ruby discovering his real identity. Owen's head jerked up when he heard Maggie's name and he almost banged it on the bottom of a kitchen chair.

"She's fine," I told him. "She's coming for supper. You'll see her tonight." He went back to nosing around for crumbs I hadn't vacuumed up yet.

Hercules, on the other hand, was giving me his undivided attention, although that might have been because he was hoping to score a bite or two of apple from my bowl.

"Here you big mooch," I said, reaching for the bag of sardine kitty crackers on the counter and giving him a couple. I handed a couple down to Owen too.

I was just putting my dishes in the sink when the phone rang. I hobbled into the living room to get it. My ankle still ached, but just putting my foot up while I was at the table had helped. It was Rebecca, my backyard neighbor.

"Hello Kathleen," she said. "I was wondering if this would be a good time to bring over that box of my mother's things you wanted to look at for the display at the library centennial?"

"Yes, it would," I said. "Are you sure you can carry the box? I don't mind coming to get it."

She laughed. "Thank you, but it's not that big and—"

"—you're not that old," I finished.

"Oh, I am that old," she said. "It's just not that far across the lawn."

"I'll see you in a few minutes, then," I said.

When I went back into the kitchen, Owen and Hercules were sitting by the back door. Clearly they were waiting for Rebecca. I had no idea how they knew she was on her way. It was just another one of their "abilities" that I couldn't explain, and next to walking through walls and becoming invisible, it was pretty mundane.

The coffee was brewing and I had a plate of date squares on the table when Rebecca tapped on the porch door. I figured after the morning I'd had I was entitled to having dessert twice. I let her in and took the cardboard file box she was carrying.

She frowned at my face. "Oh dear, that looks sore," she said. I noticed that she didn't ask what had happened.

"It looks worse than it feels," I said. "Who told on me? Roma?"

A pink flush spread across her cheeks. "I wouldn't exactly call it telling on you," she said. "And no, it wasn't Roma. It was Marcus Gordon."

"So you decided you'd bring this over"—I patted the top of the box—"and check on me."

"I was planning on coming over anyway," she said. "When Marcus told me what happened yesterday, it just seemed like perfect timing." She looked me up and down. "How's your ankle?"

"My ankle's just fine. And Marcus Gordon has a big mouth."

I glanced down at her boots. They were black with little red ladybugs all over them. "Oh, I like your boots," I said.

Rebecca stuck out one foot and rolled it from one side to the other. "Thank you. Ami gave them to me."

Ami was Everett Henderson's granddaughter. She adored Rebecca and Rebecca was crazy about her.

Rebecca put her foot back on the floor and stepped out of the ladybug boots.

"How about a date square?" I asked as we headed into the kitchen.

"Oh that does sound good," she said, patting her silver-gray hair. "And don't think I didn't notice how you changed the subject away from what happened to you." She reached into her pocket and handed me a small, brown paper bag. "Spread this on your ankle before bed. It'll help."

"Thank you," I said. I gave her a one-armed hug.

She caught sight of Owen and Hercules then, and moved across the floor to bend over and talk to the cats. For the moment at least, I was spared from having to explain for what felt like the umpteenth time that I was fine. The cats were listening intently as Rebecca spoke softly to them and I could hear the low rumble of both of them purring like twin diesel engines.

The boys really liked Rebecca. Everyone did. Everett was as smitten with her as he'd been when they'd fallen in love as teenagers. Maggie, whom she was teaching about herbal medicine, hung on her every word. Harry Taylor, Senior, shamelessly flirted with her even though he was twenty years her senior.

There was something about Rebecca, maybe it was her innate kindness, that made people care about her, that made them—me included—just a little protective, at which for the most part Rebecca just smiled. On the other hand, underneath that gray hair and angelic smile there was a steel-hard stubborn streak.

"Would you like a cup of coffee?" I asked as she came over to the table.

"Thank you, I think I would," she said, hanging her bag on the back of the chair.

I poured a cup for both of us and then took the chair opposite her, so the box was on the seat between us.

Rebecca picked up her mug and smiled at me. "Did you make a doctor's appointment?" she asked. "Just to get checked over."

"I'm going to," I said, feeling my face flush.

"Why don't you go ahead and do it right now?" she said. She smiled down at her two furry cohorts sitting beside her chair. "Hercules and Owen will keep me company."

I hesitated.

"I've found it's best not to put things off." She still had the sweet smile on her face.

I knew when I was beaten. And I felt a kind of grudging respect for Marcus, who had come up with a pretty good way to do an end run around my dislike of doctors and hospitals.

"Excuse me," I said.

The doctor's office had a cancellation for Monday morning. I took it. When I went back into the kitchen, Rebecca was sneaking some of her date square to Hercules. Owen was already sniffing his bite on the floor.

I sat down, giving Rebecca's box a quick, curious glance.

"Go ahead and take a look inside," she urged.

I wiped my hands on a napkin and pulled off the lid. Inside were books and papers that had belonged to Rebecca's mother, Ellen Montgomery. She'd acted as unofficial nurse and midwife in Mayville Heights in her day, using herbal remedies to treat kids, adults, and from what I'd heard the occasional horse, cow and house cat.

I lifted out a thick, handmade book bound with neat, Coptic stitches.

"That's her plant book," Rebecca said.

I opened the cover and for a moment I was speechless. The first page was a beautiful watercolor of a dandelion plant. There were notes in black ink and fine block printing along the bottom and up both sides of the page.

I turned the page to an equally beautiful image of a chamomile plant. I looked up at Rebecca. "These are gorgeous," I said.

She nodded. "My mother was very artistic. There are paintings and sketches of every plant she used in that book."

I had no idea how I was going to make the book part of a display in the library, but I definitely wanted to use it. I went through the rest of the things in the box—more drawings, a book of herbal remedies with meticulously detailed instructions for making various salves, infusions and poultices, a stack of black-and-white photos tied with a faded blue ribbon and several composition books that I realized had been Ellen's journals.

"Are you sure about these?" I asked Rebecca, holding up one of the black-covered, narrow ruled notebooks.

She nodded. "Yes, assuming you find anything that's useful in them." She took one of the small volumes from me and slowly flipped through the pages. "My mother kept a journal all her life. They were always 'open books' so to speak and so was her life." She looked up, a devilish twinkle in her eye. "I don't think you'll find any secrets in these books, sad to say."

"You sound disappointed," I said with a smile, as I put everything back in the box.

"Well, Kathleen, there was a time when I entertained the fantasy that I'd been left by pirates and that my real parents would someday come back for me."

"Pirates?"

"Oh yes." She picked up her cup again and leaned back in her chair. "In a huge pirate ship like the *Jolly Roger*, with a monkey in the rigging and flying the skull and crossbones of course."

"Of course." I picked up my own cup. "How exactly were they going to come for you?" I asked. "Minnesota isn't really an ocean front state."

"By sailing up through the Great Lakes system into Lake Superior," she said.

I couldn't keep a straight face. "And when the Good Ship *Rebecca* made it to Lake Superior, how exactly was it supposed to get to Mayville Heights?"

"Magic, of course," Rebecca said, laughing. She picked up her fork and took a bite of a date square. "Ummm, these are good."

"Thank you," I said, grinning back at her across the table.

Owen and Hercules were still beside her chair, watching her with their mournful no-one-ever-feeds-us look. It was so fake. And it always worked.

Roma was constantly reminding us that Owen and Hercules were cats and should be fed as such—they just didn't seem to understand that. A couple of weeks ago she'd caught Maggie feeding them grilled tomatoes and mozzarella and had ranted that in a few years the cats were going to be two overweight fur balls with bypass surgery scars. Maggie had simply nodded solemnly and gotten more careful about sneaking them food.

I *had* stopped feeding the cats pizza, but that was

mostly because it gave Owen unholy bad breath and made Hercules burp like a Pepto-Bismol tester. The cats had some decidedly uncatlike abilities and I was beginning to suspect their digestive systems were not exactly those of typical cats, either.

I topped up Rebecca's cup and her expression grew serious. "Kathleen, what about the cats out at Wisteria Hill? Will they be okay?"

"They're all right for now," I said. "Marcus has the carriage house cordoned off, but if the investigation goes on very long"—I shrugged—"it's possible they'll have to be relocated."

"I hope that doesn't happen," she said. She smiled down at Owen and Hercules. "Those cats should be able to live out their days where they feel safe."

She took another sip from her coffee. "What's the name of the little calico? Lita and I saw her when we were out at the house getting my mother's journals. She peeked around the side of the carriage house."

"That's Lucy," I said. "She's kind of the matriarch of the colony."

"She reminded me a little of Owen," Rebecca said. He meowed softly at the sound of his name.

"That's probably because they both walk around like some kind of jungle cat," I said, smiling down at Owen who was too busy watching Rebecca to spare me even a sideways glance. Hercules, on the other hand, came and leaned against my leg. I reached down to scratch the top of his head.

"You know, you didn't have to go all the way out to Wisteria Hill just to get those journals for me," I said to Rebecca as I straightened up.

"Of course I did," she said. "You've worked so hard

on the library restoration. I can't wait for the centennial celebration. And it's long past time I got my mother's things from Wisteria Hill. It was good to be out there. I have a lot of wonderful memories."

I wondered how Rebecca felt about the old estate having been abandoned. Did she know why Everett continued to leave the house empty and neglected? No one else did.

"I hate to see the house looking so lost and forgotten," Rebecca said then.

How had she known what I was thinking? "Rebecca, you make the best lemon meringue pie I've ever had and you're a whiz with scissors." I pulled a hand through my hair. "Don't tell me mind reading is one of your skills, too?"

She tilted her head to one side and gave me a sly smile. "Well, I don't like to brag." She picked up her cup and then set it down and her expression grew serious again. "It will probably seem odd to you, but I think it's nostalgia that keeps Everett from doing anything with the old place."

"What do you mean?" I asked.

"Well, you know he grew up there, and since my mother worked for Anna, in many ways my brothers and I grew up at Wisteria Hill as well. I was the youngest. I spent a lot of time out there."

"It's where the two of you fell in love."

Rebecca's cheeks turned an adorable shade of pink again. She always blushed when the conversation turned to Everett's feelings for her. He'd loved her steadily for most of his life.

"We had a charmed childhood, Kathleen, as clichéd as that may sound. If Everett sells Wisteria Hill, or develops the land himself, that last link to those times will be gone."

I ran a finger around the rim of my cup. "I'd never thought of it that way," I said.

"Everett has a sentimental streak," Rebecca said.

"That wouldn't be my first choice of words to describe him," I said with a laugh.

Everett Henderson was a very successful, self-made businessman. He was generous with both his time and his money. He was also hard-nosed and uncompromising. There was nothing soft about the man.

"He's really a pussycat."

I looked down at Owen and Hercules. "Are you trying to tell me he has fish breath and sheds on the furniture?" I said.

Rebecca laughed. "Well, he does like my tuna casserole."

I laughed and Hercules looked from me to Rebecca, probably trying to figure out what the joke was. Hercules took fish very seriously.

"Do you think you'd like to live out there?" I asked.

She shook her head. "Wisteria Hill was a wonderful place to grow up, but my life is in town now." She smiled at both cats. "I'd miss these two coming across my backyard. I'd miss visiting you. And how could I not be here to see what contraption the Justason boys were building in their backyard?" She held up both hands. "I'd miss the bright lights of Mayville Heights too much." There was a devilish twinkle in her blue eyes. "And have you ever been out there in the early summer? The mosquitoes are large enough to carry you away." She looked at her watch. "Heavens, I should get going," she said.

"Thanks for this," I said, gesturing to the box as I got to my feet. "And for the salve."

"Oh you're welcome," Rebecca said. "Use whatever you like from my mother's things. And rest that ankle." She leaned over and looked from Owen to Hercules. "Come over for tea some morning once things dry out." Both cats gave answering meows.

I walked her out to the porch door. "Do you mind if I ask Maggie if she has any ideas on how we can display some of your mother's notes and drawings?"

"Not at all," Rebecca said. "That reminds me. I was thinking of asking Maggie if she'd do one of her big collages of Wisteria Hill for me. I have some old photographs that have just been sitting in a box."

"I'm sure she would," I said. Maggie had created some wonderful collage panels of old photographs for a display during the Winterfest celebrations a few months ago. They were on permanent display now in the town hall.

"At first I thought maybe a painting or a drawing of the place would be nice. When Lita and I were out there, someone actually was sketching the old house."

There was nothing to stop anyone from being out at Wisteria Hill, other than technically they were trespassing because the land was private property. I had Owen and Hercules because I'd been wandering around exploring out there.

In fact, one day late last summer Harry Taylor—the younger—had discovered a bilious green Volkswagen camper van in the yard and two middle-aged women—as Harry described them, looking like they were on their way to a reunion at Woodstock—picking mint and bouquets of cow parsnip.

"Don't tell me those two women in the chartreuse microbus stopped by again on their way back to Manitoba?" I said with a grin.

Rebecca grinned back. "No. Though rumor has it that one of them gave Harry her e-mail address. No. I'm not sure who we saw—one of the co-op artists, most likely—he or she was wearing a big sweatshirt with a hood." She stepped into her ladybug boots. "Now I really have to get going. I'm meeting that young man who works for Eric at the café."

I looked at her blankly.

"You know," she said. "The artist. Jaeger Merrill."

10

My face clearly gave me away because Rebecca's eyes narrowed. "Did I say something wrong?" she asked.

I shook my head. "No," I said. "It's just that Jaeger slipped on the basement stairs at the co-op store. He, uh . . . he's dead."

Rebecca closed her eyes for a moment. "Oh my word," she said. "That poor man."

"Why were you meeting him?" I asked. "If I'm not being too nosy by asking."

"You're not," she said. "I was at the café having lunch with Lita, the day we'd gone out to Wisteria Hill. I was telling her about breaking my old apple peeler just as Jaeger showed up with our food. He asked if I still had it. He said he could take it apart and use some of the pieces in his masks. We started talking and I realized I had some other things—what I thought of as, well, junk really—that he might be able to use. So I told him I'd look around and see what I could find. That was just a couple of days ago."

She exhaled slowly. Then she looked at me. "How's Maggie? I know there was water in the building and she had to close the store. Now this."

Hercules had come out and was leaning against my leg. I bent to pick him up. "She's okay. A little overwhelmed, but okay."

"Does she like cabbage?" Rebecca asked.

For a moment I felt like I was talking to Marcus, the way the conversation had veered off in a completely new direction. "I've seen her eat coleslaw," I offered, wondering what Maggie liking coleslaw had to do with the store basement flooding and Jaeger falling on the steps.

"Good," Rebecca said, zipping up her jacket. "I have a lovely cabbage and pork stir fry recipe. I think I'll make her a little care package."

I squeezed her arm with my free hand. "She'll love that. She's going to be here for supper."

"Even better," Rebecca said. "Don't cook. I'll bring dinner for both of you."

"You don't have to do that," I said. Hercules immediately meowed his objection to my objection.

Rebecca patted my hand. "I'm sorry my dear. You've been outvoted. Dinner will be here at six o'clock."

"Will you at least join us?" I asked.

She smiled. "Thank you, but I already have dinner plans."

I knew by that smile that her plans had to be with Everett. She waggled her fingers at Hercules and left.

I carried Herc back into the kitchen. Owen had disappeared. "Tell your brother Rebecca is making supper," I told the little black-and-white cat as I put him back down on the floor.

I gathered the plates and cups and started running water in the sink. Maggie liked to tease me because I always did the dishes by hand. I'd told her that was because we hadn't had a dishwasher when I was growing up so it was habit—which was true. It had also been the only time I could get some time to myself in my crazy family. I did my best thinking while scrubbing crud off the bottom of a pot.

I'd just filled the sink with bubbles and water and was trying to figure out how I was going to wash everything one-handed when I heard something fall behind me. I turned around and Hercules was sitting on the edge of a kitchen chair, his head in the box Rebecca had brought over, the lid on the floor.

"Hercules!" I said sharply. He looked up, all confused innocence. "Get your head out of that box now and get off that chair."

He hesitated, looking from whatever it was in the box that intrigued him to me.

"Now!" I repeated.

He lifted a paw as though he were going to climb into the carton. I rang out the dishcloth just a little and held it up. "You really want to do this?" I asked. "From this distance there's no way I can miss."

He made a noise that was halfway between a yowl and a grumble—Roma insisted that sound was cat-speak for "Bite me"—and jumped down. "Wise choice," I called after him as he stalked away muttering under his breath.

I dried my hands and put the lid back on the box. Hercules kind of had a thing for boxes and bags. He liked to climb in the canvas grocery bags. He liked to ride around in the new messenger bag I'd bought to replace the one I'd lost last winter. In fact, the bag actually was a cat carrier bag since I knew that Owen and Hercules were going to end up in it as much as my towel and tai chi shoes did.

I took the box upstairs, setting it on top of my tall chest of drawers where I knew neither cat could get into it. Then I went back downstairs, put Barry Manilow on the CD player and cranked up the volume before I went back to the kitchen.

Halfway through the chorus of "Ready to Take a Chance Again," Hercules appeared on the edge of my vision, in the doorway to the living room, head bobbing blissfully to the music.

Owen didn't reappear until a few minutes before Maggie arrived. A gray paw slid around the basement door and nudged it open, and then he poked his head out.

"You're safe," I said. "No more Barry Manilow for now."

Owen squeezed his eyes shut and shook his head vigorously. He didn't share my and Hercules's appreciation for the man who wrote the songs that made the whole world sing.

I'd just set the table when Maggie tapped on the porch door. Owen, who had been lolling under the kitchen table, leaped to his feet and to his surprise went skidding across the freshly washed kitchen floor in his haste to say hello to her. He shook himself and then had to stop to give a couple of swipes to his face with his paw.

I picked him up. "You look like a million bucks," I assured him, smoothing the fur on the top of his head. "You look like a cat version of Brad Pitt."

Maggie smiled when I opened the door but I saw at once that she was tired. There were dark circles under her eyes and tiny frown lines on her forehead. "Hey Fuzz Face," she said to Owen. He immediately started to purr. Maggie let out a long sigh and leaned in toward the cat. "Owen, you are the only male in any species that I like right now," she said. That just made him purr louder.

She kicked off her boots, I took her jacket and she padded behind me into the kitchen. I set Owen down and hung up her jacket. Maggie dropped into one of the kitchen chairs and Owen took up his position of adoration at her feet.

"Long afternoon?" I asked, leaning against the counter.

"Very," she said. "Ruby told me about Jaeger Merrill really being Christian Ellis. How bizarre is that?"

"Ruby kept saying she remembered him, but I thought they'd just been in a class together or maybe they'd met at an exhibition."

Maggie leaned an elbow on the table and propped her head on her hand. "I don't see why he felt he needed to lie," she said.

I shrugged. "Maybe he was embarrassed. Maybe he didn't want people to know what he'd done. Would you want to tell other artists that you'd been a forger?"

She made a face. "Good point. On the other hand, did Jaeger—I'm sorry, in my mind he's Jaeger Merrill— strike you as the kind of person who cared what people thought?"

"No," I said slowly. "Ruby asked me the same thing, but I didn't really know him."

"I guess none of us did," Maggie said. She looked around the kitchen, frowning. "Hey, Kath, I don't mean to be rude, but you do remember that you invited me for dinner, don't you?"

Owen gave a loud, enthusiastic "meow" before I could answer. "Yes, we know you remember," I said. I smiled at Maggie. "Rebecca is making dinner for us. You do like cabbage, don't you? I said you did."

Maggie looked at Owen. "What do you think?" she asked. "Coleslaw maybe?"

He seemed to make a face.

"You're right," Maggie said. "Coleslaw is more of a July/August kind of thing. It could be egg rolls? Or sausage and cabbage soup?"

Owen looked up at her, his head cocked to one side as though he was trying to decide which choice sounded the best. There was a knock on the door then.

"That'll be Rebecca," I said, heading for the porch.

Maggie leaned down toward Owen. "Maybe it's corned beef and cabbage," I heard her say to him.

It wasn't Rebecca at the back door; it was Everett, in jeans and a black windbreaker, carrying a large, insulated cooler bag and a smaller canvas tote. "Hello, Kathleen," he said. Even in casual clothes, he reminded me of actor Sean Connery, without the Scottish accent.

I smiled. "Hi, Everett." I moved aside and he stepped into the porch, setting the cooler on the bench by the door and handing me the canvas bag.

He leaned in for a closer look at my face, frowning at my scraped forehead. His dark eyes met mine and his expression was serious. "Kathleen, are you sure you weren't hurt?" he asked.

I nodded. "I appreciate your concern, Everett," I said. "But I really am okay. The paramedics checked me over very carefully. It looks much worse than it feels."

"I'm so sorry," he said. "I had no idea that bank was in danger of collapsing."

"There's no way you could have known," I said. "I heard Harry Taylor say that this is the wettest spring this area's seen in more than forty years. Please don't worry about it."

His expression softened just a little. "If you need anything, I want you to call the office. Lita will take care of it."

"Thank you," I said. I reached for the nylon cooler. "And please thank Rebecca for this."

"I will," Everett said. His face closed in again and he lowered his voice. "I heard about Jaeger Merrill, Kathleen. Please tell Maggie if the co-op has any problems. Lita will know how to find me."

"I'll tell her," I said.

He nodded and left. I carried everything into the kitchen. Hercules had joined Maggie and Owen and all three of them looked expectantly at me.

I handed the canvas bag to Maggie. "See what's in there," I said. I put the nylon cooler on the counter and unzipped the top. Inside there was a large casserole dish. I lifted it out, took the lid off and inhaled the delicious smell of onions and spices. A small dish held Rebecca's homemade noodles.

"There's apple crumble in here," Maggie crowed behind me. "And cinnamon rolls."

I put both casserole dishes on the table, stuck the apple crumble in the oven to warm and stashed the cinnamon rolls on the counter. "Let's eat," I said to Maggie.

She glanced down at Owen and Hercules sitting next to her chair like two furry guardians. "You're not even going to give them a taste?" she asked.

"Roma told me to stop giving them so much people food," I said. "She told you the same thing or did you forget?"

She looked at the cats again. "I don't see Roma anywhere, do you?" Owen actually looked around the kitchen much to Maggie's delight. She made a sweeping gesture around the kitchen. "Nope. No sign of her anywhere."

I sighed and got a couple of small bowls from the cupboard. "Number one, I'm telling Roma next time I see her." I put a few noodles and a bit of meat and sauce into each bowl. There was no way I was giving the cats cabbage. That had to be a bad idea. "And number two, when they hack up something disgusting tomorrow, I'm calling you to come clean it up."

I handed her the bowls and she set them on the floor, one in front of each cat. That even got her an adoring look from Hercules. Maggie unfolded her napkin and smiled sweetly at me as she reached for the noodles.

Rebecca was an outstanding cook. I'd had meals at five-star restaurants that weren't as good as the meal she'd sent.

"Did you talk to Marcus?" I asked over my second helping of apple crumble. Owen was still by Maggie's chair, carefully washing his face. Hercules had wandered off to do whatever it was he did after supper.

She nodded. "I did. He wanted to know how Jaeger could have ended up on those basement stairs." She sighed. "I'd like to know that myself."

"Maybe he picked the lock." I didn't add that it was something I knew how to do—depending on the lock.

"Maybe he did. He didn't have my keys and he didn't have Ruby's." She pulled one leg up underneath her and leaned against the back of the chair. "Have you ever noticed that Marcus asks you a question and then a few minutes later he asks the same question again, in a slightly different way?"

"I noticed," I said. "I don't know if it's a cop thing, or just a Marcus thing."

"It's like he's testing you to see if you'll give the same answer every time."

I set my spoon down and pushed my dish away before I ended up with a third helping of apple crumble. "So what was it he kept asking you about?"

Maggie's cheeks went pink and she looked down at the table. "He heard about the fight I had with Jaeger."

"You mean at the meeting?"

"No. I mean the fight." She lifted her head and looked at me. "I didn't tell you."

"Why?"

"Because I was embarrassed."

Owen had stopped washing his face and was staring intently at Maggie, as though he could feel her discomfort.

She played with the crimson and silver scarf at her neck. "I usually handle things better than this, but Jaeger got under my skin. Between the flooding at the store, the flooding period, trying to rearrange the yoga and tai chi classes and keep up with the Web site orders and deal with him trying to incite a rebellion—" She stopped, and slid a hand over her hair. "I'm making excuses."

I shook my head. "No you're not. You've been running on herbal tea and very little sleep for over a week. I've at least had caffeine."

"I don't think any amount of caffeine would have made dealing with Jaeger any easier," she said.

There was a tiny bit of apple left in her dish. She scooped it up with her spoon, leaned over and held it out to Owen. He sniffed it carefully and instead of putting it on the floor so he could investigate it like a crime scene technician, he actually ate from the spoon.

"And, if you're wondering if I pushed Jaeger down those stairs, the answer is no."

"Let me guess. Marcus actually asked you that."

She gave me a wry smile as she straightened up. "He did. He also asked if I'd given Jaeger my keys." She held up a hand before I could say anything. "And don't call him a dipwad. He's just doing his job."

"I know," I said. "I just wish he could be a little more human when he does it." I got up from the table and put the kettle on to boil so I could make Maggie some tea. "And I wish he'd put his focus back on those remains — whoever they are — out at Wisteria Hill. Jaeger's death was an accident."

Maggie stretched, stood up, and started clearing the table. "I should call Roma," she said. "Do you think it actually is her father's body out there?"

"That ring is his. He disappeared a long, long time ago. It does make sense." I got a cup and the peppermint teabags I kept just for Maggie out of the cupboard. "I did a little research in the newspaper's archives. Thomas Karlsson had a job with a landscaping company for a while — Sam's father's company. Maybe he was working at Wisteria Hill."

Just then the phone rang. "Go ahead and make your tea," I said to Maggie as I headed for the living room.

I leaned across the wing chair, and grabbed the receiver.

"Hi, Kathleen," Roma said.

There was something flat and off about her voice. I dropped onto the footstool.

"Dr. Abbott got someone she knows who's a forensic dentist to come look at the . . . remains."

My chest tightened. "And?" I said.

"And . . . and I don't know how he did it so fast but Marcus got my—Tom's dental records."

I knew what was coming before she said the words.

"It's him, Kathleen. That's my father who was buried out at Wisteria Hill."

11

I rubbed my left shoulder, which had suddenly tightened into knots. "I'm so sorry, Roma," I said. "Are you all right?"

"I don't know," she said. "All these years I thought he'd just . . . left. Now I find out . . . I don't know."

"I know that Eddie's on the road," I said. "Why don't you come over? Maggie's here and there's some of Rebecca's apple crumble."

She hesitated for a moment. "Okay."

"We'll see you in a few minutes," I said and hung up.

I went back to the kitchen. Maggie had cleared the table, stacked the dishes at one side of the sink and was drinking her tea and talking quietly to Owen.

I dropped into the chair across from her. She studied my face. "Whoever that was, it wasn't good news."

"That was Roma," I said. "I have no idea how Marcus did it all so quickly, but those are her father's remains."

Maggie winced and shook her head. "I was really hoping it would be someone else."

"She's on her way over," I said, getting up to put more water in the kettle. I leaned around Maggie's chair to look at Owen, pointing a warning finger at the cat. "No glaring. No hissing," I said sternly. "This has been a horrible day for Roma. Remember what Flower's mother said." He looked at me, almost thoughtfully it seemed, then he headed for the living room.

"Flower's mother?" Maggie asked, clearly confused.

"The little skunk from the movie, *Bambi*," I said. "His name was Flower."

"So what did his mother say?"

"If you can't say something nice, don't say anything at all."

"I like it," Maggie said. "But somehow I doubt Owen has seen *Bambi*."

The kettle had boiled and the cinnamon rolls and the last of the apple crumble were on the table when Roma knocked at the back door. I hugged her and then she took a step back to examine my forehead. "That looks ugly," she said, "and yes I know, you're fine." She looked over to the kitchen door. "I heard about Jaeger Merrill. How's Maggie doing?"

I nodded. "She's okay."

Roma followed me into the kitchen and Maggie folded her into a hug. "I'm sorry about your father," she said.

"Hey, I'm sorry you had to find Jaeger Merrill's body," Roma countered. She looked from Maggie to me. "Can you believe the past couple of days? Two bodies and you almost ended up in the hospital."

"I've had better days," Maggie said. "At least it didn't rain." Roma and I exchanged tiny smiles, which Maggie caught. "What?" she asked.

"Nothing," I said as I hung up Roma's jacket. "It's just you're the most positive person I know."

"Do you think that's bad?" Maggie asked as she made tea for Roma.

"No, I don't," Roma said, sitting down with a sigh. "I think it's good."

"Have you talked to Eddie?" I asked, pulling out my chair.

Roma nodded. "I have. Twice. I wish he wasn't on the road."

"So what happens now? What did Marcus say?" I asked.

"Dr. Abbott and her team are going to keep looking for the rest of . . . the remains. They'll have to do an autopsy." She picked up her cup and then set it down again without drinking. "However Tom died, it wasn't natural causes. Otherwise he wouldn't have ended up at Wisteria Hill."

Maggie reached over and laid her hand on Roma's arm. "I'm sorry that you had to see those bones and then find out they were your father."

"It was more odd than sad," Roma said. "You know, I barely have any memories of the man. I can remember, of all things, playing hide and seek with him. I was two or three, maybe. He put a blanket or something over my head and told me to be very quiet and I pretended I wasn't there."

She closed her eyes briefly. "And I can remember sitting on his lap, pretending I was driving. I can still see the car. It had turquoise and white bucket seats."

"Those are good memories," Maggie said. "You don't have to give them up because of what happened."

"I know," Roma said. "For me, my father is my stepfather, Neil. I know I have a connection to those . . . bones, but what I really want is the truth. I want to know what happened." She sighed. "I have some hard questions for my mother. I think maybe the answers are going to be just as hard to hear."

"If you need anything, all you have to do is ask," I said, and Maggie nodded in agreement.

Roma gave us a small smile. "Thanks."

Out of the corner of my eye I caught movement by the living room doorway. It was Owen, carrying something in his mouth with Hercules as his wingman. So much for my speech about behaving while Roma was here. I glared at them, but as usual they ignored me.

Owen came purposefully into the room and dropped the head of a Fred the Funky chicken near Roma's feet, then took a couple of steps backward. Hercules pushed it closer with a paw. He looked at Roma and meowed softly.

"Is that for me?" Roma asked, her voice suddenly raspy. Hercules gave the yellow chicken head another nudge.

I had a lump in my throat. Was it possible that somehow they understood that Roma was upset?

She looked across the table at me. "If I didn't know better, I'd think they were trying to cheer me up," she said, her voice still low and hoarse.

"Animals can be very sensitive to emotions," Maggie said. "Maybe they do sense something."

Roma turned back to the cats and leaned forward. "Thank you," she said.

I leaned around Roma's chair and gave Owen and Hercules a nod of approval. They started around the table for the living room. Maggie gave them both thumbs-up as they passed her chair.

Roma picked up her spoon and cleared her throat. "There isn't anything more I can do about my—about Tom right now. So could we talk about something else? Please? Tell me, is it true that Jaeger Merrill wasn't in fact Jaeger Merrill?"

Gossip got around Mayville Heights faster than a speeding bullet or fiber-optic Internet service.

"It's true," Maggie said. "His real name was Christian Ellis."

Roma took a sip of her coffee. "So how did Christian Ellis turn into Jaeger Merrill and end up here in Mayville Heights?"

"I don't know why he changed his name, but he might have ended up here because his lawyer back then was Peter Lundgren," I said.

"Peter?" Roma said.

Maggie looked surprised as well. "Ruby didn't tell me that part."

I took a drink from my cup. "There's a photo of the two of them in that book Ruby has. I saw it. And I was curious, so I did a little digging into Christian Ellis's background this afternoon. I found another photo of him and Peter online." I didn't add that I knew Maggie wasn't going to be able to let the whole secret identity thing go and I'd hoped I'd find some answers so she wouldn't make herself crazy over it.

"It doesn't sound like Peter," Roma said. "He's always been the defender of the downtrodden type. His practice has been running on next to nothing for years. I think he would have gone under by now except some distant relative died about eighteen months ago and left everything he had to Peter. There wasn't a lot of money but there was a lot of very valuable land."

"Ruby said Peter was just starting out when he was Christian Ellis's lawyer," I said.

"You know I think I saw him out at Wisteria Hill last week," Roma said, tipping her bowl so she could scrape all the cinnamon-flecked apple from the bottom. "I think he was drawing the old house."

"Peter was out sketching at Wisteria Hill?" Maggie said. Sometimes the obvious escaped her.

"No," Roma said, shaking her head. "Jaeger or Ellis or whatever his name was."

Maggie frowned, tenting the fingers of one hand over the top of her teacup. "Are you sure? Jaeger was a mask-maker and before that he did paintings with religious imagery—which is probably how he got into forging religious icons. Why was he out sketching an old house?"

"It might not have been him," Roma said. "I just caught a quick glimpse of the person over by the far side of the house. Whoever it was had a hood up. It was starting to rain."

Maggie was staring off into space. "Maggie, where are you?" I said, waving my hand in front of her face.

She shook her head. "Sorry. I can't stop thinking about Jaeger. Now that we know who he really was, I'm wondering why he picked here to start over in the first place. We have a great artists' community, but he didn't exactly fit in. Most of us aren't looking for fame and fortune. We just want to make art and pay our bills."

"Maybe he just wanted to lay low," I said.

"Except he wasn't," Maggie said. "He just couldn't seem to live a quiet life, even after he'd gone to so much trouble to create a whole new identity for himself. And now he's dead."

"'It is not, nor it cannot come to good,'" I said quietly.

They both turned to stare at me.

I shrugged. *"Hamlet."*

Roma played with her tea, and then she leaned back in her chair and studied Maggie across the table. "You think he was running another scam, don't you?" she said.

In my mind I could see Jaeger, floating faceup in the water, with that ugly gash on the side of his head.

Maggie shifted in her seat. "Now that I know about his past, I do. And I can't help thinking that he might have been using—or trying to use the co-op in some way." Her long fingers played with her fork. "We're starting to do a decent business online. Some of the artists like to pack their own work for shipping. Jaeger was one of them."

"So you think what?" Roma asked. "That he was forging artwork again and using the store to ship it to somewhere?"

Maggie shrugged. "I know it sounds crazy, but yes, maybe. I don't believe Jaeger created a completely new person just because he was embarrassed about his past. He was up to something. I just don't know what."

12

Roma and Maggie insisted on washing the dishes for me. I was too restless to sleep after they left. I tidied up the kitchen and set the table for breakfast. I'd told Roma I'd take her turn out at Wisteria Hill in the morning.

I was hoping I'd get a chance to talk to Marcus. I knew it would be a while before he could piece together what had happened to Thomas Karlsson, so there really wasn't anything I could do for Roma, other than be there for her. But maybe Marcus would have some insight into what had motivated Christian Ellis to turn himself into Jaeger Merrill.

Maybe it was nothing more than looking for a new start. On the other hand, maybe Maggie was right. Maybe Jaeger—Christian—had been up to something. Now that Marcus and I didn't seem to be at odds so much with each other, maybe he could tell me something, anything that would put Maggie's mind at ease. She already had enough to deal with.

Hercules and Owen were both upstairs in the bed-room. I crouched beside them, groaning a little because my ankle really didn't want me to get down so close to the floor.

I kissed Owen's head and scratched under his chin. "That was such a nice thing you did for Roma," I said. "I'll make an extra batch of crackers for you this week-end." I stroked Hercules's fur with my other hand. "You, too," I said. "And I promise I'll figure out how to tell Maggie you are not a boot person."

Getting up again was harder than getting down to the cats' level had been. Rebecca's box was still on top of the chest of drawers. I moved it over to the table by the window, sat in the big chair, and took the lid off once more.

I set the bound book full of sketches and notes aside and lifted out one of the journals. The pages were yel-lowed, covered with the same tight, neat handwriting as the sketches.

October 19, 1960
   Spent the day making apple pies with Anna.
Must have peeled two baskets' worth of apples. De-cided I was sick of apples. Had a slice of the first pie out of the oven. Decided I was wrong.

I could see where Rebecca's sense of humor came from. I flipped back a few pages.

May 17, 1960
   Ladies Knitting Circle meeting at the library.
Anna still prefers yarn from western Canada but Mary-Lee wants to try a mill from back east. Sammy

drove me up the hill. He's such a sweet boy, nothing like his father. Thank heaven.

"The Ladies Knitting Circle?" I said to Hercules. "Remind me to ask Rebecca about them. Or Mary. And do you think Sammy is the mayor, Sam Ingstrom?"

Abigail—with some input from Maggie—was already working on a display about the various groups that had met in the library over the years. My favorite so far was the Young Women's Deportment Society from the early sixties. Abigail had unearthed five or six photos of several teenage girls walking through the stacks wearing white gloves and balancing books on their heads. She'd admitted, with pink cheeks and a self-deprecating laugh, that one of them was her.

I yawned. Suddenly all my restless energy was gone. My ankle was throbbing again, my head hurt, and pretty much everything else ached. I pushed myself up before I got too comfortable in the upholstered chair. "I'm going to take a bath," I said to Hercules.

I filled the tub with hot water. Maggie had given me a packet, made of cheesecloth and tied with string, and told me to add it to my bathwater. It smelled of chamomile and roses. I tossed it in.

I soaked until the water cooled, then spread Rebecca's salve on my ankle and wrapped it carefully with the cotton strips that had been in the bag. When I went back into the bedroom, wrapped in my oversized blue robe, I found Hercules sitting in the wing chair, his black-and-white head bent over the journal I'd forgotten to put away. It almost looked as though he was reading.

"What are you doing?" I asked.

He looked up and meowed.

"Find anything interesting?"

He lifted a paw and gently patted the book.

"Careful," I warned, bending over to look at my scabby forehead in the mirror. I had no idea that there were so many variations of blue-black.

Herc meowed again, more insistently this time. Translation: Look at this now.

I crossed over to the chair. The cat had his paw on the open spine of the journal where the pages came together. "What is it?" I said.

He dug at the inside edge of the page and then looked at me. If he could have talked he would have said, "See?" He had that kind of expectant expression on his face.

I picked up the diary. He watched me intently. At first I didn't see anything. Then as I turned the book toward the light I saw a tiny sliver of cut paper.

"Are there pages cut out of this book?" I asked Hercules.

I moved the journal closer to the lamp on the table and ran my finger along the spine where the pages came together. Two pages had been cut from the book, very carefully with what I was guessing was some kind of thin blade. The remaining tiny scraps of paper were sharp edged—there was no feathering of the cuts as far as I could see in the dim light. It looked as if the pages had been cut out recently.

"That's odd," I said. Hercules looked at me unblinkingly. I flipped slowly through the rest of the journal. There were at least three other places where pages had been removed. "Do you think Rebecca did this?" I asked. Hercules didn't so much as twitch.

No, that didn't make sense. If there were things in Ellen's diary that Rebecca didn't want anyone to read, she just wouldn't have given them to me in the first place. Secrets had kept Rebecca and Everett apart for most of their lives. If she had found something embarrassing written in her mother's diary she wouldn't keep it hidden, no matter what it was.

Hercules stood on his back legs and put his front paws on the edge of the cardboard box that held the rest of Ellen's things. The extra weight made it tip over. The carton bounced off the edge of the chair and landed on the floor, spilling the other three bound books onto the rug. Hercules landed beside them, sheepish and disheveled.

I looked at him, slowly shaking my head. "Please tell me you didn't damage those other journals," I said.

He looked at the books, and then he looked at me and murped.

"You better be right," I warned, reaching down to gather up everything.

Hercules held out his left paw and gave a pitiful meow.

"You're not hurt," I said.

He ducked his head and looked sideways at me around his whiskers, his paw still extended.

I laid the diaries on the bed and picked up the cat, setting him on my lap. "You're such a wuss. Let me see."

I gently felt all over his paw. He didn't so much as wince. "I think you'll live," I told him.

I ran a hand over the closest leather-covered book. "Do you think there are pages missing from any of these other books?"

He reached over with his "injured" paw—which didn't seem to be hurt anymore—and lightly scraped the cover.

"Good idea," I said.

Two of the remaining journals had at least a few missing pages. I'd have to look at all of them in better light in the morning to be sure. I put Hercules on the floor, gathered everything back in the box, and set it up on the chest again.

Someone had taken a great deal of care to cut pages out of Ellen Montgomery's journals. It wasn't something I could see Rebecca doing.

So who else would care about what was written in some old diaries? Everett? That didn't seem likely. He wasn't the kind of person who worried about what other people thought. He'd let Wisteria Hill sit empty and neglected for a long time now while people in town speculated about his reasons.

Lita? She was one of the few people who had access to the old house. What reason would she have to remove pages from Ellen's journals?

Could Everett's granddaughter, Ami, have done it? I wasn't sure Ami had ever even been inside the house at Wisteria Hill.

Yawning, I put the lid back on the carton. "I guess it doesn't matter, anyway," I said to Hercules who had started washing his face. "I'll call Rebecca tomorrow and tell her. Maybe this is just another one of the mysteries of Wisteria Hill."

13

Derek Craig was sitting in his police cruiser when I got to the top of the driveway at Wisteria Hill in the morning. He got out of the car and walked over to my truck.

"Good morning Ms. Paulson," he said. "You here to feed the cats?"

"I am," I said, reaching for the canvas bag of food and the jugs of water.

"Could you sign in for me, please?" he asked, offering his clipboard.

"Have you been here all night?" I asked as I signed on the line that read AM Feeding. This had to be Marcus's idea. He was über organized, one of the reasons Maggie always insisted we'd be a good match. I'd told her if we were using that reasoning, the perfect woman for Marcus would be Mary, the kickboxing grandmother who worked at the library and made the best apple pie I'd ever eaten. She actually enjoyed adding new books to the computerized card catalogue system.

"No ma'am," the young policeman said. "I got here at six."

My large metal thermos was on the floor of the passenger side of the truck. "Would you like some coffee?" I asked. "It already has cream and sugar."

He smiled. "Yes I would. I didn't think to fill one of those. Cup I brought with me was gone in the first fifteen minutes."

He walked back to his cruiser and got the thermal mug that had been sitting on the dash. I filled it with coffee and he gave me another big smile. "Thank you," he said. He gestured to the cat food and water. "Could I carry something for you?"

I wasn't nearly as stiff as I had been and my ankle felt pretty good—the combination of Rebecca's salve and Maggie's herbal soak—but I knew the path around the side of the carriage house was probably still muddy. "Do you think you could carry the water jugs around to the side door?" I said.

He set his coffee on the roof of the truck and grabbed the water. "Lead the way," he said.

It had rained a little sometime during the night and the path through the scrub at the side of the carriage house was slick and slippery, but we made it to the door without either one of us, or the cat food, ending up on the ground.

"Thanks," I said.

Derek handed me both jugs of water. "If you need anything, just yell."

I nodded. "I will."

He started back around the old building and I leaned on the door, pushing with my good hip against the moisture-swollen wood. It opened with a groaning sound—the door, not me.

I stepped inside, leaving the door a couple of inches ajar so I could see better. There was no sign that anyone had been in the space. The cats were probably still in their shelters.

I carried everything over to the feeding station, set out the food and water and then retreated back by the door. The cats had learned that the sound of someone moving around meant food, so I knew they'd be out in a moment.

A couple of minutes passed and there was no sign of any of the cats. I didn't hear anything either. Had all the people in the field behind the old carriage house scared them? Had they bolted? Then I thought about Lucy. The little cat didn't scare easily. If she was still here, then so was the rest of the colony. I leaned against the rough wooden wall of the building and continued to wait.

And finally there was a twitch of motion over by one of the support beams. I held my breath. Lucy came cautiously out of the darkness, scanning the area. She saw me and stopped. Would she go for the food or back to the shelters where the cats slept?

She did neither. She started purposefully across the floor to me, stopping maybe a dozen or so feet away. Lucy and I had a kind of rapport that I couldn't explain, other than in the unexplainable logic of cats, she just seemed to like me. Now she tipped her head to one side and looked up at me.

"Hey puss," I said softly. "I bet you wonder what's going on."

She meowed softly.

"You're safe. Marcus is taking care of everything. You know Marcus, the big, cute, annoying guy."

Lucy meowed again and then turned and headed for

the feeding station. I had no idea if she somehow under-stood what I'd said, been reassured by my tone, or if all she'd heard was blah, blah, blah and now she was hungry.

Like she'd sent off some sort of invisible signal, the other cats came out to join Lucy for breakfast. I looked each one over as usual for any signs of illness or injury. As far as I could tell in the dim light all seven cats were just fine.

I felt myself relax a little. At least one thing was going right. Maybe everything else would fall in place today.

As quickly as I had the thought, I felt the hairs rise on the back of my neck as though a slight breeze had blown over my skin. A karmic warning, maybe, that life wasn't going to work out so easily?

At the edge of my vision I saw something move be-hind me. I looked back over my shoulder. It wasn't a warning from the universe. It was Marcus. Okay, maybe it was a warning from the universe after all.

"Hi," he whispered, moving to stand very close beside my left shoulder. I could smell the citrusy shampoo he always used.

"Where's Roma?" His breath tickled my bare neck.

"There were some things she had to do," I whispered back.

Marcus was studying the cats, the same way I had, looking for any sign they weren't okay. "You all right?" he said. "How's your ankle?"

"A bit stiff," I said. "But I'm okay. Rebecca brought me one of her herbal concoctions. I have a doctor's ap-pointment on Monday, by the way."

"Good," he said. He didn't look the slightest bit guilty about telling on me. "The cats look all right."

"Lucy took her time coming out, but once she did, the

rest followed her. I'm hoping they won't get spooked and take off." He was so close to me I could actually feel the warmth coming off his body. Or maybe it was the carriage house that was getting warm and stuffy.

"I've told everyone to stay away from this building," Marcus said.

"Have you always been a cat person?" I asked.

He smiled. "I told you I had a paper route when I was a kid, didn't I?"

I nodded. It was one of the few things Marcus had shared about himself, sitting at my kitchen table having breakfast not long after we'd first met.

"I was nine. It was a Saturday morning, it was raining and I had maybe four more papers to deliver. I was on Mountain Road, just a couple of houses above yours, and there was this little ginger cat, scrawny and wet under a tree."

"And you rescued it," I said, glancing over at the feeding station where the cats were still eating.

"I put her inside my raincoat and took her home. I had this crazy idea that I could hide her in my bedroom without anyone finding out."

"I take it that didn't work?"

Marcus laughed. "Well, it might have if I hadn't had the idea to dry the cat with a blow dryer."

"You didn't?" I couldn't help laughing myself.

"It wasn't one of my better ideas," he said. "I probably scared her out of one of her nine lives. She managed to squeeze into this little space behind my dresser and she wouldn't come out." Something changed in his expression and he stuffed his hands in his pockets. "My father, in his three-piece suit and white shirt, spent a good fifteen minutes on the floor, coaxing the cat out with a sausage.

I thought for sure he'd take her to the animal shelter. But he just said, 'Put up posters and if you can't find out who owns her, you better start saving that paper money because she's going to need shots.'"

He shrugged. "No one came for her so that's how I ended up with Abner and I guess that's how I became a cat person."

I frowned, eyes narrowed. "Abner? I thought you said the cat was a she?"

"She was."

Was Marcus blushing? I couldn't tell in the dim light. "Why did you name her Abner?" I asked. "I'm not criticizing. I'm just curious."

He ducked his head for a moment. "She was wearing an old collar with a metal name plate, but all that was legible were the first two letters, 'A' and 'B.' I thought the cat's name was Abner."

"It didn't occur to you that maybe, I don't know, Abigail might have been a more likely name?" It was hard not to laugh.

"Well, now, yes. But I couldn't tell the difference between a boy cat and a girl cat back then."

"Roma did explain the difference before you signed on to help with these cats, didn't she?" I teased.

"I know the difference between boys and girls now," Marcus said, his eyes locked on mine.

For a moment it seemed as though there was no air in the room. Or maybe I'd just forgotten how to breathe for a second or two. Then from across the carriage house the yowl of a couple of squabbling cats cut the silence. Marcus took a step sideways to see what was going on and I took a breath.

One of the younger cats had tried to eat from the

same dish as an old tom. The disagreement was over almost as fast as it had started.

We stood in silence after that, until all the cats had eaten, stretched, and in the case of Lucy, washed off the remains of breakfast. She finally headed for the far corner of the old building and I stepped away from Marcus and made my way over to the feeding station. I gathered the dishes and picked up a couple of pieces of stray cat kibble, while Marcus put out fresh water.

Once we were outside again, he took both the water jugs and the bag with the cats' dishes. "Go carefully," he said. "It's a little slippery."

I put one hand on the wall of the carriage house. The old shingles were gray and cracked with age. At the truck I reached for the thermos as Marcus set the canvas tote and the empty water bottles on the passenger side floor mat. "How about some coffee?" I asked.

"Umm, please," he said.

The thermos had two cups—one nested inside the other—so I poured coffee for both of us and handed him the larger cup. I knew I could make more when I got home.

Marcus leaned against the side of my truck, wrapping both of his big hands around the plastic cup. He took a long sip and then smiled at me. "You make good coffee."

"Thank you," I said.

"Library opening today?" he asked.

I shook my head. "I'm hoping tomorrow, if we don't get any more rain." I looked around. "When will you be finished out here?"

He shrugged. "That depends on Dr. Abbott and her team." When I didn't say anything his eyes narrowed and he frowned at me over the top of his cup. "Aren't you going to ask me how Thomas Karlsson's body ended up out here?"

I took another mouthful of coffee before I answered. "No."

"No?" He shifted, crossing one long leg over the other. I could see he was trying to stifle a smile.

"You're good, but there's no way you could have figured that out yet." I smiled at him. "You were pretty fast at identifying those bones, though."

"A lot of that was luck."

"And Roma recognizing her father's ring."

His face grew serious again. "And that."

"When are you going to be finished at the co-op store?" I asked.

"I'm not sure," he said, ducking his head for another drink. "There are still some things I need to check, people I need to talk to again."

"Maggie," I said.

"Among others, yes."

I hesitated, shifting my cup from one hand to the other. "Marcus, you know that Maggie had nothing to do with Jaeger slipping on those steps? I know they'd argued, but she didn't give him her keys and she didn't let him in the basement. You know Maggie. She wouldn't lie about that. She wouldn't lie about anything."

He took a deep breath and let it out slowly. "I'm just talking to people, Kathleen," he said. "That's all. I'm not saying *I* think Maggie had anything to do with Jaeger Merrill's death."

Was I imagining his emphasis on the word "I"?

"Are you saying someone else might? Or does." I asked.

"You know I can't answer that," he began.

"Because this is a police investigation," I finished. I

sighed, pulling a hand over my neck. "I do understand that. And I really will try to stay out of it. But do you understand that I won't stop being Maggie's friend?"

Marcus took another sip of his coffee. "Yes. I've learned by now how loyal you are to the people you care about."

"Marcus, have you come up with a good explanation for why Jaeger created this new persona?" I asked. "I think the whole secret identity thing is very melodramatic."

He shrugged, but didn't say anything. It was as good as a no.

"Maggie thinks he was planning another scam and I'm starting to think maybe she's right. I did a little digging. Some people think Jaeger was a lot more involved in the whole forgery business that sent him to jail than he ever admitted. What if he was going to use the co-op in some way? What if he already was?"

Marcus's deep blue eyes fixed on my face. "Do you have any reason to think that's what he was doing?" He drank the last of his coffee, and handed the cup back to me.

"If you mean can I prove it, no," I said. I put my cup inside his and screwed the whole thing back on the thermos. "But what was Jaeger doing in the basement? And how did he get a key? During the meeting earlier in the morning, Maggie had taken everyone to see how much water had come in. If there was something he wanted to see down there, why not ask her?"

"She wasn't there, or he figured she'd say no, since they'd already had one argument."

I reached through the open driver's window and set the thermos on the seat. "Or he didn't want Maggie—or anyone else—to know what he was looking for."

Marcus stuffed his hands in his pockets, taking a quick

glance at his watch as he did so. "You think he was looking for something?"

"Have you ever been in Play it Again, Stan?" I asked.

"You mean the repurpose store out by the highway? The place with the secondhand furniture and salvaged building supplies?"

I nodded. "I was out there maybe a month ago. So was Jaeger, but I didn't think anything of it at the time. I didn't even speak to him, I just saw him. He was at the very back where all the salvaged wood and trim is stored."

"Maybe he was looking for something for his mask-making."

"Jaeger Merrill's masks were made out of metal—not wood. But those religious icons he went to jail for forging—some of those were painted on wood—old wood."

"You think he was in the basement looking for a piece of wood?" Marcus said, skepticism evident in his voice.

"Maybe. What if Jaeger was back in the forgery business? What if, when Maggie took them all down to see how much water had come in, he saw something useful and he went back to get it?"

"Okay," Marcus said. His face was unreadable. Sometime while I was talking he'd gone into police officer mode. I had no idea if he'd taken anything I'd said seriously.

"Anyway, I better get going," I said. "So, uh, have a good day."

"I will." He took a couple of steps back from the truck.

I leaned around him and raised a hand in good-bye to

Derek Craig. Then I got into the truck, fastened my seat belt and as I put the key in the ignition a shiny black pickup bumped its way up the driveway. What was Burtis Chapman doing out here?

The thermos rolled against my hip. There were at least a couple more cups of coffee in it. I picked it up and held it out the window to Marcus. He turned toward me. "Here," I said.

"You sure?" he asked.

I nodded. "You work better when you have a supply of coffee. I think you might get a little crabby without it."

He took the stainless steel flask and I put the truck in gear. "Thanks," he said. "I wouldn't want to be annoying." He stepped back again.

He'd heard what I'd said to Lucy. I could feel my face getting red. I was all the way at the bottom of the driveway before I realized that if Marcus had heard me tell Lucy I thought he was annoying, he'd also heard me say I thought he was cute.

Crap on toast!

14

The phone rang as I was hanging up my coat by the back door. "Hello, Katydid," my mother said when I answered.

"Hi," I said, sinking into the wing chair. "How are things in Boston?"

"Wonderful. The sun is shining. The birds are singing in the trees and for once your father is taking direction."

My parents taught and ran the drama program at a private school in Boston. They did a lot of theatre as well—especially Shakespeare, although my mother was moving more into directing, which meant butting heads with my father when he didn't like her suggestions. Which was only two or three dozen times in a production.

They were very dramatic people—on stage and off—which was why they'd been married, divorced and then married again.

"Is it still raining there?" Mom asked.

"Not at the moment," I said. "I don't want to jinx anything, but I may have even seen a sliver of blue sky a little while ago."

"I'll keep my fingers crossed for you, sweetie," she said and I could hear the smile in her voice. "I take it the library is still closed?" My mother read the *Mayville Heights Chronicle* online so she was usually up to date on what was happening in town.

"If the rain holds off I'm hoping we can open tomorrow." Hercules wandered in from somewhere. I patted my legs and he jumped onto my lap and stretched out on my chest. "I've been helping Maggie move things at the store. There's water in the basement," I said. "Cross your fingers that somebody finds a pump, as well."

"Fingers, toes, arms, legs and eyes," Mom said solemnly.

"Thanks," I said.

"The reason I called was to tell you I'm going to Los Angeles for a few days."

I straightened up a little, which meant Hercules had to move too. He glared at me. "Los Angeles? What for?"

She hesitated for a moment. "I'm going to do a small part—well, actually it's quite a significant part, very integral to a major storyline, what I really should call it is a limited run part"—she paused, for effect of course—"in a soap opera."

"A soap?" I said. "After the last time you said you were never going to do another daytime drama." She'd said more than that, mostly about the skills or lack thereof of the director.

"Sweetie, never is a long time."

"Yes it is," I agreed, grinning at Hercules.

"The executive producer asked specifically for me. He

said the part required an actress of my vintage with my unique skills." Then she laughed, a big, warm sound that rolled into my ear and gave me a small pinch of homesickness. "What he really meant was he was looking for an old broad who wasn't in rehab and who hadn't been tucked, tightened and Botoxed up the ying yang. And when I saw how much money they were offering, it seemed petty to say no."

I laughed. "That was very big of you, Mom," I said. "You'll be terrific."

"Well, of course I will," she said.

We talked for a few more minutes and she promised to call me again when she'd gotten to LA and been to the set.

After I'd hung up I stayed sprawled in the chair, stroking Hercules's fur. "I talked to Marcus about Jaeger," I told him.

The cat lifted his head and looked inquiringly at me. At least that's how I decided to interpret his look.

"I told him I think Maggie may be right," I said. "That Jaeger was up to something. The problem is, I don't have any proof." I pulled a hand back through my hair, sucking in a sharp breath when I touched my bruised forehead. "Ow," I said.

Hercules got up, jumped to the floor and started for the kitchen. "Good idea," I said, getting to my feet. "I need coffee."

The cat positioned himself by the counter and looked at the toaster. Cats are not subtle.

I gave him the Mr. Spock eyebrow. "How about coffee with toast and peanut butter?" I said. That got an enthusiastic "meow."

I turned around to start the coffee and Owen was suddenly right in front of me. "You have ears like a, well, like a cat," I told him. He murped his agreement.

I made coffee and toast and peanut butter and then we settled ourselves around the table—me in one chair with my ankle propped on another because who was I kidding, it still hurt a little, and the boys at my feet with their little bites of toast.

"Okay, so what do we know?" I asked. Neither cat answered. Peanut butter tended to have that effect on them. "We know Jaeger was really Christian Ellis and that he had gone to jail for forgery. He was pushing Maggie to make changes at the co-op store. I saw him at the repurpose store and digging around in a dumpster."

I took a bite of toast myself and chewed thoughtfully. It all proved exactly nothing. Nothing.

Maybe Maggie was wrong. Maybe I was wrong. Maybe Jaeger hadn't been up to anything at all other than trying to make a new life. Maybe we were seeing conspiracies where there weren't any.

Then again, maybe we were right.

I knew how hard Maggie had worked to make the co-op a success. What if Jaeger had gotten the store mixed up in something illegal? If I was going to convince Marcus, I needed a smoking gun, so to speak.

I slid down in the chair so I could lean my head against the back and that's when I saw it. Not a smoking gun. It was the little purple puff I'd picked up out at Wisteria Hill, still on top of the refrigerator. I pushed myself upright and hobbled over to retrieve it. Okay, so it probably wasn't a wig for a forest pixie. What the heck was it?

I sank back onto my chair. "Any idea what this is?" I asked the cats, holding out the puff. Owen immediately leaned in to sniff it, discovered it wasn't something he could eat and went back to his last bit of toast.

Hercules took his time, eyes narrowed, as though he were trying to think of a good answer to my question. After a minute he looked over at the sink and then turned his green eyes on me.

"You think it's something to scrub dishes with?" I asked.

He meowed his agreement.

I turned the purple puff over in my hand. It did have a rough, abrasive feel to it. "I don't know," I said. "I don't think it's big enough to scrub a pot."

Owen made a sound that sounded a lot like a sigh. He stalked over to my briefcase on the floor under the coat hooks and put one paw on top. Then he meowed. Loudly and impatiently.

I looked down at Hercules and shrugged. "I suppose we could go online and see if we can find this thing." Was it my imagination or did he give a why-the-heck-not shrug in return?

It took several tries with my favorite search engine and Hercules on my lap, "helping," before I found a photo of the tiny, purple thingamajig. It was a fine grit, abrasive buff, an attachment that worked exclusively on a small rotary tool. Imported from Sweden.

What had Ruby said when Maggie had told her Jaeger had complained that the cabinet where he kept his tools had gotten wet? *His fancy Swedish tools.*

"Jaeger was out at Wisteria Hill," I told the cats, holding up the abrasive buff. "This has to be his. How many other people in town are going to have some tool exclusively from Sweden?"

Hercules looked thoughtful, at least to me. Owen, on

the other hand, had gone into his faux-modest routine. "Yes, it was a very good suggestion that I go online," I said. He lifted his head to stare pointedly at the cupboard. "And yes, this calls for a kitty cracker." I bent my face close to Herc's black-and-white one before he could start yowling his objections. "For you too. You were a big help with the typing."

I put Hercules on the floor and got a cracker for each cat. I turned the small purple attachment over in my hand. So Roma was right about seeing Jaeger at Wisteria Hill. The old estate would be a good source of aged pieces of wood. The main house and the carriage house were over a hundred years old, I knew. It looked like Maggie was right. But was this enough to convince Marcus?

I leaned forward. "How about a road trip?" I said to Hercules. He immediately looked over to where my messenger bag was hanging next to my jacket as he licked crumbs off his whiskers. Owen, meanwhile, scurried up close to my feet and meowed loudly to get my attention.

"This job needs your brother's particular skill," I said. The cats exchanged looks. Owen made a face and shook his head. Hercules turned his back and started washing his face.

"You can go next time," I said to Owen, who refused to look at me. I pulled another cheese and sardine cracker out of the bag and held it out with a sigh. I was trying to placate a cat.

He took the kitty treat from my fingers and set it on the floor, sniffing and at the same time making sulky, grumbling noises. Hercules kept on ignoring him.

"Good to have that settled," I said, grabbing my cup and heading for the phone.

"Hey, Mags, do you have any plans for lunch?" I asked when Maggie answered her phone.

"No," she said. "What were you thinking?"

"How about Eric's?"

"Oh that would be good." She sounded a bit distracted. "Could you meet me at the shop?"

This was working out perfectly. "Sure," I said. "But isn't it still off limits?"

"Nope. I got the keys back about twenty minutes ago. The police are finished. And guess what?"

"The Pump Fairy found a pump for the basement?"

There was silence for a moment and then Maggie started to laugh.

"What?" I said.

"I'm telling Larry you called him The Pump Fairy," she giggled.

"Larry found a pump? Seriously? Where?"

"Seriously. I have no idea where. It's gas powered so we'll have to make sure it's vented properly, and Larry said it's older than Noah's grandmother, but he and Harry got it going and he swears it'll work. I'm going to meet him over there in about fifteen minutes."

I did a little fist pump in the air. "I'm so glad," I said.

Maggie let out a breath. "Me too. Why don't you meet me there in maybe an hour or so?"

"Sounds good," I said. "I'll see you in an hour."

I headed upstairs to change my old jeans for something a little more presentable. When I came back down Hercules was waiting in the kitchen, sitting underneath the hook where my new messenger bag was hanging. I lifted the bag down; he climbed inside, kneaded the bottom a little with his paws and then lay down.

There was no sign of Owen. He was probably off

somewhere pouting and gnawing on a funky chicken. "We're leaving," I called out.

No response.

"He's still sulking," I said to Herc, who murped his agreement from inside the bag.

We drove down to the library and I was happy to see that while a small part of the parking lot was still underwater, that section of street was open again. Inside the building I let Hercules out of the bag, crouching down so we were face to face. "You can look around for a while," I told him, "but please come when I call you."

He stared at me solemnly, and then he licked my nose and headed for the stacks.

I did a quick survey of both floors of the building and the basement, looking for leaks or any standing water. Happily there were none. I retrieved all the messages from our voice mail and then I cleared the book drop. I was reshelving books when Lita called to tell me the library could reopen on Friday.

As I was putting a couple of back issues of *Scientific American* in their slot, I happened to glance over at the local history section. The library had inherited a collection of Mayville Heights High School yearbooks and photographs during some renovation work at the school building.

I walked over and pulled down the volume for the year that Roma's mother, Pearl, would have graduated.

My first thought was that she looked so young and so serious in the black-and-white photo. She wasn't smiling, but no one was. She wore a short-sleeved white blouse with a Peter Pan collar and black cat's-eye frame glasses. I could see some of Roma in the way she tilted her head and looked directly into the camera.

Roma had Thomas Karlsson's coloring. He too, looked directly into the camera. There was something confident, challenging even, in his gaze.

There was an accordion file full of notes and pictures that went along with the yearbook. I flipped through several mock-up pages that hadn't made it into the finished volume. One section called "School Life," was all unposed, candid snapshots. There was a shot of a group of baseball players crowded into the front seat of a Ford Biscayne with Tom Karlsson grinning behind the wheel. On the second page I discovered a picture of Pearl and a couple of girls standing beside a 1959 T-Bird convertible. It was a beautiful car with fins and wide whitewall tires and I got so caught up in looking at it that I almost missed the young man in the photograph leaning awkwardly on the T-Bird's front fender: Sam Ingstrom. The caption read: Sam gets ready to hit the road.

Except Sam wasn't paying any attention to the road or the car at all. Sam was looking at the girls. One girl.

Pearl.

Interesting.

I checked my watch. It was time to head over to meet Maggie. I decided I'd take the yearbook and the pictures home for a closer look. I walked back to the front desk and called Hercules. After a moment he came around a set of bookshelves, crossed the mosaic tile floor and climbed in the bag. I didn't have to call him six times, threaten, cajole or even offer a bribe.

Clearly, he was screwing with me.

15

Maggie was watching for me at the front door of the co-op. I stepped inside and she smiled. "The pump's working."

"Wonderful," I said. "The street's open in front of the library so we're reopening tomorrow and"—I held out my arm and rolled my left wrist in the air—"there's no rain in the forecast for at least the next twelve hours."

Maggie laughed. "Harry said the same thing. Well, technically his leg did."

"There you go," I said. "A forecast from two unimpeachable sources."

Maggie scrunched up her face as she checked out my forehead. "That looks awful," she said.

"Thank you for sharing."

"No. I mean it looks sore."

"It's okay unless I forget and push my hair back or try to wiggle my eyebrows," I said. I could feel Hercules getting restless in the bag. "And that little packet of herbs you gave me for the bathtub helped. I'm not nearly as stiff as I was."

"You know, I have a marigold salve in my office that Rebecca taught me how to make. That would help your head," Maggie offered.

"Okay." My ankle felt better thanks to the salve Rebecca had given me. It wasn't the first time one of her herbal remedies had made a difference.

"What's in the bag?" Maggie asked. "I thought we were going to Eric's?"

"I brought you a visitor," I said. I unzipped the top of the bag and Hercules poked his head out, looked right at Maggie and meowed.

"Hey, Hercules," she said. Then she looked at me and lowered her voice. "Why did you bring him?"

"You don't have to whisper," I said. "I brought Hercules so he could make sure there aren't any other furry little visitors in the building." And do a little sleuthing for me, I added silently.

I lifted the cat out of the bag and set him on the floor. The first thing he did was shake himself and take a couple of swipes at his face with a paw. It's important to look good when one is nosing into other people's business.

"Are you sure he's not going to take off?" Maggie said.

"Hercules?" I said. "There might be dirt outside. There might be puddles. Not a chance."

Maggie bent down to the cat. "Thank you for coming, Hercules," she said. "I owe you a can of sardines all to yourself for this."

He gave her a decidedly upbeat "meow" and licked his lips.

"Maggie, you talk to them like they're people," I said as she straightened up.

"I can't help it," she said. Hercules was looking around, plotting, maybe, where he was headed first. "They just bring out that kind of response in me." She reached over and locked the door. "Anyway, you talk to them like they're people too."

Hercules meowed loudly. He was looking past me into the store space. "Go ahead," I said. "You know what to do."

"See what I mean?" Maggie said, starting up the stairs.

"The only reason I talk to Hercules and Owen as though they understand is because they have a very large vocabulary," I said, following her up the steps into the studio space. The cat was already out of sight. "They're like that dog we saw on the news a few months ago that knows over a thousand words."

"Do you think Owen and Hercules know a thousand words?" she asked.

"Absolutely," I said. "And they all have to do with food."

"So why didn't you bring Owen?" she said as she unlocked her office door.

"Because all he would have done was moon around you. The Godzilla of rodents could be in the room and he wouldn't see it. If cats can have crushes, Owen has one on you."

"I like the little fur ball," Maggie said as she unlocked the cupboard opposite her desk. "Look at how he brought that chicken out to Roma. You can't tell me he didn't know she was upset. Okay, there it is." She held up a small glass jar.

"What are you going to do about tai chi and yoga classes?" I asked.

"I'm hoping by Tuesday I can get everything out of the studio and back downstairs so we can have class again."

"That would be good," I said.

She put one hand on her hip and looked me up and down. "Have you been practicing the form?"

"Some."

Her green eyes stayed fixed on me. "A little," I said, ducking my head.

She grinned. "Maybe I'll teach some of the movements to Owen and Hercules and then you'll have someone to practice with."

I got a mental picture of the two cats doing cloud hands and laughed. "Hey, have you talked to Roma?" I asked, only partly to change the subject.

Maggie shook her head. "I called her, but all I got was her voice mail. I'll try her again later."

"I will too," I said.

She gestured to her desk chair. "Sit down." She went into the little bathroom to wash her hands, then came back, pinned my hair off my face and put a thin layer of the salve on my scraped head. "How's it feel?" she asked.

"Good," I said, "and it doesn't smell like feet."

Maggie rolled her eyes and screwed the lid back on the little jar. She—with Rebecca's help—had made a wrap for my wrist after the cast had come off last summer. It had helped the ache and the stiffness, but it had smelled, well, like feet.

"So what happens now?" I said. "Is Marcus still investigating Jaeger's death?"

Maggie sat on the corner of her desk. "I don't know. Did he say anything to you this morning?"

I shook my head. "No." I thought about what I'd said to Lucy about Marcus and felt my face flush. Luckily

Maggie had gotten up to put the salve back in her cupboard. "I did share your theory with him."

"Let me guess; he wasn't exactly enthusiastic about it."

"Marcus isn't the kind of person who's going to give much credence to a gut feeling," I said.

Maggie closed the cupboard and leaned against it. "I guess I can't fault him for that. You can't exactly take a gut feeling to court."

The tiny purple buffer was in my pocket. I pulled it out. "Mags, have you ever seen this before?" I asked.

She frowned and moved in for a closer look. Then her expression cleared. "Sure. It's one of the many, many attachments Jaeger has—had—for this little rotary tool he used for working on his masks. From Sweden. Very exclusive."

So I was right.

She looked around the crowded office. "Was it on the floor? Don't tell me I brought one of his boxes in here by mistake."

I shook my head. "It was at Wisteria Hill."

She froze, then swiveled slowly and deliberately to face me. "Wisteria Hill?" she asked.

"I picked it up right before the embankment collapsed." It occurred to me that if I hadn't picked up the little buffer pad, I might not have been so close to the edge, and the ground might not have fallen out from under my feet. Which meant Tom Karlsson's body might never have been found. One thing was connected to the other, the way so many things—and people—seemed to be in Mayville Heights.

Maggie crossed her arms over her chest and leaned against the wall. "He was out there."

"It looks like it."

Her head was going up and down like a bobble-headed doll. "He was out there, probably looking for wood so he could go back to forging those religious icons. It's probably why he was in the basement, too."

I exhaled softly. "I had the same thought."

Maggie fixed her green eyes on me. "You don't sound completely convinced. In fact, I can't believe I'm saying this, but is Marcus Gordon rubbing off on you?"

I got a mental picture of myself, running my hands along his strong jawline. I shook my head. *Where had that come from?*

"No," I said. "But I do know how he thinks. Marcus is going to say we can't prove this thing belonged to Jaeger and even if we could, it doesn't prove he'd gone back to a life of crime, so to speak."

Maggie scrunched up her face. "I hate it when you're logical and sensible."

"I'll try not to do it too often," I said. That made her smile. "And I do agree with you. Jaeger was up to something. I think we just need a little more evidence for Marcus." I didn't say I had Hercules roaming the building hunting for it.

"I can't believe Jaeger lied to all of us," she said. "I talked to Sam and helped Jaeger get this studio space and I vouched for him with Eric when he was looking for part-time work." She shook her head. "So much for my good judgment. I didn't even know the real person."

"Neither did anyone else," I pointed out.

"Am I overreacting? Do you think Jaeger had an agenda from the beginning?" she asked. "I mean, other than just a fresh start? He really was a nice guy in the beginning—or at least he seemed like one."

"I don't think you're overreacting," I said. I ran my hand

along the arm of Maggie's chair. It didn't look very comfortable but it was. "Aside from the fact that Peter Lundgren was his lawyer and Peter was from here, Mayville seems like an odd choice for a place to start over. And Jaeger changing his name, changing the way he looked, just because he'd been in prison, it seems a bit much."

"Why did Peter go along with the whole charade?" she said, stretching both arms up over her head.

"Probably some kind of lawyer/client thing."

Maggie nodded, but I realized most of her focus was on the piles of boxes in the room. "You know, there's a lot of Jaeger's stuff to be dealt with between the studio and here," she said slowly.

"I wonder if he had any family," I said.

She twisted her mouth to one side in thought. "Peter has lunch at Eric's at least a couple of times a week."

"He does."

She made a show of looking at her watch—or where her watch would have been if she'd been wearing it. "If we left now, maybe we could catch Peter and see if he knows who Jaeger's next of kin is."

"Maybe we could," I said, getting to my feet. "It's not as though you want to vent on Peter a little."

"Uh uh," Maggie said.

I did the Mr. Spock eyebrow.

She flushed. "Well, maybe just a little."

I stared at her without saying anything.

"Well, maybe a lot," she said. "I just need to wash my hands again and we can go."

"All right," I said.

Maggie stopped in the doorway. "Wait a second. What are we going to do with Hercules? We can't take a cat to Eric's."

It didn't seem like a good idea to tell her I'd actually done that once.

"We could leave him here in your office," I said. "He's nosy, but he won't damage anything. He'll probably end up sleeping in your desk chair."

"Fine with me," Maggie said.

While she went to get cleaned up, I went out into the open area at the top of the staircase where we hung up our coats and changed our shoes for tai chi class, intending to call Hercules. He was sitting under the coat hooks next to a pile of boxes and he looked, well, smug. That look generally meant he'd found something. I'd given up trying to find a logical explanation for the cats' skill at sleuthing. My best guess was that it was somehow connected to their other abilities.

I shot a quick glance back over my shoulder, and then I bent down and held out my hand. "Spit it out," I said. "Maggie will be back in a minute."

He spit out what looked like part of an old pen. I stuffed it in my pocket and wiped my hand on my pants. The cat walked over to the top of the stairs, glanced down and meowed.

I looked over the railing. There was a corpse of something gray and furry lying by the front door. "Very nice," I said approvingly. I crouched down to scratch the top of his head. "It is dead, right?" I whispered.

His response was to start washing his face with unconcerned confidence.

Maggie appeared then. "Stay here for a minute," I said to her, straightening up.

Her eyes went from me to the cat. "Why?" she asked, her voiced edged with suspicion.

"Hercules found . . . something."

She took an involuntary step backward. "Something . . . alive?"

I glanced over the railing again and gave a slight shake of my head. "Not anymore."

Hercules was still zealously washing his face. I was pretty sure I knew whose job cleaning up down by the door was going to be.

When I came back up the stairs again, Maggie was sitting on the bench, talking to Hercules who sat about three feet away from her. "You're my hero," I heard her say. He did his best aw-shucks head dip.

"Gone," I said to Maggie. Then I bent down and picked up the cat who was still doing his modest shtick, looking at Maggie sideways through his whiskers. "You're laying it on a little thick," I whispered as I carried him into Maggie's office.

I fished in my purse for the little bag of cat crackers I'd brought with me. Maggie found a small glass bowl and went to get some water. "We'll be less than an hour," I said in a low voice. "You better be in here when we get back."

Hercules pretended to suddenly be very interested in the bottom of his right front paw. "I know you're not actually going to stay in this room the entire time but don't leave the building."

He looked up, all green-eyed kitty innocence. Then he licked my chin.

"I'm not kidding," I said sternly. "I have three words for you: Animal Control Officer."

16

Maggie was in luck. Peter was sitting at a table by the end wall at Eric's, just finishing his lunch. He was dressed as though he'd just come from court, or somewhere equally formal. The jacket of his dark gray suit hung over the back of his chair, and his sandy hair was pulled into a ponytail. He'd loosened his striped tie and rolled up the sleeves of his white shirt.

Claire showed us to a table and before we could sit down, Peter had gotten up and walked over to us. "Hello, Kathleen," he said. He looked just a little uncomfortable to me, hands jammed in his pockets.

I smiled. "Hello, Peter," I said.

He turned his attention to Maggie. "Hello, Maggie," he said. "I heard about what happened to Jaeger Merrill. I'm sorry."

Maggie stood perfectly still and straight and studied Peter for a long moment. "Why did you lie about who Jaeger was?" she said finally.

Just a hint of color flushed Peter's cheeks. "He was my client."

"Was it your idea for Jaeger—excuse me—Christian Ellis to start over here in Mayville Heights?"

Peter shook his head. "No." He took a deep breath and let it out. "That case was my very first solo case. I've always wondered if I could have done better. Christian didn't deserve the sentence he got. When he showed up here using a different name, looking for a new start, I didn't see how it could hurt to let him have it. And it's not as though anyone asked me if Jaeger Merrill was Christian Ellis."

I thought about Ruby who had been so certain she'd recognized Jaeger from somewhere. What would have happened if she'd figured out who he really was when he was still alive?

"You're splitting hairs, Peter," Maggie said, her tone cool. "I vouched for Jaeger—excuse me—for Christian with Sam, so he could get studio space at River Arts"— she gestured to the counter—"and with Eric for a job, and with the other artists at the co-op, and it turns out I didn't even know who I was speaking for."

He slid a hand back over his hair. "I am sorry about that, Maggie," he said. "Christian was punished more severely than anyone else in that scam." He held up his hand. "I know he broke the law and I'm not excusing what he did, but he didn't even realize what was going on in the beginning and when he did figure it out, he stayed in because he needed the money to take care of his sick mother."

He shook his head and laughed. "I know it's a cliché, but it's the truth. Christian cooperated with the authorities when the whole scheme was exposed, he took responsibility and pled guilty, and then he ended up serving the most time because a judge threw out the plea deal."

"He wouldn't have had to serve any time at all if he hadn't broken the law in the first place," Maggie said.

Peter traced the edge of the table with a finger. "I know. But in the real world people make mistakes. And Christian didn't kill anyone. He wasn't selling drugs to kids. He faked paintings. I'm not saying it was a victimless crime, but . . ." He shrugged.

Mags took a deep breath and let it out slowly. "I know that," she said. "And I don't want to fight with you."

He smiled, the first genuine smile I'd seen from the man since we'd walked into Eric's. "Were we fighting?" he asked.

Maggie let that pass and answered Peter's smile with one of her own. "Do you know who Jaeger's executor is? There are boxes of his things at his studio and more at the store."

"I don't know for sure," he said. "Probably me." He looked at his watch. "I have to be in court this afternoon. Are those things going to be okay where they are for a day or so? I'll see what I can find out."

"They're fine," she said. "A lot of his stuff was packed in boxes already because of all the water." Her face clouded over. "If it hadn't rained so much, if those stairs hadn't been wet . . ."

"It's wet all over town," Peter said. "What happened to Christian was just a stupid, careless accident. It could have happened to anyone. It could have happened to you."

A shiver slid up my back. I remembered how Maggie had slipped on those wet, wooden steps when we'd found Jaeger, and almost ended up in the filthy water herself.

Peter looked at me. "I hear you had an accident out at Wisteria Hill. You're all right?"

I nodded. "Yes, I am. Thanks."

He held up his left hand. There was a large, bandage on most of the palm. "I did this in the parking lot of my own office." He leaned sideways and looked out the front window of the restaurant. "At least it looks like the worst of the rain is over."

He turned his attention back to Maggie. "I am sorry about all the turmoil Christian's death caused for you. If there are any repercussions—for the co-op or you personally—call me. I'll take care of anything that needs a lawyer, free of charge. And I'll find out who his executor is."

He pulled out a pen and a business card and wrote something on the back of the card before he handed it to her. "That's my cell number on the back." He looked from Maggie to me. "Enjoy your lunch," he said and then he turned and went back to his own table.

"I have a question," I said as we sat down. Claire was already on her way over with menus. We ordered and Claire poured me a cup of coffee, then she headed for the kitchen, detouring to top up Peter's cup.

"What's your question?" Maggie asked as I added cream to my coffee.

"Peter said that Christian Ellis was his first solo case."

She nodded, pouring tea into a cup from the little pot Claire had brought her.

"That case would have been five or six years ago. How long has he been a lawyer?"

"Here in town? About four years or so. Peter worked in Chicago for about a year before that. The time frame fits."

"He didn't go to law school right away," I said, sipping my coffee.

Maggie looked in the direction of the lawyer's table. "Peter didn't go to university right away. He didn't even finish high school."

"Seriously?" Peter Lundgren was so well spoken I never would have guessed he'd quit school. Being at the library and seeing what books people read, what music they liked to listen to, and what movies they were watching gave me a little peek into who they were. And often left me even more curious. For example, I'd learned that Peter liked heavy metal music, which didn't exactly fit with my image of a lawyer.

"He's literally a self-made man. There were ten kids in that family. Poor as dust. Peter quit school in ninth grade, went to work at a garage. Eventually he became a mechanic."

She picked up her cup. "You'll like this: he all but lived at the library in his free time. Eventually he got his GED. Then he got a scholarship to university. He did four years in three and got accepted to law school and he's helping three"—she held up the corresponding number of fingers—"three of his younger siblings with college right now."

"I guess it makes sense that he'd go to bat for Jaeger."

Maggie gave me a half smile. "Yeah, I guess it does."

Claire came back then with our sandwiches and more coffee and we stopped talking. I'd almost finished my sandwich—as usual Eric's sourdough bread was better than any I made—when Sam Ingstrom, Mayville Heights's mayor came in. He raised a hand in recognition to us and crossed to the counter. After he'd spoken to Claire he came over to the table.

"Hello Kathleen, Maggie," he said. Sam didn't look like a man who was almost seventy. He was heavier than he'd been in that high school photo I'd seen, but he was in good shape and there was still some dark hair mixed in with the gray.

"Hello, Sam," I said. Maggie, whose mouth was full, just nodded.

"You know that the street's clear and the library can reopen tomorrow?"

"I do," I said. "Thank you."

He studied my face and frowned. "I heard what happened at Wisteria Hill," he said. "How are you?"

"I'm fine," I said. "It looks worse than it is." I seemed to be saying that a lot.

"Glad to hear it," Sam said.

"You were friends with Tom Karlsson and Pearl Carver weren't you, back in high school?"

He shook his head. "No. I mean I knew Tom, Mayville Heights was pretty small back in those days, so we all knew each other at school, and he was a star athlete, but we weren't friends. I was a year younger. I barely knew Pearl at all."

Sam wore his own high school class ring on his right hand. I noticed he was rubbing the back of it with his thumb.

"I was surprised to hear those remains turned out to be Tom Karlsson," Sam continued. "Everyone always figured he just ran out on his responsibilities. He was that kind of man." He half turned. Claire had just come from the kitchen with what was likely Sam's order in a take-out bag. He gave me his politician's smile. "Good to see you, Kathleen," he said. He nodded at Maggie and walked back to the counter.

I was so intent on watching Sam that I didn't notice for a minute that Maggie was watching me. "You have that look," she said.

I turned my attention to her. "What look?"

"That 'something's off' look." She set down her cup and pushed her plate away. "Sam said something that didn't sit right with you."

I leaned back in my chair, thinking of the photo I'd seen in that accordion file of old high school yearbook photos at the library. "He said he barely knew Pearl, which isn't true. Why would he lie about that?"

17

"What makes you think Sam's lying?" Maggie asked, gesturing to Claire for our checks. "You didn't want dessert, did you?"

I shook my head. "I found the high school yearbook for the year Roma's father graduated. There are a bunch of pictures that didn't make it into the book, mostly candid shots. Sam's in one of them, so is Pearl and some other girls. It's pretty clear from the way Sam is looking at Pearl that he had a thing for her."

"That's probably the reason," Maggie said, getting to her feet as Claire approached the table.

I frowned. "What do you mean?"

"I think I told you that I was a little late discovering boys."

"You did." I smiled at Claire as I pulled out my wallet.

"Did you want a cup of coffee to go?" she asked as she handed over my bill.

"I did," I said. I looked at the cardboard take-out cup she was holding. "Is that for me?"

"It is," she said with a smile.

I took the coffee and gave her the money for my meal plus a tip because Claire always gave great service.

"I heard about Jaeger," she said to Maggie. "I'm sorry." She looked past us, out the front window of the restaurant where the sky looked a little lighter than it had earlier. "Maybe it's finally stopped raining and things can get back to normal." She turned back to us again. "Have a good day," she said and then she turned and headed back to the counter.

I pulled on my hoodie, careful not to catch the edge of the bandage wrapped around my thumb.

Maggie watched me. "I still think that thumb needs stitches."

"I know," I said with a small smile.

We started back to the shop. The sky really did seem less gray. Maybe Claire was right and we'd be able to get back to normal.

"Okay, so explain to me what you being slow to notice boys has to do with Sam lying about knowing Roma's mom," I said.

She brushed a stray blond curl off of her face. "My first year of college I had a huge crush on the guy who sat in front of me in my calculus tutorial." She grinned. "The back of his head was gorgeous. The front was pretty cute too."

"So what happened?"

"Nothing," she said. "He pretty much didn't know I was alive. I mooned over the guy for the entire semester. Everybody who sat near us knew I had a thing for the guy because I had that goony, love-struck look on my face all the time and trust me it wasn't because I loved calculus."

We stopped at the corner while a couple of cars and an SUV turned up the hill, then we crossed the street.

"The thing is," Maggie continued, "I literally sighed over the guy for months and never even talked to him. So even now, if someone were to ask me if I'd known him, my first reaction would be to say no, just because I still feel a bit embarrassed about the way I acted."

It was hard to imagine Maggie being tongue-tied and awkward around anyone. Last winter when we'd been trying to figure out who had killed Agatha Shepherd, we'd ended up at a club up on the highway. She so totally charmed the bartender, for a moment he'd forgotten how to do anything other than grin at her like an idiot.

"So you think Sam is just embarrassed about a teen-age crush?" I said. I knew I looked skeptical. That's how I felt.

Maggie leaned sideways. "Dried-up raisin," she said, slowly and clearly.

I stopped walking and glared at her. "Not the same thing," I said.

She was referring to a cereal commercial my dad had done years ago. He'd played a dried-up raisin in the competitor's not quite as good product. And developed a cult following. He'd actually had a fan club for a while called—you guessed it—The Raisinettes.

I'd been mortified and I admit I'd cringed a little when the company had decided to revive that ad campaign just a couple of months ago. And I hadn't exactly told many people it was my father in the commercial.

Maggie was still looking at me with the same unblinking gaze I sometimes got from the cats.

"It's not the same thing," I said huffily.

She laughed then.

"Fine. You win," I said, and started walking again.

Hercules was curled up on Maggie's desk chair when we got back to the store. He opened one green eye and studied us for a moment. I got the carrier, set it on the floor by the chair and opened the top.

"Let's go," I said. The cat made a show of yawning, stretching, and taking his time getting in the bag. I closed the top and slung the bag over my shoulder.

"I need to get going," I said to Maggie. "Susan and Mary are meeting me at the library." I'd called both of them to come in for a couple of hours so we'd be ready to open on Friday. "Call me later and let me know how the pump's working."

"I will," she promised. "And I'm going to call Roma too."

"Good," I said. "I'll try her when I get home." I put a hand on the carrier. I could feel Hercules moving inside.

"Thank you Hercules," Maggie said, leaning in to look at him through the side mesh panel.

He meowed loudly in acknowledgment.

Susan was standing by the front steps and Mary was coming from the mostly dry parking lot when I got to the library. I unlocked the door and turned off the alarm. "The first thing I need to do is put Hercules in my office," I said, putting a hand on the top of the bag.

"Did I miss Take Your Cat to Work Day again?" Susan asked. Her hair was up in its usual topknot, a silver skewer poked through it.

"I'm sorry, Susan," Mary said, all mock-seriousness. "I forgot to forward the memo."

"You two are so funny," I said.

Susan waggled her eyebrows at me. "We think so." She gestured at my bag. "Why did you bring Hercules with you? Are you planning on making him shelve books?"

I shook my head. "I was thinking that I'd get him to add new books to the system. He's a pretty good two-pawed typist."

Herc picked that moment to meow with great enthusiasm and volume. Mary and Susan both laughed.

"He was over at the co-op on rodent patrol for Maggie," I said.

"Eric told me what happened when you had the job," Susan said.

I felt my face getting red.

"What am I missing?" Mary asked, hands on her hips.

"Nothing," I said, quickly.

"Kathleen was the previous rodent wrangler," Susan said. "Turns out it's not one of her strengths."

Hercules chose that moment to meow loudly yet again. It was like having a feline Greek chorus on my hip.

"Details," Mary said.

Susan made a go-ahead gesture with one hand.

"There was a dead rat floating in the basement over at the co-op store," I said. "I fished it out and took it outside. That's all."

Susan smirked at me. "You left out the part about throwing it at Ruby."

"You threw a dead animal at poor little Ruby?" Mary said, frowning at me.

"No," I said. "I was just putting it outside and Ruby kind of got in the way."

"Now you see, the way I heard it, you used a shovel like it was a tennis racquet and the rodent in question wasn't exactly dead," Susan said, still smirking.

"Wait, wait, wait," Mary interrupted, holding up a hand. "You threw a live rat at Ruby?"

"No," I said. "Not exactly." I should have stopped talking. "At least not on purpose." I slid the cat carrier down off my shoulder. "It's complicated."

The one-cat Greek chorus took the opportunity to add his two cents. "Don't start," I said darkly to the bag.

Mary and Susan were shaking with laughter.

"Seriously," I said. "And Maggie doesn't know the rat—"

"—had more than one life to live?" Susan finished.

"Please don't tell her," I said.

They both held up their little fingers, linked them, and chanted, "I will not bend, I will not break, this pinky swear I now do make." Then they gave me big, goony smiles.

I shook my head slowly. "I swear sometimes the two of you are worse than a couple of six-year-olds."

They grinned and high-fived each other.

"Moving along, I think the first thing we need to do is open some windows and get some fresh air in here," I said, heading for the stairs.

"I'll open a couple down here," Susan said, heading for the computer area.

Mary gestured at my take-out cup. "Should I start the coffeemaker?"

I looked at her without saying a word and she mock-slapped her forehead. "Oh what am I saying? I forgot who I was talking to."

We started up the steps together. "Your forehead looks sore. I heard what happened. Do you feel all right?"

"I do, thanks," I said. "I have some pretty spectacular bruises, though."

Mary hitched her oversized, quilted tote bag a little higher on her shoulder. "As long as you weren't badly hurt, that's all that matters." She stopped on the step below me, one hand on the dark wood railing. "I didn't believe it at first when I heard Tom Karlsson's body was out there."

The image of that dirt-encrusted skull flashed into my mind. "It's difficult for Roma," I said.

"And Pearl too, I imagine," Mary said. "You know, I haven't seen her in a long time."

"You were friends?"

"Heavens yes. We were in the same class for years." She gave me a sly grin. "Don't let my girlish good looks fool you."

"So you knew Tom?" I said.

Mary nodded. "That I did. A real ladies' man. All charm and very little substance." She laughed. "My mother called him a 'slick willie.' Pretty much tells you all you need to know."

"What about Sam?" I asked. Hercules was moving in the bag against my hip again.

"Sammy Ingstrom? He was a grade behind us. Plus his father had money. Sam used to drive this aquamarine T-Bird to school. We didn't run in the same circles."

I thought about that photo again. Was I seeing something that wasn't there?

We went up the last few steps. "You know, I always thought Sam had a bit of a crush on Pearl, though," Mary said as if she'd somehow read my mind.

"Really?" I said.

"Oh yes," she said, her blue eyes twinkling. "It would

probably surprise you, given how much he likes to go on and on now, but back then Sammy didn't say much. And if he was around Pearl, well"—she gave me a knowing smile—"the boy was practically catatonic."

She headed down the hall to the staff room and I went into my office. Maybe Maggie was right. Maybe Sam had lied about knowing Pearl purely out of embarrassment.

As soon as I let Hercules out of the bag he went for my office chair, sending it looping around in a circle when he jumped on the seat.

I reached for the back and stopped it spinning and the cat looked up at me slightly cross-eyed it seemed to me.

"You like that," I said. He may not have cared for catnip the way Owen did, but it was clear Hercules liked the rush of spinning around in my chair.

I turned the seat to face the window so he could both bird and people watch. Then I hung up my jacket and changed my rubber boots for shoes.

The pen cap that Hercules had found at the co-op was still in my pocket. I took it out to look at it again. It was clearly old. It looked a lot like the pen I'd seen Everett use, which he'd mentioned once had been his mother's, but I didn't see how the cap from a pen belonging to Everett could have ended up at the co-op building. It wasn't Maggie's as far as I knew. I turned the piece of the pen over in my fingers, wondering where Hercules had found it and why he'd thought it was important enough to bring to me.

"Care to tell me why you think this is important?" I asked. The cat looked over his shoulder at me with the same unreadable gaze Maggie had given me earlier. I sighed and put the small piece of metal and plastic back in my pocket. I wasn't going to get any answers from a cat. I needed to get the library ready to reopen, not play Nancy Drew with Hercules.

"Stay in here," I warned the little black-and-white cat. "If Mary or Susan find you roaming around the library there will be way too much explaining to do."

As usual, he ignored me.

I stopped for a moment at the head of the stairs and surveyed the library space below me. The renovations had been complicated and more than once I'd thought the job would never be finished. But the building looked wonderful. The mosaic tile floors in the checkout area had been repaired. There were new windows and new flooring elsewhere in the building, as well as additional shelving and a new checkout desk that was more efficient—thanks to Mary's organization skills—and that took up less space.

Oren Kenyon's beautifully hand-carved wooden sun shone down from over the front doors, above the words LET THERE BE LIGHT, the same phrase that was over the entrance to the first Carnegie library in Dunfermline, Scotland. And now we were getting ready to celebrate the centennial of this building.

That reminded me that I needed to talk to Rebecca about the missing pages in her mother's journals as well as ask Maggie for her ideas on how best to display Ellen's sketches.

I went down to the main floor and stood looking around the computer area. My plan was to rearrange the space for the main centennial display. Maggie had already started the photo collage panels I wanted to put in the room.

Susan came to stand beside me. "Do you remember

how we were talking about displaying the photo panels on some kind of oversized easel?" she said.

"I do," I said.

"I had an idea. I don't know if you'll like it and I don't know if Oren will say it's doable." She pushed her dark-framed glasses up her nose.

"What is it?"

She tipped her head back and pointed at the high ceiling. "I don't know if you can see them or not," she said. "But there are hooks up there, in the beams, in more than one place." She pointed. "Look."

I squinted up over my head. Susan was right. I hadn't noticed them before, but there were what looked to be metal hooks fastened to the ceiling beams in several places.

"If there are enough hooks and they're in the right places, maybe the panels could be hung from the ceiling."

"I like that idea," I said. "I'll call Oren and see what he says. Thank you."

She pressed both palms together and gave me a deep bow. "I live to serve," she said.

I walked over to the desk for a piece of paper so I could write myself a reminder to call Oren ... and Maggie ... and Rebecca. The phone rang while I was standing there and I answered instead of letting the call go to voice mail. It was someone wanting to know if we'd be reopening soon. I was happy to tell the caller tomorrow.

It didn't take long to get the library ready for people again. Mary and I had kept up with the book drop and the reshelving. Now she dusted and put out the new magazines while I vacuumed and Susan checked the computers. Then I checked the e-mail again, while Mary took care of the voice mail messages and Susan dealt with the mail Mary had stopped to pick up from the post office on her way over. After about an hour we stopped for Mary's coffee and—no surprise—the conversation turned to Jaeger Merrill's death. The news was spreading fast.

"So how long is the co-op store going to be closed?" Mary asked.

"The police are already finished there." I added a bit more cream to my cup. "And Larry Taylor found a pump for the basement so if the rain holds off"—Mary was quick to rap her knuckles on the edge of the wooden table—"Maggie may be able to reopen in a few days."

"Are the photo panels she's doing for the centennial finished?" Susan asked, poking the silver skewer a little more securely into her hair.

"Almost," I said. "And I got some things from Rebecca— from her mother, actually—that I'd like to use."

"That reminds me," Susan said, shaking a finger at me. "Abigail found a list of library rules from back in the late fifties."

"Library rules?" I said.

Mary was already nodding and smiling. "They used to give them out when you got a library card. Every kid got a copy. The rules of proper library behavior. That was back in the days of 'children should be seen and not heard.'"

"Whoever came up with that saying clearly didn't have any kids," Susan said, dryly.

"So what were the rules for proper library behavior?" I asked Mary, leaning back to get a bit more comfortable.

"No voices above a whisper, for one," she said. "And everyone was supposed to wash their hands before they handled any books."

"That rule isn't necessarily bad," Susan said. "Remember the guy who was reading *Sonnets from the Portuguese* and eating the peanut butter and marshmallow fluff sandwich? I'm sorry but peanut butter and fluff are just not romantic and they're not good for books either."

"What else?" I said to Mary.

"Children were expected to step lightly, preferably tiptoe so as not to disturb the other patrons."

Susan rolled her eyes.

"And when I was in school, I can remember the teacher instructing us that we should choose books that would enrich our minds instead of ones that encouraged frivolous pursuits." Mary smiled at the memory. "*Treasure Island*, for example, was considered to be a book that encouraged too much daydreaming."

"Why do I get the feeling you read every single book that encouraged frivolous pursuits?" I said.

The smile spread into a grin. "My mother's influence. She read us *Gulliver's Travels* when I was about six."

"I'm trying to imagine trying to enforce the no books that encourage frivolous pursuits edict today," Susan said, frowning at the bottom of her cup as though she didn't know what had happened to her coffee.

"Things were very different when I was in school," Mary said, getting up and opening the cupboard over the sink. She reached up and felt around on the top shelf. "Are there any cookies?"

"No," Susan said. "You and Abigail ate them last week." She turned to me. "You have to display those library rules. People will get a kick out of them."

"I'll ask Abigail to bring them in. How about taking a look in the storage room to see if you can find anything else like that?"

"Sure," Susan said.

Mary had come back to the table.

"Do you remember a group called The Ladies Knitting Circle?" I said. "I think they might have had at least some of their meetings here and I'm wondering if Abigail has them on her list."

Mary gave a snort of laughter. "The Ladies Knitting Circle should have their own display, but they weren't the kind of group you think they were. They weren't getting together to exchange sweater patterns and try different kinds of yarn."

Susan looked at me and shrugged. Clearly she didn't know what Mary meant either.

"So what were they doing?" I asked.

"Hiding abused women from their husbands and then sneaking them out of town."

I'm pretty sure my mouth fell open. "You're not serious?" I said.

"Oh yes I am," Mary said. "My mother was part of the group." Something in her face changed. The gently teasing smile disappeared.

"Were you?" I asked quietly.

She nodded. "It was all Anna Henderson's doing."

"Everett's mother," Susan said.

"Yes," Mary said. She was sitting very straight in her chair, one finger tracing a circle on the table. "And Ellen Montgomery—Rebecca's mother—and my mother, and a few other women in town. Me, eventually. But Anna was the driving force. She knew people. She had access to her own money."

She was looking at me, but her focus was clearly in the past. "Anna would arrange for new identities—new names, birth certificates, driver's licenses. I don't know how. And trust me, it all looked like the real thing. And she'd get the women away to start new lives. A fair number of them ended up across the border in Canada."

The odd reference to yarn from Canada in Ellen's journal suddenly made a lot more sense.

"I don't know if Carson knew what she was doing or not," Mary continued. "It wouldn't surprise me if he had, but it wouldn't have mattered, he adored Anna."

"What did you do?" I asked, leaning forward, one arm propped on the table.

The twinkle came back into Mary's gaze. "Showed a little cleavage, a fair amount of leg and played dumb."

Susan laughed and tucked a stray strand of hair behind her ear. "The cleavage I believe, but I'm having a little trouble imagining you playing dumb."

"Let's just say I was kind of cute when I was younger," Mary said. "So some people didn't pay a lot of attention to this." She tapped the side of her head with one hand.

"You were more than 'kind of cute,'" I said. I'd seen photos of Mary in her twenties. She'd been a beautiful young woman, long dark hair, lots of curves and that wicked smile. She was still beautiful. Kickboxing gave her great legs and she still had that smile.

Maggie and I had accidently come across Mary doing a slightly naughty burlesque routine during amateur night this past winter at The Brick, a club out on the highway. I hoped I looked even half that terrific when I was her age, although I didn't think I'd ever be swinging a feather boa and dancing in high heels.

"Yes I was," Mary said with a sly sideways grin. "But modesty prevented me from saying that myself."

"I want to know what you mean when you say you 'played dumb.'" Susan said.

"Sometimes we needed a little diversion, to give the women time to get away. My specialty was a flat tire that I just couldn't fix. I was pretty good with a dead battery and a dry radiator, too."

Mary went on talking, but all I could think about was that Anna Henderson had been helping women disappear. Tom Karlsson's remains had been buried out at Wisteria Hill. Could Anna have had anything to do with his "disappearance"?

18

We finished getting the library ready to reopen and I sent Mary and Susan home, telling them I'd see them tomorrow. I gathered up Hercules, locked the building and set the alarm.

I had just set the cat on the seat of the truck when I heard someone call my name. I turned, pushing my hair out of my eyes and for once remembering not to touch my scraped forehead. It was Abigail.

"Hi," I called as she cut across the parking lot. "I was going to call you. We're reopening tomorrow."

"Good," she said. "If the library had stayed closed any longer, I might have had to do some housework."

Her gray hair, streaked with red, was in a braid over one shoulder and she was wearing bright yellow rubber boots covered with saucy happy faces all sticking out their tongues. Everyone had cuter boots than my plain black ones—even Hercules—which reminded me that I still hadn't explained to Maggie that boots were just not the cat's thing.

"What do you think of this?" she asked, opening the book she was carrying to a page marked with a scrap of paper.

I studied the color photograph. "I like it," I said, looking up at her with a smile.

It was a puppet theatre, at least five feet high and almost as wide.

"It's made out of a couple of appliance boxes and other recycled material. I'd like to make it for story time. Could I use the workroom to put it together?"

"Sure," I said. I looked at the picture again. "I have a little money left in my contingency fund. What do you need?"

Abigail shook her head. "Nothing. If I can't beg, borrow or scrounge what I need out of someone's recycling bin I'm losing my touch."

"Okay," I said, holding out both hands. "I don't want to take the fun out of it for you."

Her expression grew serious. "I'd like to get Maggie's opinion on reinforcing the top. I couldn't believe it when I heard what happened to Jaeger," she said. "We just saw him a couple of weeks ago at that estate sale and now he's dead."

"I don't remember seeing Jaeger at the sale," I said.

"Well he was there," Abigail insisted. "I spoke to him." She frowned. "It might have been when you went to look at those bookshelves. Anyway, he was definitely there with—I can't think of his name—the guy who does those drawings with the duck in the hat and sunglasses."

The hairs came up on the back of my neck. "Ray," I said.

She nodded. "That's him. I love his work." She looked thoughtfully past me at the building. I could tell she was already putting the puppet theatre together in her mind. "Okay, I'll call Maggie later," she said. "Thanks Kathleen."

"I can't wait to see it," I said.

"I'll see you tomorrow," she said. She headed back toward the sidewalk and I got into the truck.

I'd forgotten to ask Abigail if she'd come across The Ladies Knitting Circle in her research on the various groups that had used the library over the years. When she'd said Jaeger had been at that estate sale with Ray Nightingale, that had chased pretty much everything else out of my head.

Ray had told Ruby and me that he barely knew Jaeger. So what had Jaeger and Ray been doing at that estate sale together?

I hadn't zippered the carrier bag all the way. Hercules poked out first a paw and then his entire head. He looked at me quizzically, which might have meant he was curious about what we'd just learned from Abigail, or that he was thinking when do we eat.

"This just gets more and more complicated," I told him. "Looks like Jaeger wasn't the only one keeping secrets." I put the key in the ignition. "Oh what a tangled web we weave, When first we practice to deceive." I glanced over at the cat. "That's not Shakespeare, by the way." He wasn't impressed.

When I got to the corner I really intended to turn up the hill and go home. Really. Instead I found myself driving over to the River Arts Center.

I shot a quick glance at Hercules. He'd climbed all the way out of the bag and was sitting, looking out the windshield, seemingly checking the scenery as it went by. "If Ray's not there, we'll go home," I said.

The cat didn't even bother looking at me. And it might have been my imagination that he shrugged.

I parked on a side street and reached for the cat bag. Hercules continued to look out the window. "C'mon, get in," I said.

He didn't so much as twitch a whisker.

"You'll miss all the fun if you stay in the truck."

Nothing.

I glanced at my watch. I didn't really have a lot of time. "Ruby might be there and she usually has cookies."

That did the trick.

I pulled out my cell phone and called Ruby. She answered on the fifth ring, sounding a little distracted. "Hi Ruby, it's Kathleen," I said. "Are you in your studio?"

"I am," she said.

"Could I come up?"

"Yeah. Sure." There was a momentary silence. Then she said, "This might sound weird, but if I don't ask you now I'm going to forget; could I take some pictures of your cats?"

"Yes," I said slowly, wondering why Ruby wanted to photograph Owen and Hercules. Feeling slightly embarrassed, I said, "And as it happens, I have Hercules with me."

"Um, you do?"

"Uh huh."

"Great," she said, clearly deciding not to pass judgment. "I'm on my way down."

I closed my phone and reached for the cat bag. One furry black ear was sticking out the top. "You know what this is," I said. "Deus ex machina."

The entire black-and-white head popped up out of the opening. Herc narrowed his green eyes at me.

"That's Latin for 'God from the machine.' Or what my mother calls, 'God in a helicopter.' You know that moment in a really bad movie where the hero is about to be attacked by a grizzly bear and then the bear remembers the hero dug a splinter out of his paw back when the bear was just a cub and so he teams up with the hero and they take out the bad guys together."

Hercules pulled one paw out of the bag, turned it over and looked at it, then looked quizzically up at me.

"Yes, it could have been a cat instead of a grizzly bear." He ducked down into the bag and I reached for the strap. I shook my head. Maybe I should spend more time talking to actual people instead of cats.

Ruby was waiting by the back door in flip-flops and a paint-spattered T-shirt and jeans. Her hair was stuck in three little pigtails, one on each side of her head and one sticking straight up.

"You're not looking for Maggie, are you?" she said.

"No, I was hoping Ray Nightingale was here," I said.

She twisted her mouth to one side. "I'm not sure," she said. "He probably is. He works pretty much every day. We can go see."

Hercules decided to announce his presence then with a loud meow. I held up the bag. "Like I said, I have a cat. Do you have a camera?"

She grinned at me. "Yes. I'm not even going to ask you why you're carrying a cat around town with you." She started up the stairs and I followed.

"Rodent patrol at the co-op," I said.

"Yeah, I'm thinking Hercules would probably be better at it than you were," she said over her shoulder. "He'd at least make sure whatever he caught was dead before he threw it at someone."

"First of all, I wasn't aiming at you," I said. "Because if I had been, I wouldn't have missed. And second, how the heck was I supposed to know it wasn't dead? Check its pulse?"

I should have known Hercules would meow his opinion at that exact moment. Ruby laughed.

"No one was asking you," I said to the top of the bag.

We stopped at the second floor and Ruby pointed down the long hallway. "That's Ray's studio on the right-hand side at the end. It looks like there's a light on."

"Okay," I said. "We'll take Hercules upstairs and I'll come back down."

We went up the rest of the way to Ruby's studio and I set the cat carrier on one of the big tables she had in the middle of the room. Hercules climbed out, shook his head and looked around.

"I'm not making any promises that he'll sit still for you," I said.

Of course he immediately sat down, tipped his head to one side and gave Ruby an I'm-so-cute look.

Ruby laughed. "That cat is smart," she said.

He did his modest head duck, which pretty much worked on everyone but me.

"He certainly thinks he is," I said. "Remember not to touch him, and if you have any cookies, you should be able to get whatever photos you want."

Hercules's head had come back up at the word cookies and he was scanning the room as though he were trying to scope out where they were.

"Is it okay to give him people food?" Ruby asked.

Hercules answered with an exuberant yowl.

"Roma says not to overdo it," I said. I gestured at the cat. "They don't agree."

Ruby picked up her camera from the other table.

I ducked my head toward the door. "I'm just going to talk to Ray. I'll only be a couple of minutes." I leaned sideways so I was in the cat's line of vision. "Behave," I said sternly.

I hesitated outside the door of Ray's studio. What exactly was I going to say to him? Hi Ray, were you and Jaeger running some kind of a scam? If he had been, it wasn't likely he'd confess everything to me. On the other hand, I didn't really have another approach.

I knocked on the door. After a minute Ray opened it. "Oh . . . uh . . . Kathleen. Hi," he said.

"Hi Ray," I said. "Could I talk to you for a minute?" I was unsure what his reaction was going to be.

"Sure," he said, frowning slightly. "Does it have to do with the library centennial?"

Another of my mother's favorite sayings came into my head: Always tell the truth, it's easier to remember. "No," I said. "It has to do with Jaeger Merrill."

One hand came up and slid over his smooth scalp. There were smudges of black ink on his fingers.

Ink equals pen. I filed the thought away to chew on later.

"I don't know what I can tell you, but come in," he said.

Ray's studio was incredibly tidy. One end wall was made up of what looked like commercial shelving units, all painted black. The other wall had several glass display cabinets holding Ray's collection of vintage ink bottles. There was a long work station in the center of the room and a big drafting table with a couple of stools by the windows.

He crossed his arms over the front of his body and

gave a slight shrug. "So what did you want to know? I didn't know Jaeger that well."

"You went to the Summerhill estate sale with him a couple of weeks ago," I said.

Ray shook his head. "No. Why do you think that?"

"People saw you there."

"That's because I was there. I just wasn't there with Jaeger Merrill. I think I talked to him for a second. That's all." He was good. He didn't fidget or look away, and if I hadn't been watching for it, I probably would have missed the slight hesitation in his voice and the equally small change in his tone.

"To tell the truth, I wasn't that crazy about Jaeger. He was way too pushy about the sponsorship business at the co-op. He was the kind of person who just didn't hear no."

To tell the truth: Why did so many people who were lying use that expression?

"Do you know what he was looking for at the sale?" I asked.

He shrugged and his gaze flicked away momentarily. "He was probably doing the same thing I was doing, the same thing every other artist there was doing: looking for stuff to use in his work." He studied me, eyes narrowed. "Why all the questions?"

"I was with Maggie when she found Jaeger's body. Him being down in the co-op basement doesn't make a lot of sense to me."

"You think he was running some kind of scam." He gave me a half smile. "I heard about the whole secret identity thing."

I stuffed my hands in my pockets, trying to keep both

my body language and my voice casual. "It's crossed my mind, yes."

Ray stretched and looked out the long windows to the water. Then he looked at me once more. "If he was, I don't have a clue what he was doing." He held out both hands. "Sorry."

"Thanks anyway," I said.

He opened the door and leaned against the edge of it with one hand on the knob. "If I think of anything, I'll let Maggie know."

"Great," I said.

I started back up to Ruby's studio. Okay, so Ray Nightingale was lying. What exactly was I going to do with that information?

I could call Marcus and tell him I was certain Jaeger Merrill/Christian Ellis was working some kind of scam— maybe out of the co-op—because I'd found a little purple buffer attachment at Wisteria Hill, and Ray was involved somehow, which I knew because he'd used the phrase, "to tell the truth," and because his voice had changed while he was talking to me about Jaeger.

Oh sure, that would convince him.

I stood in the hallway outside Ruby's door. If I was going to convince Marcus of anything, I was going to have to figure out what exactly Ray was lying about and what exactly he and Jaeger had been up to. No big deal. Right?

Ruby was on her laptop, looking at pictures of Hercules she'd already downloaded from her camera. He was sitting to one side, eyeing the screen and chewing something.

"That was fast," I said.

They both looked up at me, then Ruby smiled at the cat. "Hercules is very photogenic."

The look the cat gave me was decidedly proud.

I crossed to the table and scooped him up. There were crumbs on his whiskers and I caught the faint smell of peanut butter. Clearly the cat had had a peanut butter cookie—or two.

"What are you going to do with these pictures?" I asked, reaching for the carrier.

"They're for a pop-art workshop," Ruby said, closing the top of her computer. "I'm going to do a pop-art painting of Hercules. I'm thinking lime green and Big Bird yellow."

I set Herc in the bag and zipped the top just in case he decided to go look for more cookies.

"Did you get what you needed from Ray?" Ruby asked, standing up and brushing her hands on her paint spotted jeans.

"Yes, I did," I said. I swung the bag up over my shoulder.

"Thanks Kathleen," she said. "Maggie says we should be able to have class on Tuesday. I'll see you there if I don't see you before."

"Oh boy, cloud hands," I said with a roll of my eyes. "I can't wait."

She laughed. I waggled my fingers at her and headed for the stairs.

Back in the truck I unzipped the top of the bag and Hercules stuck his head out. I reached over to stroke the fur at the top of his nose. "It was very nice of you to pose for Ruby," I said.

He made a low rumbly noise in his throat.

I started the truck, turned and headed for home. "You

know, it occurs to me that pen cap you found might have belonged to Ray," I said. "Is that what you were trying to tell me? Jaeger was up to something and Ray's tied up in it too?"

The cat gave a curious murp. It may have meant what are you going to do now? Or he may have been asking, what's for supper?

Either way the answer was the same.

"I don't know," I said.

Owen was sprawled on the floor under the kitchen table when we got home. He got up, shook himself and headed for the back door. He liked to prowl around our yard and Rebecca's every day.

I put the carrier bag on the floor and the two cats exchanged a long look. I had no idea if it was some kind of cat connection or just a random stare-down.

The phone rang as I shut the porch door behind Owen. I slid across the kitchen floor in my sock feet, almost doing a header into the refrigerator, while Hercules watched. "Don't worry, I'll get that," I told him. You'd think I would have known by now that the only thing sarcasm got me from the cats was ignored.

It was Roma on the phone. "How are you?" I asked.

She paused before she answered as if she needed to consider the question. "I'm all right," she finally said. "What about you?"

"I'm all right, too," I said. "I have some spectacular bruises but my ankle's okay and so is my hand."

"Good," Roma said. "How were Lucy and the others?"

"They all came out to eat and they all looked good."

She gave a small sigh of relief. "Thank you for taking my shift this morning."

"You're welcome," I said. I sat down on the footstool, stretching my legs out in front of me. "Any time you need someone to feed the cats for you, just let me know."

"Actually what I need is for you to come to supper tonight."

"Okay," I said slowly.

"You're sure?" Roma asked.

"Absolutely. What time and would you like me to bring dessert?"

"Six o'clock and you don't have to bring anything."

"I know I don't have to bring anything," I said. "But would you like me to bring dessert?"

She hesitated. "Truthfully, yes."

"Done then," I said. Hercules peeked his head around the doorway.

"Kathleen, my mother and father will be here," Roma said. "I need to ask some awkward questions and I'd uh, just like a little moral support."

"You have it," I said. I looked over at the doorway. Hercules had disappeared back into the kitchen. Or through a wall for all I knew. "I may not be a big, tall, cute hockey player, but I'll do my best."

"Just don't body check anyone into the furniture and we'll be just fine," she said with a laugh.

"Well, okay," I said with an exaggerated sigh. It was good to hear Roma sounding more like herself. We said good-bye and I hung up the phone and went back to the kitchen.

Hercules was sitting by his dish. He looked pointedly from the cupboard where I kept the cat treats to the re-frigerator and then meowed loudly in case I didn't get the point.

"Yes, I know I owe you," I said. I patted my pocket.

"I'm not sure what the pen top means but nice work on the mouse."

He reached over and swatted the side of his dish with one paw.

"Sardines or kitty crackers?" I asked.

He immediately went over and put one paw on the fridge door.

"Sardines. Good choice," I said, opening the door to get the remains of the can I'd opened the day before.

Hercules watched intently as I dumped the little fish into his bowl. "Why didn't you eat the mouse?" I asked him.

He lifted his head, closed his eyes and scrunched up his nose. "Maybe we should have brought it back for your brother in a—what do you call a doggy bag for cats?"

Herc dropped his head and went back to the sardines and at the same time he flipped the end of his tail. I was pretty sure the gesture meant the same thing as it did when a person made the motion. That's what I got for using my best lines on a cat.

I made lemon coffee cake to take to Roma's and while it baked I put in a load of laundry and washed the kitchen floor. And since Owen was still outside I played an entire Barry Manilow CD, which meant Hercules followed me everywhere, bobbing his head, grooving to the music. We made a pretty darn good pair of backup singers for a little black-and-white cat and a librarian who couldn't carry a tune if it came in its own bag with a handle.

Roma's small, gray house was at the far end of Mayville, out past the marina. She smiled when she opened the door and she seemed more relaxed.

"You talked to Eddie," I said.

Her cheeks got pink and she nodded.

Roma's mother and her father—I couldn't think of Neil as anything else—were in the living room.

Neil Carver, even in his seventies, was the type of man who always commanded attention, imposing without being intimidating, if that made sense. His hair was on the longish side, white and waving back from a high forehead and the proverbial steely gaze. His beard was mostly white as well, and closely cropped. And he had a beautiful voice, not surprising since he'd had a long and successful career as a TV journalist.

Neil got to his feet and we shook hands. "Hello, Kathleen," he said. "It's good to see you again."

"It's good to see you too, Neil," I said.

I turned to Pearl. She had the same warm smile as her daughter but other than that they looked nothing alike. Pearl was tiny and wore her hair short, very similar to Maggie's, with the same kind of beautiful, natural curl. She was soft-spoken and serious and on the two previous times I'd met her I'd gotten the impression that she thought carefully about every word before she spoke.

"Hello, Pearl," I said, meeting her smile with one of my own.

"Kathleen," she said. "I'm so glad you could join us." She tipped her head—Roma often used the same gesture—and studied my scraped forehead. "I hope that feels better than it looks."

"It does. Thank you," I said.

We talked about everything but Wisteria Hill and Thomas Karlsson over supper. Roma had made a chicken and rice dish and salad with lettuce and tomatoes from her kitchen window garden. Everything was delicious.

We moved into the living room for dessert. Roma sat on the edge of a brown leather tub chair and I took the matching seat beside her. I'd seen that look of determination on her face before and I knew the conversation was about to get a lot more personal.

"I know it can't be easy," she began. "But we need to talk about my father." Her gaze went to Neil. "Thomas," she added.

"You can ask me anything," Pearl said. Neil's hand slid over hers but he didn't say anything.

Roma swallowed hard and I wanted badly to do something to make it easier for her. "Did you lie to me about him? About Thomas?" she asked her mother.

"Yes," Pearl said, nodding almost imperceptibly.

"Was there . . ." Roma cleared her throat. "Was there anyone who would have wanted to kill him?"

"Yes," Pearl said again.

Roma's eyes never left her mother's face. "Who?"

"Pretty much anyone who knew him," Pearl said.

19

The words hung in the air like a fine haze of smoke from a cigar. Pearl edged forward on the sofa. "I'm sorry, sweetie," she said. "I shouldn't have put it so bluntly. It's just that Tom made a lot of enemies."

"What do you mean?" Roma asked. There was no emotion in her voice, but I could see her left hand, against her leg, clenched into a tight, knotted fist.

"For a while Tom worked for Idris Blackthorne."

"Ruby's grandfather."

"Idris Blackthorne was the town bootlegger," Pearl said. "Tom delivered and drove for him. There was some kind of dispute about money." She shook her head slowly. "Idris wasn't the kind of man to take kindly to being cheated."

"Who else?" Roma asked.

"He had some kind of fight—not just words, punches— with old Albert Coyne. Albert had been cutting pulp up beyond Wild Rose Bluff for years. A couple of days later someone put bleach in the engines of every one of his vehicles."

"Tom," Roma said.

"No one could prove anything, you understand," Pearl said. "But it was the kind of thing he'd do."

Neil picked up his wife's cup and handed it to her. Then he looked at Roma. "Are you sure you want to hear all this?"

She smiled. It just didn't quite make it to her eyes. "I do, Dad."

He nodded and didn't say anything else but I could see the pain this was causing him in the tight line of his jaw and the rigid set of his shoulders.

Pearl took a sip from her coffee and set it down again. Roma had picked up her own cup. She toyed with it, shot me a sideways glance and then, finally, looked at her mother again. "Do you have any idea why Tom might have ended up buried out at Wisteria Hill?" she asked.

Pearl rubbed the back of her narrow, gold wedding ring with her thumb. "I've been thinking about that since you called," she said. "The only thing I can tell you is that Tom was a day laborer at Ingstrom's for a little while. I don't think they were working at Wisteria Hill. I think they were out at the old boat club, but I don't remember for sure. And then Tom did something, or got in an argument with someone and they let him go. So he wasn't working when he disappeared."

She looked away for a moment. "I mean, when he died," she added softly.

Roma stared at the floor, her lips pressed tightly together. Finally she lifted her head. "Why . . . why did you accept that he'd just run off so easily? Weren't you suspicious, even a little bit?"

Pearl took a breath and let it out. She was still fingering her wedding ring. "I probably should have been," she said. "But Tom was the kind of person who didn't deal with things head on. He passed the blame or he did something sneaky, underhanded." Roma was about to say something but Pearl lifted a hand to stop her. "It wasn't all his fault, either. I want you to know that."

Neil still had his hand over hers. She gave it a squeeze. "I told you that Tom played baseball," she said.

Roma nodded. "They were state champions his senior year."

"That's right," Pearl said. "Your . . . Tom was good. Very, very good. And in those days baseball and hockey were a big deal around here. He'd started playing when he was about six. By the time he was twelve he was a summer league star. There's no doubt it went to his head."

"The high school team had never even been to the regional championships," Neil said. "Let alone state. Tom could belt a pitch into the parking lot."

"As long as he was hitting, no one cared about how he was behaving or whether he passed algebra," Pearl added.

"So if he was that good, why wasn't he playing professional baseball?" Roma asked. She took another drink of her coffee.

"He was invited to spring training by the Milwaukee Braves," Pearl said. She looked at Neil beside her on the sofa. He smiled, but like Roma's smile it didn't go all the way to his eyes. "He only lasted a week and a half."

"He had the ability," Neil said with a shrug. "There's

no doubt about that. He just didn't have the discipline to play pro ball."

Roma propped an elbow on the arm of the leather chair and leaned the side of her head against her hand. "Why did you marry him?" she asked. "Was it because of me?"

Pearl looked at me. "Kathleen, Neil and I are in the spare bedroom. There's a small box on the bed, tied with silver ribbon. Would you get it for me please?"

"Of course," I said. I stood up, gave Roma what I hoped was an encouraging smile, and went down the hall to the room she used as a guest bedroom.

The box looked like an old stationery box, the kind that a set of pretty sheets of writing paper and matching envelopes had come in. It was tied with a wide silver ribbon, more to keep the lid on and the battered box together, than for decoration. I took it back to Pearl.

"Thank you Kathleen," she said. I sat back down and she untied the satin bow and lifted the top of the box. She took out two documents and handed them to Roma. One was Roma's birth certificate. The other was Tom and Pearl's marriage license.

"I know my birthday," Roma said.

"I know you do," Pearl said. She sat back a bit and moved just a bit closer to Neil.

Roma studied the marriage license. Then she held it out to me. I did the math in my head. "Nine months and two days," I said.

Pearl nodded. "There was no shotgun at our wedding, Roma. And you weren't there either, my dear."

I handed the document back to Roma. Her gaze went from it to her mother and back again. "I thought that . . ." She let the end of the sentence trail away.

Pearl reached across the space between them and patted her daughter's knee. "I'm sorry, sweetie. If I'd realized, I would have shown you that years ago."

"So why did you marry him if you didn't have to?" Roma asked. She seemed more relaxed now.

Pearl leaned all the way back against the sofa cushions. "I was the good girl. Tom was the bad boy." She and Neil exchanged warm smiles and their obvious connection seemed to somehow chase away a lot of the tension in the room.

"I got straight A's and sang in the church choir," Pearl said. "He was handsome, charming and just a little reckless. It was exciting at first." Her smile faded. "Then it got old."

Roma leaned forward, both elbows on her knees, chin propped on her laced fingers. "Why did you stay?"

"I didn't," Pearl said. "The night before Tom disappeared, I left him."

20

"You left him? Why didn't you ever tell me?" Roma asked. There was no anger in her voice, just curiosity.

Pearl folded her hands in her lap. "Because he was your father. I didn't want you to ever believe his mistakes were somehow part of who you were."

"But where did you—where did we go? I don't remember being somewhere else and then coming back to Mayville."

Something changed in Pearl's expression. Her eyes were suddenly wary. "We didn't really go...far," she said.

I knew what she wasn't saying. "The Ladies Knitting Circle," I said.

Pearl turned her gaze to me and her cheeks were tinged with pink. "I'm not sure what you mean, Kathleen," she said slowly. Roma was looking at me as well.

"I know that The Ladies Knitting Circle didn't actually knit very much. I know that Anna Henderson and a few of her friends were helping women in" — I hesitated, looking for just the right word — "difficult circumstances."

"You mean like some kind of underground railroad?" Roma said.

I nodded. "Yes."

She looked at her mother for confirmation and after a moment's hesitation Pearl nodded as well. "I was going to take you and disappear, with some help from Anna and the others."

"Pearl, who told you about The Ladies Knitting Circle?" I asked.

She frowned. "You know, I don't remember. I'm sorry, Kathleen. That's a long time ago."

"Why then?" Roma asked. "What happened? What changed for you?"

Pearl shrugged. "I don't have an answer for that, either. So much happened in such a short amount of time, there are some blank spots in my memory. I can tell you that we were about to be kicked out of the little house we were renting. We were behind in the rent and Tom hadn't kept up the place. He was in a dark, ugly mood that night. He decided he was going to drive over to Red Wing to buy beer. I knew he'd be gone for a couple of hours. I knew Anna would take us in. I grabbed some things and walked over there with you."

She twisted her wedding ring around her finger. "We hid out at Wisteria Hill for close to a week. I thought Tom would look for us — you for certain — but he'd disappeared. They found his car abandoned out by the highway and it looked like he'd decided to hitchhike."

"You didn't wonder why he didn't come back?" Roma asked.

"No," Pearl said with a shake of her head. "It sounds

silly, doesn't it? I didn't want . . . I didn't want to run away, change our names, and always be looking over my shoulder. With Tom gone, I felt I could stay. Every day that went by, life got better. Eventually I saved enough money to divorce him and start again." She smiled once more at Neil.

"Someone found Tom's car abandoned out on the highway?" I asked.

Pearl nodded. "Sam Ingstrom and another man on their way to a landscaping job found it early the next morning. You know where the road turns off to Wild Rose Bluff? It looked like Tom had run out of gas."

All roads may have led back to Wisteria Hill, but Sam Ingstrom seemed to be doing the driving, so to speak.

Pearl's expression turned thoughtful. "I've been thinking about those days since Tom's body was found and I think now that he had to have died that night after I left. And before you ask, there's no way Anna or any of those women had anything to do with it."

I had to agree with her. I'd seen pictures of Anna Henderson and of Rebecca's mother, Ellen. They'd both been tiny women. How could they have killed Tom out behind the house? Based on what I'd heard about Wisteria Hill in those days, there was always someone around and it wasn't like he would have obligingly bent down so they could hit him over the head.

Even if he'd been killed elsewhere, there was no way Anna and Ellen could have carried Thomas Karlsson's body across the field behind the carriage house, up onto the ridge, then dug a hole and buried it. Why would they? And even if they could have come up with a way to move the body of a man twice their size, someone would have seen something or heard something.

Pearl and Roma had been hiding at Wisteria Hill.

Carson was coming and going. Everett was there. Rebecca was at the house a lot with her brothers. It wasn't like the women could have killed Tom—for whatever reason—rolled him up in a rug and carried it on their shoulders across the yard without anyone noticing.

"Do you have any idea what might have happened?" I asked.

"I truly don't know," she said. "I mentioned that Tom worked for Idris Blackthorne for a while and I can tell you that those woods behind Wisteria Hill were a short cut to a hunting camp Idris had. And there was another camp nearby, more of a shack really, where some of the men in town used to go to play poker and get drunk. The fact that it was so close to Idris's place made it very convenient. Tom was pretty much a regular at those games for a time, until he got caught cheating."

"So . . . so he could have gone to see Idris Blackthorne or gone to the poker game, ended up in some kind of . . . altercation with someone and . . ." Roma didn't finish the sentence.

"I think there's a good chance the remains being found where they were has more to do with the people Tom was associating with and probably nothing to do with Wisteria Hill, other than it was a convenient spot for someone to dispose of a body," Neil said.

Pearl nodded in agreement. "I'm sorry all of this happened, Roma. And I'm sorry that I lied to you about Tom. I didn't think there was any harm in letting you think well of him. And for what it's worth, I never saw him as happy as he was the day you were born. Not before. Not after. Not even when they won the state championship."

Roma swallowed and nodded. "Thank you," she said, her voice a little raspy with emotion.

Pearl smiled at her daughter. Then she looked at me. "How did you know about The Ladies Knitting Circle, Kathleen?" she asked.

"You know that we're celebrating the centennial of the library this June?" I said. Neil had gotten up for the coffeepot and I held up my cup for a refill, smiling my thanks at him.

"Roma told me."

"As part of the celebrations we're planning some displays about the history of the town as it ties in to the history of the library. I found a reference to The Ladies Knitting Circle in an old journal and one of my staff—Mary Lowe—told me more about the women."

"How is Mary?" Pearl asked. "I haven't seen her in such a long time."

"Still kickboxing, still making the best pie I've ever eaten," I said.

"I'd love to see her," she said.

"She's working tomorrow at the library."

"I'll try to make it in to say hello." Pearl took the fresh cup of coffee Neil handed her as I put cream and sugar in my own.

"There are so many people I want to see while I'm here," she said.

Roma smiled. "You can stay as long as you want to."

"Maybe an extra day or two?" Pearl said, looking at her husband.

"Fine with me. I'm sure there are people who would like to see you too." Then he gave Pearl a sly sideways glance and arched an eyebrow at her. "His worship, the mayor, for example. You know, if you hadn't married me, you could be the first lady of Mayville Heights now."

Roma and I exchanged confused looks and Pearl blushed.

"First lady of Mayville Heights?" Roma said. "Do you mean Mom and . . . and Sam Ingstrom?"

"He's just being silly," Pearl said, giving him a poke with her elbow.

"No I'm not," Neil retorted. "Sam Ingstrom had a crush on you." He looked over at Roma and me. "From what I heard, whenever Pearl was around Sam pretty much lost his senses."

Pearl made a dismissive gesture with one hand. "Sammy and I were just friends. He was younger and he wasn't carrying any torch for me, no matter what Mr. Romance Novel here says."

I laughed along with everyone else, but I was remembering that photo of Sam looking at Pearl and her friends. Looking at Pearl with longing written all over his face.

Pearl gestured at me then. "Kathleen, there is one thing I remember from the night I left Tom. Oddly enough, Sam was there, at Wisteria Hill."

I frowned at her. "He was?"

She nodded. "He'd driven out with a load of old railway ties they'd salvaged from some job for Carson, and Sam stepped on a nail while he was taking them off the truck. It went right through his boot into his foot. Ellen was bandaging it when Roma and I got there. The doctor's office was closed and well, she was as good as any doctor."

I'd noticed that Sam had an almost imperceptible limp when he'd been on his feet a lot. Maybe it was because of that old injury.

I wondered if Maggie was right. Had Sam lied about knowing Pearl because he was embarrassed about a teenage crush? Or could he have had something to do with Thomas Karlsson's death?

No. That didn't make any more sense than thinking Anna had killed Tom and buried him at the edge of the tree line. Working for his father's landscaping company would have given Sam lots of good places to hide the body if he'd had anything to do with Tom's death. It made no sense for him to take a body to Wisteria Hill. What would he have done? Hidden it in among the old railway ties? It wasn't as though he would have been able to walk through the yard unnoticed carrying a dead body.

It seemed lame, but Maggie's explanation was probably the right one. And given the amount of time that had passed, maybe no one would ever figure out how Thomas Karlsson had ended up buried at Wisteria Hill.

The doorbell rang. Roma got up to answer it and I leaned sideways in my chair to see who it was. When she opened the door Marcus Gordon was standing on the stoop.

21

"Hello, Roma," I heard him say. "I'm sorry for stopping by at this time of night, but I was hoping to talk to your mother. She's here?"

I knew the tone of voice and the body language well. Marcus was in cop mode. I stood up and walked over to the door before Roma could invite him in.

"Hi Marcus," I said. "It's kind of late. Do you have to talk to Pearl tonight? She only got here a little while ago."

Out of the corner of my eye I could see Roma was frowning at me.

"Kathleen," he said. "I didn't expect to see you here."

"I was invited," I said, stressing the word *invited* just a little. "For dinner."

We stood there for a long moment doing the same kind of stare-down thing I sometimes did with the cats. Of course with them I was always the first to look away. This time, here, it was Marcus. I felt a tiny surge of very childish satisfaction when he did.

"So could you wait until the morning to talk to Pearl?" I asked.

He exhaled slowly and for a second I almost thought I saw a smile tug at the corners of his mouth. "I guess I could." He pulled one of his cards out of his pocket and gave it to Roma. "Would you call me first thing and we'll set up a time"—his eyes darted to me for a moment—"that works for everyone."

"I will," Roma said.

"I really should get going myself," I said. I glanced at Marcus still in the doorway. "Could you wait and walk me to my truck?" I asked. "It's dark."

The truck was parked in Roma's driveway only a few steps away from the door, but Marcus didn't so much as turn his head in that direction. "It is dark," he agreed. "I'll just wait out here for you. Take your time." To Roma he said, "I'll speak to you in the morning." He moved down the steps to the bottom and leaned against the newel post, crossing his arms over his chest and one incredibly long, strong leg over the other.

Roma closed the door and turned to me. "What was all that between you two?"

"Nothing," I said. "It's just that it's late and your mom must be tired. Why not let her get some sleep? This has to be hard on her." Pearl was still on the sofa, turned toward Neil, talking to him in a low voice.

"You're right," Roma said, tipping her head back to stretch her neck. "I should have thought of that."

I reached over and gave her arm a pat. "It's been hard on you too."

She looked at the little cardboard rectangle in her hand and then put it in her pocket. "I'll call Marcus in the morning and we'll take care of it first thing."

"I think you should . . . uh . . . take a lawyer with you."

"A lawyer?" She made a face and shook her head. "Why would we need a lawyer? Marcus is my friend. I thought you thought of him as a friend too."

"This is still a police investigation and Marcus has to do his job. Call Peter Lundgren. Call somebody. Please, Roma." I waited.

"All right," she finally said.

I walked back to Pearl and Neil. "It was so good to see you," I said.

Pearl stood up and took my hands in hers. "You too, Kathleen," she said. "My daughter is very lucky to have you as a friend."

"I'm lucky to have her," I said and I realized how much I meant the words as I said them.

"It looks as though we're going to be here for a few days. I hope we'll see you again."

I smiled at her. "I would like that very much." I gave her hands a gentle squeeze and said, "Good night," to Neil.

"Call me if you need anything," I told Roma.

She had one arm folded across her midsection but she wrapped me in a one-armed hug. "Thank you for coming tonight."

"Anytime," I said.

Marcus was still at the bottom of the steps. He straightened when I stepped out and walked silently over to the truck with me. Then he made a point to check the front seat and the bed. "Everything looks all right."

"Thank you," I said.

He didn't smile, but I could tell he wanted to. "You're welcome," he said. He made no move toward his car, which was parked on the street in front of the house.

"Are you going to give me the 'stay out of my case' lecture?" I asked.

"Will it work?" He was standing with his feet apart, hands behind his back.

"No."

That made him laugh. "You're honest, Kathleen," he said. "I'll give you that."

I smiled at him. "I'm not trying to interfere in your investigation."

He raised his eyebrows.

"All right, I admit it doesn't exactly look that way."

"No, it doesn't."

"What was Burtis Chapman doing out at Wisteria Hill this morning?" I asked.

He hesitated.

"I can ask Burtis myself," I said.

"Yes you can," he said. "It's not a secret. Burtis knows those woods better than anyone else in town. I asked him to give me the lay of the land back there, that's all."

So did that mean he knew about the poker game and Idris Blackthorne's business operations? I knew he wouldn't answer that question.

I stuffed my hands in my pockets. "Do you know what The Ladies Knitting Circle was?"

"No. I'm guessing they were knitting?"

I shook my head. "That's what I thought. Years ago — at the time that Thomas Karlsson disappeared — they were operating a kind of safe house, hiding women from their abusive husbands and helping them get away to start new lives."

"And how do you know this?" he asked.

My hair was slipping from its ponytail and I reached back and pulled out the elastic. "I've been researching some of the groups that used to meet at the library. The Ladies Knitting Circle was one of them."

"So you think, what? That a group of little old ladies buried Thomas Karlsson out at Wisteria Hill?" Clearly he wasn't taking what the women had been doing seriously.

"They weren't exactly little old ladies. Anna Henderson was the leader of the group. When Tom Karlsson disappeared, when it looked like he'd abandoned Pearl and Roma, they were already being hidden by Anna and her friends."

Marcus glanced back at the house.

My ankle was aching and I shifted more of my weight to my other leg and made a mental note to use Rebecca's herbal salve on my ankle again before bed. "I'm not telling you this to point the finger at Anna Henderson," I said. "Pearl had an out and she'd taken it. She was safe. Her child was safe. She had no reason to kill her husband."

"I didn't say that Thomas Karlsson was murdered," he said.

"Oh c'mon," I said, my exasperation showing in my voice. "I saw his remains. I don't think he hit himself in the head and then lay down and scraped dirt and leaves over his own body with his last bit of energy. At best he hit his head accidentally and someone hid the body."

Marcus stared past me, down the driveway. I knew what was coming. Finally he looked at me. "Kathleen, this is an active police investigation," he said.

"So stay out of it," I finished. This was the point where I usually got aggravated at him and left in a huff. But I really didn't want to do that anymore. "Could you stop being a police officer and just be a person for one minute?" I asked.

"No," he said. "Being a police officer is part of who I am. As far back as I can remember, it's the only thing I ever wanted to be. If you and I are going to be friends, you're going to have to find a way to accept that." He shifted position, folding his arms across his chest. "I can't go easy on someone who's part of an investigation just because you're friends with them."

"And I just can't ignore it when one of my friends is in trouble," I said, pushing that annoying tendril of hair back off my face again. "You're going to have to find a way to accept that, if we're going to be friends."

I pulled my keys out of my pocket and unlocked the driver's door. "I'm going to leave now," I said. "Because I'm kind of mad right now."

"Are you still going to be mad Saturday morning when we go feed the cats?"

Right. I'd forgotten that I'd traded a shift with Harry Junior so I'd be out at Wisteria Hill again in another couple of days.

"I don't know," I said. "Maybe." I wanted to stay mad. It just wasn't working for some reason.

I climbed in the truck, started it, and backed carefully out of the driveway, making sure my seat belt was fastened. Marcus watched me from the driveway. I raised one hand in good-bye. I was annoyed.

Not rude.

22

I thought about everything Pearl had said all the way home. Could Ruby's grandfather have had something to do with Tom Karlsson's death? Then there were the men Tom had cheated at poker. Did Tom go back to the game? Did something happen there?

I hoped Roma really would call a lawyer before they went to talk to the police in the morning. It wasn't that I didn't trust Marcus, it was just that as he himself had pointed out to me back in Roma's driveway—he was a cop. That wasn't just what he did; it was part of who he was. I'd seen firsthand that when he was on a case he could be even more single-minded than Owen on the hunt for Fred the Funky Chicken parts.

There was no sign of the cats in the kitchen when I got home. I kicked off my shoes, hung up my jacket and padded into the living room. Owen was the picture of an adorable house cat, sitting next to the big wing chair.

"I'm not fooled," I said. "I know you were lying on the footstool." It was his favorite place to nap, which meant

I was always vacuuming cat hair off the top. I could just never catch him up there.

I bent down, swept him up, and sank into the chair. He sat on my lap and studied my face. "Guess who showed up at Roma's?" I said.

"Meow?" he said.

"Uh huh. He wanted to talk to Pearl." Okay, so Owen hadn't actually said . . . err . . . meowed Marcus's name. On the other hand, we weren't actually having a conversation. I told him what I learned from Pearl, turning over each bit of information in my mind. Owen listened intently, or at least pretended to.

"I keep coming back to Tom's body being buried out at Wisteria Hill and Anna hiding Pearl and Roma at the same time. For those two things not to be connected is a bit of a coincidence." I was slumped down in the chair, the cat stretched across my chest. "On the other hand, coincidences do happen." Owen muttered his agreement.

I pictured the dirt-encrusted skull I'd found myself sprawled next to when the embankment had collapsed. It had been caved in, fractured on the left side.

By my estimation, based on the photographs I'd seen of her, Anna Henderson had been more than a foot shorter than Tom Karlsson. "There's no way she could have hit the man," I said to Owen. "What did she do? Ask him to wait while she got something to stand on? I don't think so."

Plus what reason did Anna have to hurt Tom, I asked myself. She was helping women get away from abusive men, not do away with them. Even if Tom had shown up at Wisteria Hill looking for his wife and daughter, there was no way he could have gotten to them. The Hendersons were the most prominent family in town. Tom would have ended up in jail for any kind of threat against Anna. Assuming he'd survived Carson's wrath.

I tipped my head to look at Owen, who was lazily washing the end of one gray paw. Or possibly licking a bit of leftover food off of it. "Am I being naïve for not considering the possibility that Pearl had something to do with Tom ending up buried at Wisteria Hill?"

The cat paused, paw in the air, as though he were actually mulling over my question. Then suddenly he turned his head and licked my wrist before going back to his laissez-faire paw cleaning. That could be a no, I decided.

"Okay, let's say for the sake of argument that Pearl did kill Tom." Owen's eyes flicked up to mine. "By accident," I said, moving my hand so I could scratch behind his ear. "How did his body get all the way to Wisteria Hill? If Anna had helped her—"

Owen lifted his head again, eyes narrowed. For a second it almost seemed like he was following what I was saying. "If," I said. "If."

That seemed to satisfy him.

"So if Pearl had killed Tom and if Anna had helped her with the body, why on earth would they have taken it to Wisteria Hill? That makes no sense."

I shook my head and shifted to scratching behind Owen's other ear. He gave up on his paw, closed his eyes, and started purring.

"I just don't think Pearl had anything to do with what happened to Tom," I said thoughtfully. "I didn't get any sense that she wasn't telling the truth tonight. Yes, she lied about Tom so Roma wouldn't know her father was a deadbeat. But she wouldn't have killed him. She wouldn't do that to Roma."

I closed my eyes. So if the killer wasn't Pearl and it wasn't Anna Henderson . . . I clenched my teeth. I didn't like the idea, but could it have been . . . Sam?

It was clear Sam had had a thing for Pearl. Those old photos that hadn't made it into the Mayville High yearbook pretty much confirmed that.

"So when she showed up at Wisteria Hill with Roma, did Sam go to confront Tom?" I asked Owen.

He didn't seem to have an opinion.

"No, wait, Tom wasn't there."

What had Pearl said? She felt she had time to get away because Tom had gone to Red Wing on a beer run—I was guessing because Idris Blackthorne wouldn't sell to him. The car had been found abandoned at the side of the highway, out of gas, right by the turnoff to Wild Rose Bluff. It would have been a long walk back to Mayville.

Of course, that didn't mean Sam couldn't have come across Tom later that night. Sam would have been big enough to hold his own in a fight with Tom. Tom had been an athlete, but Sam had been working in his father's landscaping business. He was more than strong enough to swing whatever had fractured Tom Karlsson's skull.

"Except he couldn't drive," I said to Owen. I sat up straighter and slid the cat down onto my lap. "Pearl said Sam had taken a load of old railway ties out to Wisteria Hill for Carson, and run a nail through his foot. He wouldn't have even been able to drive the truck. It would have been a standard."

I looked at Owen. "I have to get up." He made grumbly noises but he jumped down to the floor and trailed behind me into the kitchen. Hercules came through the door from the porch. Literally through. The energy in the kitchen seemed to change somehow and there he was. It still made me jump.

Owen looked at my keys on the table and meowed. "We're trying to figure out what happened to Tom," I said to Hercules.

I shook my head at Owen. "No," I said. "Sam would have been driving one of the Ingstrom trucks—I'm guessing maybe a one-ton. It would have been a standard. He couldn't manage the clutch."

I hooked one of the chairs with my foot and pulled it out so I could sit down. I stretched out my left leg and rolled my ankle in big, slow circles. "How about this?" I said to the cats. "Pearl shows up with Roma. Ellen is bandaging Sam's injured foot. Tom didn't actually go to Red Wing, so he shows up looking for his wife."

Hercules interrupted my recitation with a loud meow.

"I don't know how he knew Pearl was at Wisteria Hill. He just did."

The cat didn't raise any more objections.

"Tom shows up. Pearl won't leave with him. Sam and Tom get into a fight. Sam whacks Tom with one of those railway ties and everyone helps him bury the body out behind the carriage house and never speaks of it again."

I looked at them. Even cats know stupid when they hear it.

"Okay, so maybe that's a little too far-fetched." I stretched both feet out across the floor. "I'm thinking Pearl may be right. Maybe Tom ended up out there because of someone who was connected to Ruby's grandfather or even that poker game."

So how was I going to find out more about a dead man and a group of nameless, high-stakes card players from more than forty years ago? I knew Marcus would say it was none of my business, but I also knew Roma needed answers.

"I need to make a phone call," I said.

I found the small red book I kept addresses and phone numbers in. I went back to the living room, sat down again, and reached for the phone.

Harry Junior answered at his father's house. "Hi Harry," I said. "It's Kathleen. Is your dad around? I was hoping I could pick his brain."

"Hi Kathleen," he said and I could hear a hint of exasperation in his voice. "He's right here, arguing hockey stats with me. Hang on a minute."

I waited, picturing Harry taking the phone over to his father in his chair by the woodstove, with Boris, his German shepherd at his feet.

"Hello, Kathleen," Harrison Taylor, Senior said, his deep voice warm in my ear. "My son says you want to pick my brain. I should warn you, the pickin's are slim."

"I doubt that," I said with a laugh.

"What can I do for you?" he asked.

I leaned my head against the back of the chair. "Tell me about Idris Blackthorne."

"Meanest son of a bi- . . . gun I ever met," he said.

"Is it true he wasn't the kind of person you wanted to be on the wrong side of?"

The old man gave a snort of laughter. "No one ever crossed old Idris twice."

"Was he capable of killing someone . . . or having someone killed?" I asked.

"Ahh . . . this has to do with Tom Karlsson, doesn't it?" he said. "I heard you found what was left of him out at Wisteria Hill. How are you?"

"I'm fine, Harry," I said. "But I am curious how Roma's father ended up buried out there."

"Well, I'm not saying Idris had nothing to do with that," Harry said slowly, and I pictured him fingering his snowy beard. "But it wasn't his way. And if he was responsible for what happened, I can't see him burying the body out at Wisteria Hill. Too close to his business enterprises, if you know what I mean."

"I do," I said. "I've heard about Idris Blackthorne's business."

"Then you know he wouldn't have been doing anything to draw attention to himself."

I stretched my legs across the footstool. "Harry, did you ever hear about some kind of high-stakes card game going on in a cabin in the woods out behind Wisteria Hill?"

"That was another one of Idris's business ventures," he said. I could hear his dog, Boris, sniffing the phone.

"High stakes?" I asked.

"From what I heard. The closest I ever got to a high-stakes card game was nickel poker around the kitchen table on a Saturday night." He laughed. "My wife thought gambling was a waste of money. Didn't mean she didn't clean out my friends on a regular basis though."

"Do you think it's possible someone at that poker game did something to Tom?"

"It's possible," he said. He was silent for a moment. "You should talk to Burtis Chapman if you want to know more about things to do with Idris. He worked for the man for a lot of years." Harry lowered his voice. "In fact Burtis took over a small bit of Idris's business. But you could keep that to yourself."

"Yes, I could," I said.

"If you can get down to Fern's about six tomorrow morning, you're likely to find Burtis having breakfast. Tell him I told you to talk to him."

"Thank you Harry," I said. "I just might do that."

"You take care of yourself, Kathleen," he said.

"I will," I said. "Good night."

Breakfast with Burtis Chapman was not my idea of a good time. "Maybe Marcus is right," I said out loud. "Maybe I should just stay out of this."

The phone rang then. It was Maggie.

"Hi," she said. "I just wanted to check in and make sure Roma is okay."

"She's good," I said, leaning forward to brush a clump of cat hair off the footstool. "Pearl answered all her questions, but I'm not sure Marcus or anyone else is going to be able to figure out what happened to Roma's father. It's just too long ago." I exhaled slowly. "He showed up after supper."

"Really?" she said. "Did you have some kind of séance?"

"Not Tom," I said. "Marcus. He wanted to ask Pearl a few questions. We convinced him to wait until tomorrow morning."

"I'm glad Roma's all right. It's been a rough couple of days for her."

"For you, too," I said. "How's the basement?"

Owen appeared in the kitchen doorway and started across the floor to me. He had some kind of kitty intuition that told him when it was Maggie on the phone.

"Almost dry last time I checked, and Harry took a look at the back wall for me. He's pretty sure he knows where most of the water came in and he thinks it's an easy fix."

"Oh Mags, that would be terrific."

"It would, because there isn't very much left in the contingency fund."

I looked down at Owen whose eyes were fixed on the phone's receiver. His right paw was over his left one. "Owen has his paws crossed for you," I said.

Maggie laughed. "Give him a scratch for me. If we were just the same species, he would be the perfect guy."

I reached down and scratched behind the little gray cat's ears. He closed his eyes and started to purr.

"Kath, I've been thinking," Maggie said. "Do you think someone from Jaeger's past could have tracked him down, and convinced him to go back to his old life?"

"It wouldn't have been that hard," I said. "I know he changed his name, but he wasn't exactly keeping a low profile around town—at least not lately. And look where he ended up, in the same small town his lawyer came from."

Maggie grunted her agreement and I pictured her stretching one arm behind her head, or hanging from the waist with her hands flat on the floor. "His old life was very different from waiting tables at Eric's and working a few shifts in the co-op store, you know."

"What do you mean?" I asked.

"I e-mailed one of my old profs," she said. "Before he got caught—before he went to jail—Jaeger, Christian, was living quite the ritzy life: fancy apartment, gallery openings, the best tables at restaurants—all the clichés."

"Wait a minute. That doesn't fit with what Peter told us," I said. "Remember? He said that Jaeger needed the money to take care of his sick mother."

Owen jumped onto my lap. I pointed at a tuft of cat

hair stuck to the edge of the stool. He looked blankly at me.

"I'm not so sure Jaeger was the person that Peter seems to think he was," Maggie said.

"Were Jaeger and Ray Nightingale friends?" I asked. Owen kept putting his paw out to the telephone receiver as though he wanted to take it away from me.

"Not as far as I know. Why?"

I shifted sideways a little so I wasn't sitting directly on one of my many bruises. "Remember when Abigail and I went to that estate sale in Summerhill a couple of weeks ago?"

"Uh huh."

"Jaeger was out there. Abigail saw him and she says Ray was with him."

"So what did Ray say? Did you ask him about it?"

"He said he bumped into Jaeger at the sale, that's all."

There was silence on the other end of the phone for a moment. Then Maggie said, "You don't believe him."

I sighed. "No, I don't."

"Ray's not the kind of guy to get mixed up in some kind of scam, Kath. He just isn't. I've known him for years. He was one of the first artists to get behind the idea of the co-op."

"I didn't say he was involved in some kind of scam. It's just . . ." I hesitated. "When I asked him about Jaeger he didn't tell me the truth. I know a lie when I hear one, Maggie, and Ray was lying, about something."

She made a small sound on the other end of the phone. "Do you think I should talk to him?"

"No," I said. "Not yet at least. Maybe, maybe I'm wrong." Owen bumped my hand because I'd stopped scratching the side of his head. "Would you like a date square?" I asked.

"What?" she said, clearly confused by the abrupt turn the conversation had taken. It occurred to me I was sounding like Marcus.

"Would you like a date square?" I repeated.

"Umm, okay."

"Would you like some company with your date square?"

She laughed. "I would. I'm at the studio."

"I'll be there in ten," I said.

Owen jumped off my lap and headed purposefully for the kitchen. "No," I called after him.

He didn't alter his path. He didn't even glance back at me. I got to my feet and followed him. I knew what was in his furry little mind.

He went directly to where the cat carrier bag was hanging next to my jacket and sat underneath it. I stood, arms folded, by the kitchen table. "I know you understand the word no," I said.

He continued to ignore me and instead tried to swat the bag with one paw. He didn't even come close.

"You're not coming with me," I said.

Nothing. Clearly I was on permanent ignore. I went upstairs and brushed my teeth and my hair, and then I came back down and put half a dozen date squares in a container to take to Maggie's. Owen was still sitting underneath the bag.

I bent down closer to his level. "Owen, I'm sorry but you can't come." He glared at me for a moment then turned his back on me, flipping his tail straight up in the air so I suddenly had a face full of furry kitty backside.

Had I just been mooned by a cat?

I straightened up. "I'm leaving," I told him. "I won't be long."

His response was a slitted-eye glare. Then he headed for the living room and disappeared.

Literally.

I knew he'd sulk for a while and when I came home I'd find bits from one of his catnip chickens all over the kitchen floor.

I was almost at the stop sign at the bottom of the hill when a flash of movement caught my eye, just at the edge of my field of vision. A small white dog darted into the street. I jammed on the brakes and turned the wheel toward the sidewalk as the back end of the truck fishtailed, waiting for a thump and hoping it wouldn't come.

It didn't, although there was a noise from the passenger side of the truck and the right front tire bounced off the edge of the curb.

The dog bolted across the empty left lane and disappeared up someone's driveway.

I put the car in park and leaned my head back against the seat, eyes closed. My heart was pounding a cha-cha rhythm in my chest.

After a moment I opened my eyes again and looked over at the passenger seat. "I know you're here, Owen," I said. I waited for him to pop into view, so to speak.

He didn't.

"I'm not moving this truck until I can see you."

Nothing.

Okay, so he wanted to play hardball.

"When we get home I'm going to gather up all the cheese and sardine kitty crackers and give them to Harry to take out to Boris."

Boris was a big and intimidating German shepherd that looked like he ate small cats for lunch. In reality he was, well, a pussycat. However, he'd once woofed in Owen's face, which made him dog non grata in the cat's eyes.

I waited, and in a moment Owen winked into view on the seat beside me.

23

He didn't exactly look innocent—that's hard to do when your fur is all messed up, you have dirt on your nose, and one ear is turned inside out—but he tried.

I glared at him. "You are a very bad cat," I said in my sternest voice, although it was a struggle not to laugh with his ear like that. "I'm taking you home and shutting you in the bedroom."

The moment the words were out of my mouth I knew they were a mistake. He just vanished again.

If I couldn't see him I couldn't grab him. I knew from experience that even if I lunged over to the passenger side, Owen would just jump out of the way. He wasn't above meowing and then moving just to throw me off. Not only had I apparently been mooned by a cat; it also looked like I'd been bested by one in a game of wits.

"Fine, you win," I said, "but if you're coming with me the least you can do is nose around and see if you can find some kind of clue about what Jaeger Merrill was up to."

The cat appeared beside me on the seat again. His ear was still turned inside out but his demeanor had changed from faux-contrite to cocky.

"Ear," I said, pointing.

He swiped at it with one paw, turning it right side round again.

I tightened my seat belt, backed up and then pulled out onto the road again. "And you can't let Maggie see you." I turned right, watching the road carefully because there were still patches of standing water. "You'll have to do your look of adoration from afar."

I heard muttering noises from beside me but at least he didn't go invisible again. "You know one of these days someone is going to catch us having one of these conversations and that's going to be very hard to explain," I said. Then I laughed because here I was having a conversation with a cat about having a conversation with a cat.

I pulled into the tiny parking lot behind the River Arts building and Maggie waved from the back door. I grabbed one of the canvas bags I kept in the truck for grocery shopping and scooped Owen into it before he could pull yet another disappearing act. I put my purse in next to him, grabbed the date squares and got out of the truck.

"Peter called," she said, holding the door open for me. "He'll be here in a minute. Do you mind if we wait for him?"

"I don't mind," I said, handing her the date squares. "Did he say what he wanted?"

"No." Maggie slid a hand over her hair. "Just that it had something to do with Jaeger—well, Peter calls him Christian."

"Maybe Peter found some family." Owen was moving restlessly in the bag and I set it on the floor between my feet before Maggie noticed and asked me why the tote bag was squirming.

Peter's four-wheel drive SUV pulled into the lot then and he got out and walked across the pavement. He was wearing jeans and a denim shirt, his hair back in its usual ponytail.

"Hi Kathleen," he said when he saw me. "How's your head?"

"All right," I said. "Not nearly as bad as it looks." I gestured to his hand, which was still bandaged. "How's your hand?"

He smiled. "Not nearly as bad as it looks." He turned to Maggie. "Maggie, it looks as though I'm definitely going to be taking care of Christian's estate. Could we set up a time so I can see what's in his studio?"

"What's tomorrow morning like for you?" she asked. "Is eight too early?"

She shook her head. "No. That works for me."

His face grew serious. His mouth worked and then he said, "Maggie, do you have a lawyer?"

"Why? Do I need a lawyer?" Maggie said, frowning.

He brushed a hand over his neck. "The police did a routine check of Jaeger's car—it had been towed because it was left parked on the street. There were a couple of masks, packed to be mailed in the car."

Maggie looked at Peter. She was clearly puzzled. "I know," she said. "Some of the artists like to wrap their own artwork when it's going to be sent somewhere. Ruby does. Jaeger did."

"Do some of the artists use twenty-dollar bills instead of Styrofoam peanuts for padding?" he asked, dryly.

Maggie went completely still. I couldn't even see her breathing. "What?" she finally said.

"There was ten thousand dollars stuffed in the back of the two masks. The address they were being sent to is a mail drop in Chicago." He studied her face. I couldn't tell what he was thinking from his expression. "You're sure that Jaeger did all the packing?" he asked. "Not you?"

"Of course I'm sure," Maggie said slowly.

"Peter, what's this about?" I asked.

He held up a hand, but his eyes never left Maggie's face. "Give me a minute, Kathleen," he said. "What about the packing supplies?"

"Other than the money?" she said, anger adding an edge of sarcasm to her voice. "Those all came from the co-op. And there would have been an invoice and a mailing label."

"Did you print those?"

"Yes, on the store's computer."

"Okay," Peter said thoughtfully and I got the impression he was cataloging everything Maggie said in some mental filing system.

"Wait a minute," she said. "The police don't think I had anything to do with that money being hidden in Jaeger's masks, do they?" Her shoulders were rigid.

He shrugged. "That I don't know. But before you talk to them again—because they are going to want to talk to you—I think you should get yourself a lawyer."

"Peter, no one's going to seriously believe Maggie was involved in some sort of scam with Jaeger are they?" I asked.

"I can't say for certain," he said. "I wouldn't have believed he was forging artwork again, but I can't come up with any other explanation for that much money stuffed in a couple of masks."

"Okay, let's start from the premise that Jaeger was doing something illegal again." I looked directly at Maggie for a moment before turning my attention back to Peter. "That doesn't mean Maggie was his partner in crime. Ask anyone. They weren't exactly getting along. If"—I held up a hand—"if he was working with someone, it's more likely someone from his past. That's where the police should be looking, at the people Jaeger— Christian—knew back then." I didn't see the point in saying anything about Ray Nightingale to Peter.

"Good to know I have your trust," Peter said dryly.

"I'm sorry, Peter," I said. "I didn't mean you."

"I know what you meant," he said. He focused on Maggie again. "I've heard there are some . . . inconsistencies in Christian's finances. Are they going to find anything off in his sales through the store?"

"No," Maggie said.

He studied her face and seemed satisfied with whatever he saw there. "All right," he said. "If the police want to talk to you again, I'd be happy to represent you. You have my card."

She nodded.

"I'll see you in the morning, then," he said. He nodded at me and left.

"That little . . ." Maggie shook her head and pressed a fist against her mouth. She didn't swear and she was struggling to find words to describe Jaeger.

I put a hand on her shoulder. "Mags, Peter is a lawyer. I'm not saying he's overreacting, but keep in mind it's his job to take everything, every small detail, very seriously. Just because that money was hidden in the masks doesn't mean the co-op is involved in any other way. And no one, no one—not even Marcus—is seriously going to buy you as Jaeger's cohort."

"I have to talk to Ray, Kath," she said. "If there's any chance he knows anything . . ."

"Okay," I said. "Tomorrow. I'll come with you."

She nodded and pushed the sleeves of her T-shirt up to her elbows. "So do you really think Jaeger's past caught up with him somehow?"

"I think it is possible. Like I said to Peter, he wouldn't have been hard to find. That auction that Abigail and I went to had some nice artwork, as well as old photographs and rare books. I'm pretty sure there were people from out of state there, as well as from out of town. Jaeger could have easily met someone who knew him as Christian, maybe just by chance."

There was a loud crash from upstairs, just as I realized the bag between my feet, where Owen was supposed to be waiting, had gone limp.

24

Maggie looked up over her head and then she looked at me. "If there's another . . . furry trespasser up there I'm going to scream."

I was pretty sure the noise had been caused by a furry trespasser, just not the kind she meant.

"I'll go look," I said, reaching for the bag by my feet and slinging it over my shoulder. If I saw—and I did mean saw—the fur ball I was certain had caused the noise, he was going back in the bag and back in the truck.

Maggie took a deep breath and swallowed. "Okay, I'm coming too."

That would make it hard to grab Owen, assuming he was visible. I thought about coming clean, but Maggie was already resolutely climbing the steps. I started up after her.

There was no sign of the cat in the empty hallway, but a large cardboard box was lying on its side, the contents half spilled on the floor. It had clearly fallen off the stack of boxes pushed against the wall next to the door of

Maggie's studio. I was happy to see there was no squashed cat underneath it.

Maggie made a face. "I think I stacked those too high," she said.

"Probably," I agreed, thinking Owen jumping on the pile and rummaging around inside the top box hadn't helped.

She was already crouched down, gathering papers.

"What are all these boxes doing out here?" I asked, bending down to help.

"Another leak; in the storage space this time. We had to move everything out. And I just brought these things over from the co-op a couple of days ago."

There were boxes stacked by Ruby's door and Jaeger's former studio as well.

"Oren is supposed to come in the morning to see if he can fix it," she said. She picked up a dark brown leather portfolio that had been partly covered by a couple of her sketches and turned it over, clearly puzzled. "This isn't mine."

She reached for the cardboard carton, still lying on its side. Inside among the papers and photographs was a wooden box, with an inlaid geometric design on its lid. Maggie sat pack on her heels with the box resting on her lap. "This isn't mine, either." She tipped the box sideways. "I don't even see how to open it."

I took it from her. The box was about the size of a small jewelry box, low and flat, made of smooth honey-colored wood. The intricate design set into the cover had been made from several different kinds of wood. There were no hinges and no catch. "It's a puzzle box," I told Maggie. I swallowed a couple of times and studied the small box. It was well made.

She reached over and ran her fingers over the top, feeling the design. "It's very nice work. I thought puzzle boxes were a lot smaller than this."

"Not always," I said. I gestured at the leather portfolio on the floor by Maggie's knee. "Look inside and see if you can figure out who it belongs to. Maybe the same person owns this box too, and just put their stuff with yours by mistake."

Maggie undid the snap closure and opened the folder flat on the floor. The top piece of paper inside was a sketch for a mask. The page was covered with notes written in a tight, cramped handwriting.

She blew out a breath. "This is Jaeger's," she said slowly. She flipped through the papers underneath the top one, nodding her head. "Yeah, this is definitely his." She looked over at the puzzle box. "Do you think that belongs to Jaeger as well?"

"What are the chances two different people would accidently put something in one of your boxes?" What was the chance even one person would?

"When did you put these boxes in the storage room?" I asked.

"Tuesday night, after the meeting with the town council. Ruby helped me."

Jaeger had died on Wednesday. "Was Jaeger here?"

"He was in and out," Maggie said. "Lots of people were."

It was way too big a coincidence that the puzzle box would belong to anyone but Jaeger Merrill. "Jaeger's masks were made from metal and found objects, weren't they?" I said.

She nodded, still shifting through the papers. "They were. He had a great eye." She pointed at one sketch.

"That mask for instance. It was in the store and there was something unsettling about it." She flipped through the papers underneath that top one, and then suddenly she stopped and turned to look at me. "He did do one piece and the basic face—the base if you will—was made out of wood, several different pieces that he carved and fitted together."

"It's possible Jaeger made this," I said, turning the box over. If he had, he did very fine, meticulous work. "There are hours and hours of work in this."

"How do you know so much about these boxes?" Maggie asked.

I ducked my head, brushing my hair gingerly off my forehead. "A . . . friend of mine gave a puzzle box to my dad, and then Dad and Ethan found one at a yard sale and spent an entire weekend trying to get into it."

I remembered the two of them coming home with their two dollar treasure and I smiled at the memory.

"What is it?" Maggie said.

"I'm just remembering Dad and Ethan, they couldn't get that box open and pretty soon they were fighting about it. My brother was trying to make this chart with arrows to 'map the process' and my father wanted what he called an instinctual approach—in other words, trial and error." I couldn't help laughing.

"Finally, my mother came sweeping out from the kitchen—I remember she had some kind of long gold scarf flowing behind her, very dramatic—carrying a wooden meat mallet she'd gotten from who knows where—probably one of the neighbors—threatening to 'open' the box herself if they didn't stop arguing over it."

Maggie grinned at me. "Did they?"

"No," I said, shaking my head.

"Did they ever get it open?"

"Someone, uh, opened it for them," I said. I slid my finger over the end of the box and then pushed on an edge. A small section of the side panel extended itself forward. I pushed it back into place and felt along the bottom edge. It took a couple of tries but finally I managed to slide out a thin bottom panel.

"Oh wow," Maggie said. "Could I try?"

I handed the box over to her. "Go ahead," I said. "I don't know how many moving pieces there are and the trick is that you have to move them in the right order or you won't get the box open."

She moved her long fingers over the polished wood, sliding the bottom in and out and moving the side section again.

"We should call Marcus," I said. I looked over the stack of boxes, wondering where the heck Owen was. He could be sitting on the top watching us for all I knew. Given his massive kitty-crush on Maggie I knew he had to be close.

"Right," she said, so engrossed in playing with the puzzle box, she didn't even look up. Then my words seemed to register and her head snapped up. "Wait a minute. Why?"

The portfolio was glove-soft leather. The puzzle box had been beautifully crafted by someone, Jaeger, maybe? I had no way of knowing.

I did know neither item seemed to go with Jaeger's starving artist persona, although they probably fit right in to Christian Ellis's more lavish lifestyle that Maggie had described to me.

"Because these things ended up in a box of your things less than twenty-four hours before Jaeger died," I said. "I don't know why. Maybe it's as simple as he stashed them in the wrong box. Maybe he was hiding them. Given that we know it looks like he was up to something hinky, I think Marcus needs to know what we found."

Maggie laced her fingers and squeezed her palms together. "Kathleen, do you think there was something 'hinky' about Jaeger's death?"

"I don't know," I said. "Maybe. All I can tell you is, in my experience, it's not a good idea to keep secrets from Marcus."

Maggie nodded. "You're right. I just wish we could call your dad or your brother and maybe get this thing open."

I gave her the Mr. Spock eyebrow. It's very impressive. "I didn't say we couldn't do that as well." I pulled out my cell phone. "Do you want to call Peter, first?" I asked, holding it out to her.

"No."

"Are you sure?"

"Yes, I'm sure," Maggie said with certainty. "I'm not going around acting like I need to protect myself when I haven't done anything wrong." She dipped her head toward the phone. "Call him."

I hesitated. While I felt it was important to let Marcus know about the box and the portfolio, I wasn't sure we should keep Peter out of the loop.

Maggie narrowed her eyes at me and gestured to the phone. "Call Marcus," she said. "Or I will."

I punched in the number for Marcus's cell, which I had memorized for some unknown reason, and he answered on the fourth ring. I explained that Maggie and I had found something at the studio that he needed to see. He didn't ask what or how or why. All he said was, "I'm about ten minutes away." I told him one of us would be at the back door to let him in and hung up.

"I'll go down and wait for him," Maggie said. She handed the puzzle box to me and stood up, brushing her hands on her pants. "That thing's worse than Rubik's Cube."

She headed down the stairs. After a moment I got to my feet and looked around for Owen. I couldn't see him anywhere.

"Owen!" I hissed.

Nothing. Where the heck was he?

I looked around all the boxes and then walked to the far end of the hall. "Owen, where are you?" I whispered. Why did he have to pick now to prove I had zero control over what he did?

It occurred to me that maybe he'd knocked that cardboard box off the top of the pile because there was something he wanted me to see inside. Had he been able to somehow smell that the leather portfolio had belonged to Jaeger Merrill? Heaven knows he could smell a catnip chicken over in Rebecca's kitchen.

I crouched down in the middle of the hall. I heard Maggie letting Marcus in downstairs. "Owen!" I hissed again. "Stop messing with me!"

Almost as fast as a finger snap he was there in front of me, with the same smug smile as the proverbial cat that swallowed the canary, although in this case it was a piece of paper, not a yellow bird. And Owen hadn't swallowed it. It had just been in his mouth.

He spit the torn piece of paper at my feet and put a paw on it for emphasis.

"I see it," I said. "Now go get in the bag." I could hear Maggie and Marcus on the stairs. He looked at the canvas bag on the floor where I'd left it by Maggie's door. I swear he smirked at me.

And then he disappeared.

25

"Thanks for calling me," Marcus said. He was wearing jeans and a short-sleeved blue T-shirt over a long-sleeved gray one.

I'd gotten to my feet and was waiting, holding the portfolio and the puzzle box when he got to the top of the stairs.

"You're welcome," I said. I handed him the leather case.

"Maggie said you found this in a box of her things?"

I pointed to the cardboard carton, still on its side on the floor. "It definitely belongs . . . belonged to Jaeger. Maggie recognized the top sketch."

He flipped through some of the other papers without comment, then looked at the puzzle box. "And the box? What's in that?"

"I don't know," I said.

He smiled. "You didn't look?"

"We couldn't." I handed him the box. "It's a puzzle box."

He frowned. "Seriously?"

"Seriously."

Maggie reached over and took the box out of his hands. "See? There's a piece here that slides out. And another on the opposite side."

I took a few steps away from them and pulled out my phone. I counted eleven rings before my father answered.

"Hello, my sweetheart," he said. "I knew it was you."

"No you didn't," I said, smiling at the sound of his voice.

"I did," he insisted. "You're the only person who wouldn't hang up when I didn't answer right away."

That was true. "So what took you so long?"

"I was trying on my leather pants."

It wasn't quite as odd as it sounded, given that my dad had played a number of dashing, leather-clad swordsmen over the years. Still . . . "Do I want to know why?" I asked.

He laughed. "Probably not." My dad had a great laugh, deep and rumbly. I could almost feel the vibration in my chest and for a moment the longing to be back in Boston with my family took my breath away.

I had to swallow a couple of times before I could speak. "Dad, um, I called because Maggie and I have a puzzle box we need to get into. Do you think you could help?"

"I can try sweetheart. I'm assuming you don't know who made the box or anything about it."

I glanced back at Maggie and Marcus. Marcus had his cop face on and Maggie looked very serious. "No, Dad," I said, quietly. "I don't. But this is important."

There was silence on the other end for a moment.

"Katie, there's something you're not telling me. Probably more than one thing, but interrogating you is your mother's job so all I'm going to say is please be careful, whatever it is you're doing."

"I will, Dad," I promised.

"Describe the box," he said.

I walked over to Marcus and Maggie and silently held out my hand. Marcus gave me the box. I described what I was looking at to Dad.

"It's not an antique, is it?" he asked.

"No, it's not. I think it was made fairly recently."

"How far out does the piece on the right side move?"

I worked at it and told him.

"Okay, let's see what we can do," he said.

We probably tried six or seven different combinations of moves, but the box didn't open. I could see Marcus was getting impatient, shifting restlessly from one foot to the other. Finally I shook my head and handed it back to him, taking a few steps away.

"I'm sorry I can't help you, Katie," Dad said.

Marcus had turned the puzzle box over and was studying the underside.

"I'm guessing it would be a bad idea to try to pry it open."

"You could damage what's inside," Dad said. "My advice would be to either keep trying—maybe there's a part we missed—or"—he hesitated—"if you really need to get this box open, ask someone who knows a lot more about them than I do."

Roma's wonderful meal suddenly felt like a piece of stone from Wild Rose Bluff in my stomach. "I don't really want to do that, Dad," I said in a low voice.

"I know," he said.

"Thanks for trying." I wished that he were a lot closer so I could hug him.

"I'm sorry I couldn't help. Call your mother when you have time. I love you."

"I love you too," I said.

I disconnected the call and looked over at Maggie. Owen adored her. Hercules liked her and I had no idea how I would have adjusted to life in Minnesota if we hadn't become friends.

I walked back over to her just in time to see her shake her head angrily at Marcus.

"I don't know how to open that box," she said, enunciating each word slowly and carefully. "I don't know what Jaeger was doing, but whatever it was, I wasn't part of it."

She reached over and grabbed the top carton from the pile by her door and thrust it at Marcus. "Here. You want to search my things for evidence? Go ahead!"

"Maggie, I'm just trying to do my job," Marcus said. There were tight lines around his mouth.

I took a deep breath and let it out. I put one hand on Maggie's shoulder and the other on Marcus's arm. "Stop," I said. My voice was louder than I intended and it bounced off the walls of the hallway.

"I might have another resource," I said. I was surprised that my voice didn't shake. It was the only part of me that wasn't. "Just give me a minute."

I opened my phone and dialed a number from memory and my heart pounded as it rang on the other end. He answered and for a moment I literally couldn't breathe, I couldn't speak. Then somehow I remembered how to do both.

"Hi Andrew," I said. "It's Kathleen."

26

Maggie's mouth actually dropped open a little.

Marcus was watching me and I had to work not to let my emotions show on my face or creep into my voice.

"Kathleen." I heard Andrew swallow on the other end of the phone. "How are you?"

We hadn't spoken in a year. I could see his face even without closing my eyes, his sandy blond hair, blue eyes and just a hint of a smile warming up his face. Was he in his office with his feet on the desk, tilted back in the old wooden office chair? Or was he upstairs sitting on the edge of the bed?

I gave my head a little shake to chase away the images because it didn't matter. "I'm well," I said. "How are you?"

"I . . . all right. It's starting to get busy, work I mean."

It felt so awkward to be making small talk with him. I needed to get to the point. "I, uh, need your help with something," I said. Quickly, I explained the bones of the problem and that Dad hadn't been able to help. Andrew didn't ask why I needed to open a puzzle box that clearly didn't belong to me. He didn't even ask why I'd called him, although he had to have guessed what it was costing me.

"Describe the box," he said.

I took it from Marcus again and explained what it looked like, trying to give him as much detail as possible.

"Any chance you could send me some photos?"

I looked at Maggie. "Can we take some pictures of the box with your phone and e-mail them to Andrew?"

"Sure," she said.

"Do you have the same e-mail address?" I asked.

"I do," Andrew said. "Nothing's changed."

No. Nothing had changed, including the fact that he'd taken off on a fishing trip with his buddies after we'd had a fight and had come back married to a waitress from a fifties diner that he'd met on the second day of the trip. The fact that a fair amount of alcohol had been involved hadn't made me feel any better about it.

Maggie snapped the pictures and e-mailed them.

"Got them," Andrew said after a minute. I heard a creak, the kind of thing that sounded like a horror movie sound effect. I knew it was his old chair, which meant he was in the downstairs office.

"Whoever made the box does nice work," he said approvingly.

"Do you know how to open it?" I asked.

"I think so. It looks like a pattern I've seen before." He gave me instructions and I relayed them to Marcus who followed each one precisely.

"Cross your fingers," Andrew said, finally. "Let's hope I'm right."

He was. Marcus twisted the bottom panel and the top of the puzzle box opened. He nodded, and Maggie, who'd alternated between watching Marcus and watching me with troubled eyes, gave a small smile.

I moved away from them again.

"Thank you, Andrew, your help means a lot," I said. The conversation was back to being awkward.

"Are you happy Kathleen?" he said quickly, probably thinking I was about to go.

"I am," I said. "I really am."

It was true. Maggie was my best friend, and while I didn't have a clue what exactly Marcus was, I was happy to have him in my life, even when he annoyed the heck out of me—which was at least fifty percent of the time. And I had Roma, and Rebecca, and everyone at the library, and the Taylors and of course Owen and Hercules. I didn't know what was going to happen when my contract with the library board was up, but if they did ask me to stay, it would be very hard to say no.

"I miss you," Andrew said, so softly I almost didn't hear him. "I screwed it all up and I'm sorry."

"I have to go," I said. I took a deep breath and let it out. "Take care of yourself."

"You too," he said.

I closed the phone and turned back to Mags and Marcus. They were looking at the contents of the puzzle box. There were some photographs and sketches inside, along with an old fountain pen and that was it.

"Is that Santa Claus?" I asked, pointing to one drawing.

"Looks like it," Marcus said.

Several of the photos were images of the Coca-Cola Santa. There were a couple of a bearded older man who felt familiar, maybe because of his resemblance to the Coke Santa in his red suit.

The sketches had obviously been done by Jaeger Merrill; they were his style and every bit of extra white space was covered with notes in his crablike handwriting.

"Why did Jaeger have a bunch of drawings of Santa Claus?" I asked.

"Don't you get it?" Maggie asked. Her eyes danced and her cheeks were flushed.

It took a moment, but then I remembered decorating the library the previous Christmas with Mary and Abigail and hearing about Mayville Heights's alleged connection to the iconic Christmas image. "Of course," I said, nodding my head.

Marcus looked blankly at us.

Mags gestured at the pictures of the bearded man. "Does he look familiar?"

"No. Who is it?" Marcus asked.

I held up a hand. "Wait a second." I leaned in a little closer. "Look. Take away some hair and thin the face a little." He still didn't see it. I looked at Maggie. "This is Everett's father, Carson, isn't it?"

She grinned her approval. "And these pictures and sketches, they just prove that the rumors were right."

"What rumors?" Marcus said. There was a touch of irritation in his tone.

"That Carson Henderson was Santa Claus, of course," Maggie said.

27

"Santa Claus?" Marcus said, frowning in confusion. "You mean North Pole, elves and flying reindeer?"

"Kind of," Maggie said.

"Take another look," I said to Marcus, pointing from the old black-and-white photos, to the sketch he was holding, to the soft drink ad. "Do you see it?"

He studied the images and then looked up at me. "It does look like the same person."

"Exactly," Maggie said. "There have been rumors around Mayville Heights for just about forever that Carson Henderson was the inspiration—at least in part—for the Coca-Cola Santa paintings done by Haddon Sundblom." She narrowed her eyes at Marcus. "I can't believe you've never heard that story."

He shrugged. "There's always some kind of story going around town."

Maggie's gaze slid over to me. "Let me guess, Mary told you, right?"

"And Abigail, when we were putting up that big cardboard Santa in the children's section." I pointed to the Coke Santa photos. "I thought Sundblom always said he was inspired by a friend—a salesman—let me see, Prentiss, Lou Prentiss."

She nodded. "He did. And I think Prentiss was the inspiration, at least in part. But Haddon Sundblom and Carson Henderson had been friends since they were kids. Carson's mother—Everett's grandmother—had family in Muskegon where Sundblom grew up. Carson spent part of every summer there when he was young."

She looked at Marcus and pulled both hands back through her hair. "According to my grandmother, who knew pretty much every bit of gossip in Mayville Heights, Carson wasn't the kind of man who would want to go through life as Santa Claus. Anna and Everett were pretty much his only two soft spots."

"So you think Jaeger Merrill knew about this Santa Claus thing?" Marcus asked. He didn't even try to keep the skepticism out of his voice.

"Why not?" Maggie countered, an edge in her voice. "He was an artist. People tend to tell us stories about art."

"And he was working at Eric's, remember?" I added. "The whole town is in and out of the café. You can get more news there than in the newspaper." I looked more closely at the photographs of Carson Henderson. They weren't copies. They were original snapshots. I was pretty sure where Jaeger had gotten them.

"That's what Jaeger was doing out at Wisteria Hill," I said slowly.

Maggie nodded. "He was going back to forgery, just not those icons."

"He was looking for those pictures of Carson." I gestured to the box. Then I remembered the pen cap Hercules had found at the co-op. Did it belong with the fountain pen lying in the puzzle box? I tried to take a closer look without being obvious about it.

"Or possibly sketches Haddon Sundblom may have given to Carson." She pointed at the drawings. "Jaeger was incredibly talented and because he knew how to forge all the provenance it was a pretty much foolproof plan." She glanced at Marcus. "Provenance is all the documentation that proves the authenticity of a piece of art."

He nodded without saying anything, and I got the feeling he already knew what the word meant. Even though he didn't have a library card he did seem to know a lot about a lot of things.

"Do you think he was working alone?" I asked Maggie. With Marcus standing there I didn't want to ask if she thought Ray could have been helping somehow.

"I don't know," she said. "He could have reconnected with someone from his past." She turned her attention to Marcus. "Or maybe it was me." She made a dramatic sweeping gesture with one hand. "Maybe I just staged all of this to draw suspicion away from myself."

"Did you?" Marcus asked, looking around the hallway.

Maggie's mouth twisted sideways and she gave a slight shake of her head.

"I'd like to take the rest of those boxes," he said.

For a moment Maggie didn't say anything, but I saw her jaw tighten as she clenched her teeth together. She put a loose fist flat on her chest and took several deep breaths. Then she looked at Marcus. "I'll need to call my lawyer first," she said. She pulled her cell phone out of her pocket and walked down the hall several paces.

I turned to Marcus. "Why are you picking on Maggie?" I asked.

"All I'm doing is my job," he said. "I'm following the evidence—wherever it leads. It doesn't really have anything to do with Maggie."

I looked over at her; she had her back to us, talking quietly, I was guessing, to Peter Lundgren. I turned back to Marcus, shaking my head. "It has everything to do with Maggie," I said.

Before I could say anything else, she snapped her cell phone shut and walked back to us. "I'm sorry Detective Gordon," she said, her voice cool and formal. "My lawyer has advised me not to give you these boxes unless you can show me a warrant."

"I understand," he said. If he was angry I couldn't see it. "I can get a warrant. Until then I'm going to need to have someone keep an eye on all of this." He gestured at the stack of cardboard boxes.

"It's a town building," Maggie said with a slight shrug.

This time it was Marcus who stepped away and took out his phone.

"I can't believe you called Andrew," she said as soon as he was out of earshot.

"It's not a big deal," I said, and as the words came out I realized it really wasn't. Hearing Andrew's voice hadn't hurt the way I'd anticipated it would anytime I thought about talking to him again. And I hadn't thought about it for a while.

"Was that Peter you were talking to?" I asked Maggie, keeping my voice low so Marcus wouldn't hear me.

She nodded. "He said that Marcus will be able to get the warrant. The idea is just to make him do all the paperwork so everything is documented properly." She looked over at the detective. "Anyway, there isn't anything in these other boxes."

"Mags, you don't know that for sure."

She actually smiled at me then. "I do," she said. She pointed to the carton still on its side on the floor. "Someone took the tape off that box—Jaeger I guess, when he put his things inside it—otherwise everything wouldn't have fallen on the floor. There's tape on the tops of all the other boxes. I think I'm safe."

I blew out a breath. I felt better. "What about the puzzle box and the portfolio?"

"Marcus gets to keep those. And for what it's worth, you were right. I should have called Peter when you suggested it."

I stretched my arms over my head and yawned. "I would have pushed if I'd realized Marcus was going to—"

"—do his job?" Maggie finished.

I stopped in midstretch and stared at her. "He's looking for a way to tie you to Jaeger and that money they found."

She shook her head. "No he isn't. He's doing his job. He's aggravating, but he's just doing what he's supposed to do. He's a cop." She put a hand on my arm. "You two butt heads because"—she smiled at me—"well, you know why I think the two of you always have a little conflict going."

Maggie had been trying to get Marcus and me together—romantically—for months, although she'd eased off recently. I had to admit he was easy to look at, if you liked the tall, broad-shouldered, chiseled jaw type. And maybe, *maybe* I did. A little.

"But the two of you also have totally different ways of looking at life," she continued. "Marcus is all about facts and logic. You pay attention to feelings and all the little nuances of what people don't say. Which makes sense, by the way, given that your parents are both actors."

For a long moment I didn't say anything. Finally Maggie gave me a quizzical look. "No argument?"

I shrugged. "You're right. I'm just not sure how to stop butting heads, as you put it."

"How about focusing on the fact that it's a very cute head you keep butting, not to mention the actual bu—"

"—I get the picture," I interjected.

Marcus came back over to us. "I have an officer on the way to keep an eye on the building. I'll walk you two down to your cars if you're ready to leave."

"May I get my purse and lock my studio?" Maggie asked.

"Of course," he said.

While Maggie got her things, I rescued my bag, happy to see by its lumpy shape that Owen was inside. The date squares were still on top of the pile of boxes and Maggie picked them up when she came out. She showed the container to Marcus. "These are date squares. I'm not trying to sneak evidence out of the building. Kathleen brought them for me. I'd offer you one, but I wouldn't want it to be misconstrued as a bribe."

"I appreciate that," Marcus said, and I thought I saw his lips twitch. We headed down the stairs.

"Call me in the morning," I said to Maggie, wrapping her in a hug.

"Thank you for calling Andrew," she whispered.

"Anytime," I whispered back.

Maggie's bug was parked several spaces away from my truck. She looked around the lot. "No bogeyman," she said to Marcus. "Talk to you tomorrow," she said to me and then she pulled out her keys and walked over to the car.

Marcus walked me the few feet to the truck. He gave a quick once-over to the truck bed and then glanced into the cab.

"Good night, Kathleen," he said.

I looked up at him. Mags was right. That head I kept butting my own against was kind of . . . cute. "Good night," I said. I put the key in the lock and he walked back to the building. I couldn't help watching him over my shoulder. He was kind of cute from every angle. *Stop thinking that*, I told myself as I set Owen on the seat and slid in beside him.

The canvas bag wriggled and Owen stuck his head out. His fur was kind of disheveled and there was a sour look on his face. He meowed loudly.

"We'll be home in a minute," I said as I backed up and pulled out onto the street. "Are you hungry?"

He meowed even more insistently, cat for, "Of course I'm hungry."

He was silent as we headed over to Mountain Road and started up the hill. "So, I'm assuming you heard all the stuff about Carson Henderson," I said. Owen was staring out the windshield as though he really was riding shotgun.

I shifted my eyes back to the road, squinting into the darkness at the edge of the range of my headlights just in time to realize there was a vehicle coming down the hill without any lights on.

On the wrong side of the road.

Headed straight at us.

28

I tightened my grip on the steering wheel as my stomach lurched and my heart thudded in my chest. Instinct took over.

By some miracle, there was nothing coming down the hill in the opposite lane. I hit the horn and at the same time yanked the steering wheel hard to the left. The truck lurched across the road and onto the grass between the curb and the sidewalk, just missing a telephone pole. I floored the brakes with one foot and hit the clutch with the other, knocking the gearshift into neutral.

Then I sucked in a breath, stretching my right arm across the seat in front of Owen, my left hand clutching the seat belt, and braced for the impact of the other vehicle colliding with the end of the truck bed. I didn't see how it could miss us, and then somehow it did, speeding past, still with no lights, with what seemed like just inches to spare.

I slumped against the back of the seat, heart pounding in stereo in my ears, a hand pressed against my mouth and the sound of my ragged breathing filling the truck. Beside me Owen was crouched wide-eyed and very, very angry, fur standing on end, claws dug into the seat.

There was some kind of noise behind the truck and I looked in the rearview mirror. A vehicle had pulled behind me, which meant I couldn't back up. Had the other driver stopped? I didn't care if it was a couple of joyriding teenagers or someone who'd been stupid enough to drive after drinking, whoever it was had almost gotten all of us killed. I didn't really want to hear an apology. I was angry enough that what I really wanted to do was yell at someone.

Still operating on autopilot I tossed my sweatshirt, which was lying on the seat, over the cat, I guess mostly to protect him. Owen yowled his annoyance but he didn't move. There was a wrench under my seat along with a couple of other tools in case I had a flat tire. I locked the truck door with one hand and grabbed the wrench with the other. Mayville Heights might be a very safe place but I was suddenly aware that I was a woman alone, except for a small gray cat.

I looked in the rearview mirror again. Someone was walking toward my truck, head down, hands in his—his, judging by the build of the person—pockets. I felt the acid burn of anger in my throat. Owen gave a couple of sharply angry meows from under my hoodie. It would have been better if whoever that was just turned and walked away. We were a mightily pissed off woman and small cat.

I tightened my grip on the wrench, ready for what, I wasn't sure.

Then Marcus appeared by the driver's door of the truck. I literally sagged with relief. I leaned over, unlocked the door and opened it.

"Are you all right?" he asked. There were tight lines of worry etched between his eyes.

I nodded.

"Can you get out?"

"I'm fine," I said, but I slid down off the seat onto the grass, glancing behind me to make sure Owen was still undercover. "Did you see the other driver?"

"Just his or her taillights," Marcus said. "I called it in, but I wanted to make sure you weren't hurt." He noticed the wrench that I was still clutching in my right hand. "Wait a minute. You thought I was . . ." He hung his head for a moment. "I'm sorry. I didn't mean to scare you."

I held up the wrench and maybe it was relief or the last bit of adrenaline zipping through my body, but I started to laugh. "It's okay, Marcus," I said. "I wasn't scared. I was mad. Very, very mad."

He smiled. "I'm suddenly glad you've never been very, very mad at me," he said.

We both turned at the sound of a police cruiser pulling to the curb behind us. "I'll be right back," he said.

I leaned back against the seat and pushed the wrench back underneath it. "Are you all right?" I asked the lump under my shirt. I got a soft murp as an answer. "Hold tight. We'll be home in a couple of minutes."

After a minute or so the police car pulled into the street again and Marcus walked back across the grass to me. "They didn't catch whoever it was, did they?" I said.

He shook his head. "I'm sorry." He leaned forward and looked closely at the driver's side tire, which had gone up over the curb. "This tire looks okay. I'm just going to check the other one and the front end."

I waited while he walked around the front of the

truck, examining the bumper and crouching down to take a closer look at the passenger side tire.

"Everything looks okay," he said when he came back to me. "It wouldn't hurt to have it put up on the hoist and get the undercarriage checked, just in case."

"I will."

He jerked his head back toward his SUV. "I'm going to follow you the rest of the way up the hill."

"You don't have to," I said, rubbing the back of my neck with one hand.

"I know," he said.

He pulled into the street and I backed carefully off the curb. Everything seemed to work the way it was supposed to and there were no new rattles or mysterious sounds in reverse or in drive.

I started up Mountain Road again. Out of the corner of my eye I could see my shirt moving, kind of like there was an alligator wrestling match going on underneath. Finally Owen poked his head out. "Two minutes," I said, "and we'll be home."

The look he shot me was decidedly sour.

I pulled into the driveway and Marcus's SUV slipped in behind me. I got out of the truck and walked back to him and all at once I realized how quickly he'd been on the scene after I was forced off the road.

He got out of the car.

"You were following me home, from the arts center, weren't you?" I asked.

"Yes I was."

"Why?"

He leaned one hand on the hood of the SUV. "When I first got there, I saw a vehicle drive by. It didn't have any lights on." He shrugged. "Sometimes that's nothing more than someone who's had a few and doesn't want to get caught driving home."

"But," I said.

"Whoever it was, drove by more than once." He made a face. "And I didn't tell you because I wasn't sure it mattered. I could have been wrong."

"In other words you were acting on instinct. On a feeling." It was hard not to smirk at him.

He shook his head, smiling. "See. I knew you were going to say that."

"Don't worry," I said. "I know this is just a one-time aberration." Then I remembered Maggie. "Marcus, what about Maggie?"

"It's okay. I had a car follow her home as well."

"Do you think this has something to do with Jaeger Merrill?"

He flexed his fingers up and down on the hood of the SUV, like a spider doing pushups. "I don't know."

Since for once he wasn't evading my questions I decided to ask another. "Thomas Karlsson's death—that was murder." I crossed my arms over my chest. It was cool without my hoodie.

He nodded. "You saw the skull. There's no way that was an accident."

"I know you have to talk to Pearl tomorrow," I said. "I get that. Just please be . . ." I hesitated.

"Nice?" he offered.

"Okay." I held up my thumb and index finger, just a tiny space apart. "Just a little bit?" Another yawn slipped out.

"You're tired," he said. "I should get going."

I took a couple of steps closer to him and he straightened up. "Thank you, for getting me home safely."

He pulled in a deep breath and let it out and suddenly the air between us seemed somehow charged, electric, the way it did when Hercules walked through a wall or a door.

"You're welcome," Marcus said, his eyes locked on to my face. "I'm very glad you're okay."

I could feel myself moving toward him, imperceptibly, but I could feel it. Abruptly he cleared his throat and whatever the heck had come over me was gone. For the most part.

"Good night, Kathleen," he said. "Stay safe."

I stood there watching him drive away, hugging myself. Then I went back to get Owen out of the truck, shaking my head to chase away the last of the discombobulated feeling. I had not been going to trace the curve of Marcus's unbelievably manly, chiseled, stubbled jawline with one finger. And I had most certainly not been thinking about kissing him. No I had not.

I scooped Owen off the seat along with my purse and my sweatshirt. Then I unlocked the back door and carried him all the way to the kitchen before I set him on the floor.

His fur was still sticking out in every direction. He walked around the room making grumbling noises, clearly in a major bad mood.

I washed my hands, put bread in the toaster and milk to warm in the microwave. Hercules appeared from somewhere. He watched Owen walking around and grumbling for a moment, then walked over to me and gave me a quizzical look, head cocked to one side.

"Long story," I said. "Just wait until I get the toast made and I'll fill you in." He sat down.

Once the hot chocolate and toast with peanut butter

were made I pulled out a chair and gave Hercules the Cliff's Notes version of the evening, while Owen worked on a little pile of kitty treats and added a grumbling comment from time to time.

I didn't tell the cats about the little "moment" between Marcus and me in the driveway. It was an adrenaline comedown. It was tiredness. And it hadn't meant anything.

It hadn't.

I had a bath, spending a long time soaking in the hot, lavender scented water. Then I did an inventory of my bruises to see what colors they were now. They went from greenish yellow, through various shades of red to deep purple. I put a layer of Rebecca's salve on my ankle and used the last of the cotton strips to wrap it.

I was too wired to sleep. So, apparently, was Owen. He wandered in and out of the bedroom, too restless to stay for more than a minute. Hercules, on the other hand, jumped up onto my lap the minute I sat down in the big chair by the window.

"There's nothing I can do to help Maggie," I told him, stroking his fur. "I'm going to have to leave things in Peter's hands for now. But maybe I can do something to help Roma. She needs answers and I think I know where to get them."

I leaned my head against the back of the chair and closed my eyes for a moment. "I'm going to have breakfast with Burtis Chapman."

When I opened them again, Herc's furry black-and-white face was just inches from mine. His way, I was guessing, of asking, "Have you lost your mind?"

29

At quarter to six I was in the truck on the way over to Fern's Diner. I didn't know if it was a good idea or a bad idea, mostly because I knew if I thought about it too long I might just talk myself out of going.

The diner wasn't somewhere I went very often, although I had been a couple of times with Roma for meatloaf Tuesday. According to Roma, Fern's had been restored about five or six years ago back to its 1950s glory, or as she liked to put it, "Just like the good old days only better." The building was low and long, with windows on three sides, aglow with neon after dark. Inside there was the requisite jukebox, booths with red vinyl seats and a counter with gleaming chrome stools.

Burtis's black truck was in the back parking lot and he was perched on a corner stool inside, elbows on the counter, head bent over a heavy, white china coffee mug. He was wearing a green plaid shirt and his Twins hat. His hands were massive, I noticed, big enough that he could probably squeeze my head between his thumb and index finger and make my brains come out my ears, but I tried not to think about that as I took the stool beside him.

"Good morning," I said.

"Morning, Kathleen." If he was surprised to see me, it didn't show.

The waitress slid a mug in front of me and held up the coffeepot with an inquiring look on her face. At the same time she put a huge, oval dish in front of Burtis that could best be described as a heart attack on a plate.

I nodded and she poured my coffee. "What can I get you hon?" she asked. She was wearing red pedal pushers, a short-sleeved white shirt with—I kid you not—PEGGY SUE stitched over the left breast pocket and red-framed glasses. Her hair was in a gravity defying, bouffant updo. I eyed it, wondering if there was any way Rebecca could get my hair to do that.

My stomach rumbled, reminding me that not only had I not had any coffee yet, I hadn't had any food, either. I dipped my head toward Burtis's plate. "I'll have what he's having," I said.

The waitress nodded and went through the swinging door into the kitchen.

I put cream and sugar in my mug and took a long sip. The coffee was strong and hot, just the way I liked it. I gave a small smile of pleasure and wrapped my hands around the cup. I could feel Burtis's eyes on me and I turned my head to smile at him.

"What brings you out here so early?" he asked. "I thought you favored that little place by the water."

"I came to talk to you," I said.

That got me a smile. "Oh did you now?" he said. He speared a half a sausage and it disappeared into his mouth. "I'm kinda tied up with my breakfast at the moment."

"Take your time," I said, picking up my coffee again.

I'd finished about half my coffee when the waitress came back with my plate, as loaded as the one she'd brought for Burtis. There were scrambled eggs, sausage and bacon, fried potatoes with onions and tomato, and raisin toast. She topped up my coffee and headed down the counter to three men who had just walked in.

Burtis was watching me out of the corner of his eye. I picked up my fork and started eating. The eggs were fluffy, the bacon was crisp and I found myself wondering where they had gotten tomatoes that actually tasted like tomatoes at this time of year.

I was mopping up the last bits of potato and onion from my plate with a corner of bread when Burtis said, "What did you want to talk about?"

"Idris Blackthorne," I said. "Harrison Taylor told me you were the one to ask what Idris was like back in the day."

"Oh did he now?"

"He said you might be able to tell me about the way Idris did business."

"Seems to me you're friends with old Blackie's grand-daughter," he said, staring down into his cup. "Why don't you ask her?"

"Seems to me it would be bad manners to ask someone if her grandfather whacked a man over the head and buried his body out at Wisteria Hill," I said, taking a long drink from my mug.

The words seemed to hang there for a moment and then Burtis laughed. "I guess it would at that," he said.

I shifted sideways on my stool so I could look at him a little easier, leaning one elbow on the counter.

"Roma Davidson is my friend," I said. "Tom Karlsson was her father and she wants to know how he ended up out in that field."

"So you thought you'd poke your nose in and ask a few questions."

"Pretty much."

He gave another snort of laughter. "You're honest girl, I'll give you that." Burtis wasn't nearly as intimidating when he laughed.

The waitress came back and topped up our cups again. I added another packet of sugar to mine. "Burtis, I know Idris was...an entrepreneur. I know Tom worked for him and then suddenly he didn't. What I don't know is—"

"—whether Idris did have him whacked over the head and buried out behind the Henderson place," he finished.

"Did he?"

He shook his head. "No. You see Idris had a reputation. It wasn't what he did, it was what people thought he did that kept 'em in line, if you get my drift."

I did. I poured a little cream into my coffee and stirred it. "I hear there used to be a fairly regular poker game happening out in those woods back then," I said.

"There may have been."

"I hear Tom Karlsson was a cheat."

Burtis picked up his mug and drained it. "I don't care for cheaters myself," he said, putting his cup on the counter and sliding off the stool. "But I've heard that story. I also heard Tom broke a couple of fingers and had to give up playing cards." He shrugged. "Those things happen sometimes."

He pulled his keys out of his pocket. "One more thing. Back then, there was a road of sorts, rough but passable, that cut through those woods up there behind the Henderson place. If someone wanted to get back there they didn't necessarily have to go past the house." He tipped his hat to me and smiled. "You have a nice day, Kathleen. Come back and have breakfast again, sometime."

He headed toward the cash register and I picked up my coffee. So if I believed Burtis, neither Idris Blackthorne nor the poker players had anything to do with Tom Karlsson's death. And there had been a way to get Tom or his body up onto that ridge without anyone in the main house seeing anything.

Was Burtis telling the truth?

Was there any reason for him not to?

I slipped off my stool and walked over to the cash register. "Mr. Chapman took care of it," the waitress said with a smile.

I walked back to the counter and left a generous tip. Then I went out to the truck. Assuming Burtis hadn't been stringing me a line, I was back at square one.

So now what?

There was no sign of either cat when I got home. I headed upstairs to make the bed. Hercules came out of the closet as I was pulling up the spread.

"What do you do in there?" I asked. He looked at me blankly.

I dropped into the chair by the window and pulled the carton with Rebecca's mother's things closer. With all the turmoil of the previous few days I hadn't done any more planning for the library centennial celebration. I hadn't even asked Maggie for her ideas on what to do with Ellen's drawings.

Hercules jumped into my lap, ducking his head under my arm so he could look too. I reached into the box, pulled out one of the journals and opened it. Hercules shifted so he could see the pages. Maybe he was reading too for all I knew.

Now that I understood what The Ladies Knitting Circle had actually been doing, Ellen's oblique comments about the women made more sense. After reading a few pages I put the diary back and looked for the journal that spanned the time period when Tom Karlsson had probably been killed. It would have been easier if Hercules hadn't decided to help. He kept moving around on my lap, trying to poke his black-and-white head inside the box.

"Just sit still for a second," I said in frustration. "And I'll get it."

He made a huffy noise, but he pulled his head back and I was able to find the book I wanted. It started about six months before Pearl and little Roma had ended up at Wisteria Hill. A couple of times Ellen even wrote about seeing Pearl with Roma, and I wondered if she was the one who'd told Pearl about The Ladies Knitting Circle. And she mentioned Sam several times. It was clear she'd liked him and that she hadn't thought much of Sam's father. The day Tom disappeared there were several pages carefully cut out of the diary. The entries picked up more than a week later. Hercules put a paw on the seam.

"I see it, too," I said. I looked down at the little tuxedo

cat. "Do you think it was just a coincidence that Tom's body was buried at Wisteria Hill—that it had nothing to do with what Anna and her friends were up to?"

He covered his face with a paw.

"Yeah," I said. "Me neither."

30

I put the journal away, curled my feet up under me, and settled Hercules a little more comfortably on my legs. I thought about the few memories of her father that Roma had shared, like that game of hide and seek with Tom tossing a blanket over her head and telling her to be quiet and then "pretending" to look for her.

Owen wandered back in, stretched out on the floor in front of my chair and started washing his tail. He was acting just a little spacey, which meant he'd been into his stash of catnip chicken parts. He seemed to have gotten over our near accident the night before. I was pretty sure he was most annoyed about having my old sweatshirt tossed on top of him.

My shirt thrown over Owen to hide him.

A blanket thrown over Roma. Part of a game or an attempt to hide her?

Maybe Tom hadn't been playing a game with Roma.

Maybe he'd been going to take Roma away from Pearl. Maybe that's what had caused Pearl to pick that particular day to run. Was I wrong about Roma's mother?

"Could Pearl have killed Tom to protect Roma?" I asked Hercules. What else had Roma said about Tom? "He sat me on his lap and let me drive," she'd said. "I can close my eyes and see the car. It had turquoise and white bucket seats."

Could those memories be from the same night? The night Tom disappeared?

I stroked the top of Hercules's head. There was a connection I couldn't quite make. I glanced at the box of Ellen's things beside me on the table and suddenly tab A dropped into slot B.

"I have to put you down for a second," I said to Hercules. I set him on the floor and hurried downstairs to the living room where I'd left my briefcase. I took it back up to the bedroom with me, sat down on the rug with the cats and pulled out the old yearbook and the envelope of photographs.

I started with the pictures. Hercules put both paws on my leg and poked his head in to check out each photo. Owen was content to watch and crane his neck for a better look from time to time.

It took a while, but I eventually found what I was looking for, not in the photos but in the yearbook under the heading TRAVELIN' MAN.

"That's piece number one," I told Hercules. "Cross your paws that I can get piece number two."

He held out his paw and looked at it.

I pulled the phone down and thought for a moment. "She should be home," I said to the boys. I dialed Mary's number and crossed my own fingers that she was home and would have the answer. I was hoping the fact that she was a bit of a pack rat would work in my favor.

It did.

I hung up, set the telephone on the floor, and leaned back against the side of the bed. Hercules climbed up onto my legs and put his paws on my chest.

"I think I know what happened to Tom," I said. "It's a bit of a stretch—okay a lot of a stretch—but I think I know who killed him.

"And why."

31

The phone rang and I almost jumped out of my skin. It was Pearl.

"I need a favor from you, Kathleen, if you have time," she said.

"What do you need?" I asked.

"I want to go out to Wisteria Hill before we go talk to Detective Gordon. Roma's going to drive out there with me, but Neil has an appointment. Is there any chance you could join us?" She hesitated for a moment. "I think it would help Roma to have a friend."

"Of course," I said. There were things I needed to ask Pearl, and Wisteria Hill seemed like a good place to have that conversation. It was where everything had started and ended in many ways. We agreed to meet at the old estate in half an hour.

"Wish me luck," I said to Owen and Hercules.

I tucked the truck in next to a muddy, nondescript SUV out at Wisteria Hill and Roma pulled in right beside me. I thought she looked tired. The past few days had been pretty horrible for her and I was impressed by how well she'd handled everything.

Pearl got out of the passenger side of the car. "Hello, Kathleen," she said. "Thank you for coming."

"You're welcome," I said.

Her attention was already being drawn to the carriage house and the field behind it. "I'm just going to look around a little," Pearl said. "It's been a long time since I was out here."

I nodded and walked over to Roma.

"Thanks for coming out here," she said. "She wouldn't exactly take no for an answer." She stood with her arms tightly wrapped around her body and for a moment I wondered if I should just keep what I suspected to myself. "I think she just wanted to see where . . . he was, all these years."

I put a hand on her arm. "Why don't you go check on Lucy and the others? I'll walk around a bit with your mom. I don't mind."

She exhaled slowly. "I uh, thank you. I think I will."

"Take your time," I said.

Pearl was standing by the side steps to the old house. I walked over to her.

"It makes me sad," she said without turning around. "This house used to be full of life and now it's just . . . lonely." We stood there in silence for a minute. "Show me where he was," she said.

I hesitated.

"Please, Kathleen," she said, softly.

I nodded. "All right."

We made our way along the edge of the field. I could see that Dr. Abbott and her team had measured out a grid that covered most of the back end of the grassy area.

"There?" Pearl asked.

"Yes," I said, pointing at the slope. "I was standing at the edge of the trees. The earth gave way. It was just so wet." I remembered the feeling of the ground falling out from under me. I sucked in a breath and closed my eyes for a moment.

When I looked at Pearl again her eyes were fixed on some distant spot across the grass. I glanced back over my shoulder for any sign of Roma. Sam Ingstrom and a man I recognized from Everett Henderson's office were getting out of a town truck that had pulled up by the old house.

"Why don't we go find Roma?" I said to Pearl.

She had a look in her eyes that I couldn't decipher and all the color seemed to have drained out of her face.

"What is it?" I asked.

"All these years he was out here and I didn't know. I walked around in those woods and Tom was . . .underneath my feet."

My heart started to pound. "Let's go sit down," I said. I led Pearl over to the steps at the side of the old house. We both sat down. She folded her hands in her lap and I covered them with my own. "It's not your fault," I said.

She'd been staring past me, focused on nothing really, maybe the past, but she looked at me then. "He didn't deserve that." She gestured toward the embankment. "He wasn't a bad person."

"He wasn't a good person," a voice said. Sam's voice. He was standing just a few feet away. He shook his head emphatically. "He was a lousy husband and a lousy father, Pearl. Don't make Tom out to be some kind of saint just because he's dead."

Pearl got to her feet and I did as well.

Sam came and stood in front of us, ignoring me, focusing only on Pearl. "Whatever happened to him has nothing to do with you. You did the right thing for you and for Roma. If Tom had been a good man, you wouldn't have had to sneak away with the supper dishes on the table and just the clothes on your back. You wouldn't have had to depend on Anna's kindness."

"We know what Anna and the other women were doing," I said quietly.

Something flashed quickly across Sam's face. "Okay," he said. "That doesn't change anything."

Pearl kept her eyes fixed on Sam, one hand clenched into a tight fist at her side. "You told me it would be all right Sam, but you lied, didn't you?"

"No, I didn't," Sam said. His focus was completely on Pearl. "It was all right. You've had a good life."

"That night, he threatened to take Roma, trying to scare me," Pearl said. "He twisted her arm, she was crying and I . . . I told him I'd do whatever he wanted." Her voice gained strength. "I made his favorite meal—liver and onions—when it was ready he said it tasted like an old boot, and he went out looking for beer because Idris wouldn't sell any to him anymore."

Roma had come up behind Sam and she stood there, arms wrapped tightly around her body again, one hand pressed against her mouth.

"I grabbed Roma and I ran," Pearl continued. "I knew Anna would help us so that's where I went. You were there. You said it was over, Sam. But it isn't."

She seemed to be aware of only Sam, towering over her, his mouth pulled into a thin, tight line.

He swallowed and gave her a smile of sorts. "It's been

over for a long time, Pearl." He reached toward her and then abruptly pulled his hand back.

"Turquoise bucket seats," Roma said then, to no one in particular.

We all looked at her. She was shaking. I pulled off my sweater and put it around her shoulders. She looked at me. "The car had turquoise bucket seats. I was in the driver's seat turning the steering wheel, driving the car. I remember. Then my dad came and he sat me on his lap and I was still driving the car. He smelled like cinnamon gum."

Her hands were clenched into tight, knotted fists. She took a couple of steps closer to Sam. "It was you. You let me sit on your lap and drive. It wasn't Tom. It was you."

32

Sam acted like Roma hadn't even spoken. All of his attention was concentrated on Pearl.

"Just leave this all be, and trust me," he said. "You didn't kill Tom. You couldn't." His body language didn't give anything away but I could hear an edge of desperation in his voice.

"You helped Anna, didn't you, Sam?" I asked.

His gaze flicked in my direction.

"I don't know why," I went on. "Maybe your father hurt your mother. Maybe you stumbled onto what Anna and the other women were doing and it made you feel good to help. Really it doesn't matter why you were helping. You were doing it."

"So what if I was?" Sam said. He made a dismissive gesture like he was shooing away a fly. "Pearl didn't kill Tom."

"No, she didn't," I said.

Pearl was shaking her head. "I just wanted to get Roma away from him." She reached for her daughter, putting a protective arm around her shoulders. It made my chest hurt, thinking about a young Pearl, all those years ago, desperate to keep her child safe.

"I know," I said. I kept the emotion out of my voice as much as I could and I didn't take my eyes off of Sam, who met my gaze with no problem.

Roma was still staring at Sam. "I remember the car," she said. "It was parked over there, by the carriage house. I remember *you*."

Sam's eyes flicked over to her. "I know you do. It just wasn't that night," he said, gently.

"Tom talked with his fists, didn't he?" I said.

"That he did," Sam agreed. He stood with his arms loosely at his sides. He was a big man, strong. More than forty years ago he would have been more than a match for Tom Karlsson.

My throat was dry and I swallowed a couple of times. "I'm guessing you drove by that little house a lot."

"We had work in the area. I drove by a few times."

"But not that night."

Sam shrugged. "I don't know what you mean."

"That night, by some accident of timing—good or bad—you saw Tom come back. Idris Blackthorne wouldn't sell to him, but someone else in town did. And you could see Pearl walking up the side of the road. You knew what would happen when Tom found her."

"I was delivering a load of railroad ties at Wisteria Hill."

"No," I said. "You did that earlier. You were in your car, the one with the turquoise bucket seats, on your way to check on Pearl. You'd probably heard they were going to be evicted. Maybe you knew Tom was drinking. Or you guessed he would be. You knew there'd be trouble."

"I don't remember seeing the one-ton that night," Pearl said, slowly. "I remember that pile of railroad ties, but not the truck."

I kept looking at Sam thinking, *say the words*, but he didn't. And I knew I was going to have to.

Except Pearl beat me to it.

"You didn't have to kill him, Sammy," she said.

I looked at Roma and Pearl. Then I looked back at Sam. He gave his head a little shake.

"I couldn't figure out how you did it," I said, "because your foot was injured, and I didn't see how you could get around, but you didn't go see Tom after Pearl showed up out here, you were there *before* she got here.

"You saw Tom before you put that spike through your foot," I continued. "In fact, I think that's where you did it. Not here."

His jaw tightened, but that was the only visible reaction.

"I can't blame you, Sam. I don't know what I would have done in your place."

Pearl's face was still drained of color. Her back was straight and she held tight to Roma. She was strong enough to get through this. And so was Roma.

"I didn't tell anyone that I walked out and left supper on the table," Pearl said. "You were there at the house, after we were gone. That's the only way you could have known the dishes were still there."

Sam and I continued to lock eyes. "Has there ever been a time that you didn't love Pearl?" I asked gently.

Sam smiled then, giving me a glimpse of the young man who'd carried a torch for a pretty girl who thought of him only as a friend.

"No," he said. "There hasn't." He looked at Pearl. "He

didn't deserve you or Roma. I know, *I know* you were leaving him, but do you really think he would have ever let you go, let you be?"

He held out his hand to her and she took it, giving it a squeeze. "He'd banged your head so hard against the wall you probably had a concussion. And the marks of his fingers were on Roma's little arm."

He looked at me. "The nail through my foot did happen out here. I came the long way around. Got here just before they did. I wasn't looking where I was walking. I dumped the load earlier. That's what I was doing on the road that night, coming back here to stack it all up." He turned to Roma. "You were in my car that night, 'driving' it while Anna took a look at your mother's head."

I shifted from one foot to the other, wishing I'd wrapped my ankle this morning. "You told Ellen what happened, didn't you?" I said to Sam.

He didn't answer.

"She bandaged your foot and she helped you make it look like Tom had just walked away from Pearl and Roma. I'm guessing it was her idea."

Sam's mouth moved but he still didn't say anything. Pearl never took her eyes off of him.

"There's no way you could have driven Tom's car out to the highway. You couldn't have managed the clutch with your foot bandaged. Ellen drove and she helped you clean up and bury the body . . . here. I'm guessing sometime in the middle of the night. So you both knew where it was. So you could both make sure no one found it. The women couldn't have carried Tom. But you could. Ellen knew this whole area. You probably brought the body in through the woods some way. I know there was a road back there."

"Why, Sam?" Pearl asked. "Why did you kill Tom?"

He looked at her and all the years fell away. All I could see was a young man looking at his first love. Maybe his only love really.

He smiled. "So you'd be safe. I'm sorry you had to find out this way. I'm sorry you had to find out at all. But I can't be sorry Tom's dead."

33

"Call Marcus Gordon," Sam said to me without turning his head, but before I'd punched the number into my phone, Marcus had arrived anyway.

I walked across the yard to meet him. All I said was that Sam wanted to talk to him about what had happened the night Tom Karlsson disappeared. Sam should be able to tell the story his own way, I figured. I owed him at least that.

I stayed where I was, out of the way, as Marcus walked over to Sam and Pearl. Roma had moved a few steps away from them. Pearl stood with one hand on Sam's arm. They were talking. I had no idea about what.

Marcus stopped to say something to Roma. He looked back at me for a second. Roma turned as well and then she came across the grass to me.

"I can't believe Sam killed my father," she said.

I put my arm around her shoulders, the same way Pearl had. "I'm not making excuses for Sam," I said. "But he was young. He loved your mother." I tipped my head to look at her. "And you."

After Marcus had talked to Sam and Pearl for a couple of minutes, he moved away from them and pulled out his phone. Roma went back across the yard to her mother and they walked back to me, arm in arm.

"Wait here with Kathleen for just a minute," Roma said to Pearl. "I'll be right back."

I assumed she was going to speak to Marcus, but instead she returned to Sam, who was half turned, staring out at the field behind the carriage house. Roma touched his arm and he swung around to look at her.

"How did you figure it all out?" Pearl said to me.

"Roma told me about 'driving' with Tom," I said. "It was one of the few memories she had of him. She was so specific: turquoise bucket seats. I'd seen a picture of Tom's car. I was thinking about what Roma had said and I remembered that Tom's car didn't have bucket seats."

Pearl nodded. "No it didn't." She held her hands out, studying them as though she was looking for answers in the fine web of lines on her skin. "How could I not know, Kathleen?" she asked.

"You had no reason to think Tom was dead," I said, gently. "Let alone that Sam had killed him. And you most likely had some kind of a concussion that night that mixed up your memory a little."

She looked over at Sam and Roma, just as Roma put her arms around the older man and gave him an awkward hug. "I wonder how things would have been different if I'd returned Sam's feelings." Pearl said.

I reached for her hand and enfolded it in mine. "I don't know," I said. "My mother always says that doing one thing differently isn't like pulling a single thread on a sweater and having the whole thing unravel. Our lives are a little more complicated than that. And if you'd done things differently there would be no Roma." She was headed back to us, shoulders squared, head held high. "I like the world a whole lot better with Roma in it."

Pearl smiled at me. "So do I."

Roma and Pearl drove down to the police station and I followed them, mostly because it made me feel better. Roma hugged me in the parking lot and I told her I'd be at the library later if she needed me.

Hercules was waiting for me in the porch when I got home. I picked him up. "I feel bad about Sam," I said. "He shouldn't have killed Tom, or covered it up, but it makes me sad that he never got past his first love." The cat nuzzled my neck. Across the backyard I could see Everett's car in Rebecca's driveway. Susan was covering for me at the library so I had time to fit the last piece of the puzzle into place.

I went upstairs and found the journal I wanted. Owen was in the kitchen when I came down. "I'm going to Rebecca's," I said. "Want to walk me over?" He made a beeline for the back door. Hercules decided to stay inside the porch on the bench where he could look out the window. He didn't like a lot of "out" in his outdoors.

Owen led the way across the grass, making noise all the way. I said, "Uh huh," at intervals just in case he was talking to me, although it occurred to me that I could have been agreeing to a month's worth of catnip chickens or wild salmon for breakfast instead of cat food.

Owen headed for a spot in the sunshine in Rebecca's gazebo and I knocked on the back door. She smiled when she saw me. "Hello Kathleen," she said. "Everett and I were just having coffee. Do you have time to join us?"

"I do," I said. "If you don't mind."

"Of course not," she said. Then she noticed the diary I was carrying. "Did you find something you want to use?"

I looked at the hardbound journal. "There's something I wanted to ask you about."

"Come in, dear," she said. She glanced past me, caught sight of Owen on the gazebo railing and waved at him. He bobbed his head in return.

Everett was sitting at Rebecca's tiny kitchen table. His jacket was hanging on the back of the chair and his tie was loose. He got to his feet when I walked in.

"Hello, Kathleen," he said. His eyes flicked to the journal.

Behind me Rebecca was pouring me a cup of coffee and cutting a piece of her cinnamon coffee cake; coffee at Rebecca's never meant just coffee.

Once we were all seated at the table I turned to Everett. "I should tell you that Marcus Gordon will be in touch. In fact he may have already left a message with Lita. He knows what happened to Tom Karlsson, and how his body ended up out at Wisteria Hill."

Everett's eyes narrowed, but otherwise there was no change in his expression.

Rebecca's face grew serious and she shook her head.

"I'm sorry," I said. "It turns out it was Sam."

Rebecca looked at me, clearly surprised. "Sam? Sam Ingstrom?"

"Yes."

"You're certain?" Everett said.

I nodded.

I could see Everett relax, just slightly. "I'm glad it's over," he said. "For Roma and for Pearl."

I could hear my heart pounding in both my ears and for a moment I thought about just drinking my coffee and going home. Then I thought about how Wisteria Hill's secrets had hurt Roma.

Sam, Ellen, Anna, and who knows how many others had kept the secret of what happened to Tom to protect Roma and her mother. But it had hurt Roma when the truth was uncovered. The truth had a way of working itself to the surface, no matter how carefully it was buried, just like those bones had.

"What your mother was doing is going to come out," I said to Everett. I had to put my hands in my lap because suddenly they were shaking.

I was never going to play poker with Everett Henderson, I promised myself. He had no tells. "You know about the knitting circle," he said, picking up his coffee.

Rebecca looked from me to Everett. "What are you two talking about?"

He gestured at the diary, on the table between us. "I think Kathleen figured out that my mother was doing more than running the house and knitting blankets for the orphanage."

"She was helping women whose husbands were hurting them," I said.

Rebecca smiled again. "Oh that sounds like your mother," she said. "And it explains some things my own mother did." She looked at Everett. "She was involved, wasn't she? She had to have been."

"Yes," I said, before he could answer.

"There's something else, isn't there?" Rebecca asked, her smile fading.

I waited for Everett to speak. To say no. To say yes. To say anything. But he didn't. It seemed as though I was the one doing all the talking today.

I swallowed because there was suddenly a lump in my throat. "Rebecca, your mother helped Sam. She helped him bury Tom's body and clean up. And she drove Tom's car up to the highway. Sam had put a nail through his foot and he couldn't manage the clutch."

"I'll talk to the county attorney," Everett said immediately. "And Sam's lawyer. It doesn't have to come out."

Rebecca shifted to look at him, her head on one side. "I want it to come out," she said.

Everett's mouth tightened and she reached across the table for his hand. "I'm proud of my mother," she said. "Not that she broke the law, but for trying to help the people she cared about: Pearl, Roma, Sam." She turned to face me. "There were no women's shelters then. If your husband hit you, that was just part of life."

She patted Everett's hand. "I don't need to be protected from what my mother did—good or bad." She gestured at the journal. "I'm looking forward to reading what she wrote about it all." She turned her attention to me again. "She did write about it, didn't she?"

I didn't look at Everett, but I could feel his eyes on me. "There are some pages missing," I said.

"How did that happen?"

When I didn't answer right away, Rebecca repeated her question.

"I cut them out," Everett said.

She looked at him across the table. "Why?" There was nothing but curiosity in her voice.

He hesitated and I realized his reasons, even though I was pretty sure I knew what they were, were none of my business. I pushed my chair back from the table. "I'll let you talk," I said.

Rebecca touched my arm. "You don't have to go anywhere, Kathleen," she said. "I don't have any secrets. Not anymore."

Everett took a deep breath and let it out. "I found the journals after my mother died. I read them." He pulled a hand over his face. "I missed you," he added softly. "I'd heard rumors about my mother and I knew that she'd never said no to anyone in need, so it wasn't that hard to figure out what she'd been doing and that she'd gotten your mother involved." He stared down into his coffee, running one finger around the rim of the cup. "It took me a long time to read them all." He looked up at Rebecca. "Ellen loved you."

"You thought my mother killed Tom," Rebecca said.

He nodded. "She wrote about burying the body, but nothing about Sam being involved. I was going to burn the journals, but I couldn't bring myself to do it. They were my connection to you. I put them back in the attic. I thought if I left everything the way it was, you wouldn't ever have to know."

"Were you going to leave Wisteria Hill empty forever? So no one would find Tom's body?" she asked.

"If I had to," he said.

"You could have told me the truth."

Everett pushed his cup away and shook his head. "Tell you your mother killed someone? No. I wouldn't hurt you that way."

"No more secrets," Rebecca said. "Do you understand? A secret kept us apart for a long, long time. I'm not ever going to let that happen again."

She covered the hand on his coffee mug with hers and

she turned her head toward me. "No more secrets, Kathleen," she said. "Tell the whole story."

"All right," I said. "We'll go through the journals together. I'll call you later."

"Thank you," she said.

I nodded, touching her shoulder as I left.

I walked back across the yard to my house. Everett and Rebecca had looked at each other with so much love I couldn't help feeling just a tiny pinch of envy.

34

I called Maggie when I got home to let her know what had happened at Wisteria Hill.

"Roma's really okay?" she asked.

"She is," I said.

"So I was wrong about Sam?"

"Not completely," I said. "He was downplaying his feelings for Pearl, just not for the reasons you thought." I was sitting on the footstool and I stretched my legs out in front of me and scissored them up and down. My ankle felt pretty good this morning. "Did Abigail call you?" I asked.

"She did," Maggie said. "We're going to get together next week. Do you think Rebecca would talk to me about her mother?"

"I know she would," I said. "And that reminds me, could you take a look at Ellen's drawings? I want to display some of them but I'm not exactly sure how."

"Absolutely," she said.

Marcus had gotten his search warrant and the police had collected Maggie's boxes and the ones that belonged to Jaeger. "Do you still want to talk to Ray this morning?" I asked.

"I do," she said. "And you're not going to believe this. *ARTnews* is going to do a piece on his work. Do you know who Galen Lee is? Or I should say, was?"

"He was a pop artist, wasn't he? Like Roy Lichtenstein only with kind of neon bright colors."

"That's him. Turns out he mentioned Ray in a letter he wrote just before he died. It's generated some interest in Ray's work."

"That's good," I said.

She exhaled slowly. "It is—for Ray and maybe even for the co-op."

"Except you think they're going to ask questions about Jaeger."

"I guess I'd like to ask the questions first."

There were two furry faces peeking at me around the kitchen doorway. "Do you still want some company?" I asked.

"Please," she said. "Have you had breakfast?"

"Very early this morning, over at Fern's with Burtis Chapman—sausage, eggs, the works. But I wouldn't say no to another cup of coffee."

"You never say no to a cup of coffee," Maggie said, dryly. "And I do want to hear why you had breakfast with Burtis."

"Half an hour?"

"Yes. Ray should be here by then."

"You're at River Arts?" The cats were still staring at me.

"I'm here."

"I'll see you soon," I said and hung up.

The cats crossed the room and sat in front of me. "I'm not making you two any snacks," I said.

They exchanged glances and resumed staring at me. I got up and went into the kitchen and got a glass of water. Owen and Hercules were right on my heels.

"I'm serious," I said, looking down at them. "Both of you eat way too much peanut butter. Roma said I should just be feeding you cat food and the occasional sardine."

Owen's face twisted into a cranky pout. Despite his gift of Fred the Funky Chicken parts, Roma was still not his favorite person.

I bent down to pet him. He sniffed my hand, reared back in a kind of kitty double take and then sniffed me again. Hercules watched, puzzled. Owen looked at me, golden eyes narrowed.

There was no way he could smell sausage on my fingers. I'd washed my hands at least twice since I came back from Fern's, and brushed my teeth. Clearly, he'd been eavesdropping while I talked to Maggie.

He gave a snippy meow. Hercules leaned in for a sniff and his gaze narrowed as well.

I pulled back my hand. "Stop sniffing me," I said.

They couldn't fold their paws across their chests, but everything else about their body language said pissed-off cat. I could feel their eyes on me as I moved around the kitchen. I knew who was going to win this one.

I got a can of sardines from the cupboard and put half of one in each of their dishes. "I'm admitting nothing," I said.

They exchanged quick glances—and started eating. I went upstairs to wash my hands. Again.

In the bedroom I put the lid back on the box of Rebecca's mother's things and set it up on the dresser just in case Hercules decided he wanted to "read" the journals again. The pen cap that he'd found was on the table and I picked it up, turning it over in my fingers once again. Did it mean anything, I wondered? It was old and as far as I could tell it was the cap from a fountain pen. It looked as though it belonged to the pen that had been in Jaeger's puzzle box. I stared at it and ideas began to link together in my head.

It had to have something to do with Ray. He collected and sold vintage ink bottles. I'd seen them in his studio. Maybe he had some old pens, too. Maybe the cap—and the pen that had been in the puzzle box—belonged to Ray.

I was certain he'd lied about being at the Summerhill auction with Jaeger, but the pen didn't prove anything.

Or did it?

What had Maggie said to Marcus about Jaeger? He knew how to forge all the provenance. Jaeger knew how to forge documents, like a letter from a respected and dead artist.

I looked around for the piece of paper Owen had found. All that was on it was the same signature written over and over, five times on the small scrap. The handwriting was tight but shaky, like someone very old had written it. It was part of whatever Jaeger Merrill had been up to. I just wasn't sure how it fit. I slipped the bit of paper in my pocket for now. It was time to meet Maggie and get some answers.

I made sure the litter box was clean and the cats had water. "I'll see you later," I told them and headed out.

Maggie was sitting on the front steps of the arts center in the sunshine. "Isn't this beautiful?" she said, holding out her hands and looking skyward.

"How are things at the store?" I asked, walking across the sidewalk to her.

"Dry," she said with a grin. "I might—might—be able to do a makeup tai chi class tomorrow."

"It doesn't seem right to be doing cloud hands when the sun's out," I said.

"Nice try," she said, getting to her feet. "I expect you to be there. I know you haven't been practicing the whole form, but you have been working on your cloud hands, haven't you? And snake creeps down?"

"Sort of," I said, following her inside.

"Sort of yes, or sort of no?" she asked as we started up to Ray's studio.

"Define 'working on.'"

"Okay, so no," she said.

"Let's change the subject," I said. "I think I've figured out what Jaeger was doing."

"Seriously?"

"Seriously."

She stopped and leaned against the railing. "Since we're on our way to Ray's studio he must be involved in some way."

"He is," I said. "I think."

"Tell me," Maggie said.

So I did.

"You don't think that Ray could have . . . pushed Jaeger down the stairs, do you?" she asked after I'd finished explaining.

I shook my head. "No. I don't."

"Okay," she said. "What do we do?"

I started up the steps again. "Go talk to Ray and find out for sure."

The door to his studio at the end of the hall was open. Ray, in jeans and a denim shirt, was studying several large drawings he'd leaned against the wall. Maggie knocked on the door frame. "Hi," she said. "I heard about the interview. Congratulations."

"Thanks." He smiled and walked over to us.

I pulled the pen cap out of my pocket and held it out. "Does this belong to you?" I asked.

"It does," he said. "Thank you. I thought I'd lost it at the store."

"You're welcome," I said. "The rest of the pen is in a box that was Jaeger's. The police have it."

Ray frowned, not missing a beat. "I don't know what you mean. Why would Jaeger have one of my pens?" He was doing a better job of lying this time. He remembered to meet my gaze and he didn't twitch or fidget.

I handed him the cap. "You loaned it to him, along with some ink. Did you get the paper he needed at the estate sale?"

"Paper? For what?" He crossed his arms over his body and continued to look me directly in the eye.

"For the letter that Jaeger forged for you. The one that Galen Lee is supposed to have written in which he said he liked your work."

He swallowed and looked away.

"Ray, what were you thinking?" Maggie asked.

His head swung around. "I was thinking that I'm sick of working my ass off just to see some kid, whose idea of art is spray painting squiggles on the side of buildings, become the new darling of the art world, while artists—real artists—continue to be ignored."

"So what?" she retorted. "You fake a letter from a dead artist to get noticed?"

"My work will stand on its own merits. All I'm doing is getting someone to pay attention for a minute," he snapped.

"By lying," I said.

He looked at me then. "It's one letter and Galen Lee is dead. Who's it going to hurt?"

"All of us," Maggie said. Her face was flushed with color and one arm was up over her head, almost as if she was trying to hold herself back. "You've damaged the reputation of this center, and the co-op and all the artists who work here. You said your work will stand on its own merits. You should have let it do that."

Ray's mouth moved but no sound came out. His face was flushed as well.

"You figured out who Jaeger was," I said.

He cleared his throat and made an effort to focus on me again. "Purely by accident. I was in Chicago. One of the local stations did a piece on the forgeries. It was the anniversary of the arrests. I recognized him. I have a good eye for details."

"And he offered you a trade, your silence for a letter that could make your career."

Ray nodded.

I glanced at Maggie standing stiffly beside me. "You had the pens and the ink. You went to the estate sale to find the right paper. Galen Lee was a bit of a tightwad. He never threw anything out. He wouldn't write a letter on new paper."

"No," Ray said, shaking his head. "I mean yes, you're right about Galen Lee, but Jaeger already had the paper for the letter he wrote for me. He was looking for paper for something else."

"What?" I asked.

"I don't know."

"Did you know he was going to fake a Sundblom Santa Claus?" Maggie asked.

"Yes. I'd told him the rumors about Carson Henderson being the model for the Coke Santa. I think he went out to Wisteria Hill to look around a couple of times."

"He did," I said.

"But he gave up the idea. He had something else going. I don't know what it was. All I can tell you is that he wanted to use a couple of other pens and some black ink. I swear I don't know what for."

Ray turned to Maggie. "Maggie, I'm sorry," he said.

She took a deep breath and exhaled slowly. "So am I, Ray," she said.

I left Maggie to deal with the fallout of what Jaeger and Ray had done. Ruby was in her studio and after we'd brought her up to date they started calling the other artists to arrange a meeting to decide how they'd handle things.

I got to the library just before eleven. It seemed as though everyone had run out of things to read or watch or listen to. I was happy to know the library usage numbers were staying up. It made all the work and turmoil of getting the building renovated worth it.

Roma came in with lunch for both of us a few minutes before one, just when I realized that I was hungry and had forgotten to pack anything to eat.

"Claire said you hadn't been in, so I took a chance and brought something," she said, holding up the take-out bag.

I smiled at her across the checkout desk. "Thank you." Right on cue my stomach made a loud rumble. "My stomach thanks you too."

I got a cup of coffee for each of us from the staff room and we settled in my office.

"How are you?" I asked after I'd taken a big bite of my turkey and tomato sandwich.

"Stunned, mostly," she said. "Marcus talked to my mother, mostly to confirm what Sam told him. I went over what I remembered about being in the car with Sam and about my father getting me to hide under a blanket." She picked up half her sandwich and put it back down again. "I don't know what's going to happen to Sam."

"He thought he was protecting you and your mother," I said. "That should count for something."

Roma stared at her shoes. "I thanked him," she said in a low voice. "I thanked him for loving my mother and caring about me."

She took a deep breath and slowly breathed out. Then she looked up at me. "I'm going to have Tom's remains buried with the rest of his family." She put a hand flat on her chest. "In my heart and my mind Neil is my father, but Tom gave me life and I want him to have a proper burial."

"Let me know when the service is," I said. "I'll be there, if you'd like some company."

She had to clear her throat before she answered. "Thanks," she said.

We ate in silence for a few minutes. "How's your mother doing?" I asked when most of my sandwich was gone.

"Surprisingly well," Roma said. "I think she feels guilty about Sam."

I nodded.

"And me."

"You're not angry," I said, shifting in my seat and tucking one foot underneath me.

"I'm not." She reached for her coffee. "My mother's stories about Tom always made him out to be a little bit too good to be true. I guess somewhere inside I never totally believed them. The truth didn't hurt as much as you'd think it would." She took a long drink from her cup. "I owe you a thank you."

"What for?" I said

"For finding Tom's remains."

"That was an accident." I picked up my own coffee. "I wouldn't have even been standing there if I hadn't seen something and gone to pick it up. The embankment might not have collapsed without my extra weight."

"So what did you see?"

I held up my fingers, about an inch apart. "A little, purple buffer."

"You mean for a manicure?" Roma asked, glancing down at her short, unpolished nails.

"No. I mean for working on a mask."

Her eyes widened. "Jaeger."

"Yeah," I nodded, slowly. "Maggie was right. He did have some scam going. Maybe more than one. It looks as though Ray Nightingale was involved, too."

Roma shook her head. "I'm guessing Maggie is on damage control."

"She is," I said. "It's going to be a messy few days for the co-op."

"That reminds me. I have a vet to cover for me for a few days starting tomorrow—I'm going to see Eddie on the road. Could you take a couple of my shifts at Wisteria Hill?"

I smiled. "Absolutely."

We talked about the cats as we finished eating, then Roma looked at her watch. "I need to get to the clinic. Someone brought in a stray with chemical burns to her feet. We're having a heck of a time keeping the bandages on and clean."

"Boots," I said.

She shook her head. "No. She doesn't look like a Boots. She's all white. I've been calling her Snowy."

"I don't mean Boots for a name," I said. "I mean she needs boots, to wear over the bandages."

She thought about it for a moment. "Interesting idea, but where am I going to find a pair of cat boots?"

I smiled at her. "It just so happens Hercules has a pair and I'm pretty sure he'd be willing to donate them to a cat in need."

Roma smiled at me. "I'm not even going to ask you what Hercules is doing with boots. I'm just going to say yes."

"I'll drop them off at the clinic," I said. "Thank you for lunch."

She hugged me. "Thank you for, well, everything."

After Roma left I went out to give Susan a break at the front desk, pulling on my sweater because the building still seemed a bit chilly after having been closed up for several cool, damp days. I was stacking books on one of the carts to be reshelved and when I bent to put a couple of magazines on the bottom something crackled in my pocket. I straightened and put my hand inside, pulling out the piece of paper Owen had found at the studio.

I squinted at the cramped, spidery writing. The name looked like Gerald Sherriff. Ray had said that Jaeger had given up on faking the Coca-Cola Santa for something else. Maybe Gerald Sherriff was connected somehow. Marcus would say, "Leave it alone," but I couldn't. I knew Maggie wouldn't relax until she knew for sure what Jaeger had been up to.

I turned to the computer and typed the name in a

search engine. Nothing. I couldn't find a Gerald Sherriff connected with the art world or any kind of scam.

I frowned at the scrap of paper. Maybe it was meaningless. Maybe Owen had picked it up because it smelled like tuna to him, not because it was some clue that would solve the Jaeger Merrill/Christian Ellis mystery. He was just a cat after all. Okay, a cat with some pretty good sleuthing skills that I was probably never going to be able to explain, but in the end just ten pounds of furry feline with fish breath and lots of attitude.

Mary came over with an empty book cart. She glanced at the corner of paper on the desk. "Who's Carroll Stennett?" she asked. "The name's familiar."

"That doesn't say Carroll Stennett," I said. "It says Gerald Sherriff."

Mary shook her head at me. "I may need glasses, but I can see. Whoever that is writes like my mother did. I think it's some style of penmanship they used to teach in school. Look." She pointed to the first letter in the name. "That's a C not a G, and that's an L at the end, not a D."

I held the piece of paper up to the light. The shakiness of the writing made it hard to distinguish the letters, but now that she'd pointed it out, I could see she was right about the C and the L.

"Mary, you're a genius," I said.

She patted her gray curls. "I know. It's a curse sometimes." She exchanged the empty cart for a full one and went back to the stacks.

I typed Carroll Stennett into the search engine box. It took a while to find the connection and I probably would have missed it altogether if the source of the story hadn't been the *Mayville Heights Chronicle*. I leaned back in the chair and reread the article on my screen.

Carroll Stennett had lived and died—about a year and a half ago—in the house he'd been born in, the old family homestead out near Wild Rose Bluff. He had no close family other than a great-nephew by marriage. An eccentric, reclusive old man, most people figured he barely had two cents to rub together. Of course they were wrong. He owned all the land around his run-down farm—several hundred acres—and had a stash of government bonds in a safe deposit box. The bonds had been left to a church-run summer camp for underprivileged kids. The land had been left to the great-nephew.

Peter Lundgren.

Peter, who had kept Jaeger Merrill's secret about who he really was.

Peter, who had jumped in to help Maggie after Jaeger's death.

Both Maggie and Ruby had said the reason Jaeger had been successful as a forger for so long was his ability to forge the provenance for his artwork—the documents that provided their authenticity.

He'd forged a letter for Ray. Was it possible that Jaeger had created a document for Peter too?

I looked at my left hand. I'd needed only a small bandage this morning on the place where I'd torn the skin on the basement railing at the co-op. I thought about the bandage I'd seen on Peter's hand. He said he'd fallen in his office's parking lot.

That's what he said.

Was I wrong? I wanted to be. Peter had been advising Ruby about the money she was inheriting from Agatha Shepherd. He'd even uncovered a piece of evidence in the case against Agatha's killer. And he was helping three of his younger siblings get an education. Then I thought of what Roma had said about her mother's stories about Tom: *They always made him out to be a little bit too good to be true.*

Like Peter.

I pulled a hand back through my hair. I remembered Jaeger's body, mostly submerged in the cold, filthy water in the co-op basement. What if . . . what if that hadn't been an accident? What if . . . someone . . . had pushed him down those stairs or held him under the water. Whatever Jaeger had done, he didn't deserve that.

I'd told Maggie I didn't believe Ray had pushed Jaeger, but could Peter have done it? The problem was, I didn't have any real proof tying Peter to anything illegal, just a piece of paper my cat had found in the hall outside Maggie's studio. Even Erle Stanley Gardner and Perry Mason couldn't make a case with that.

I could call Marcus and tell him what I suspected. Would he take me seriously with no evidence?

Or I could call Peter and try to find out a little more about his relationship with the dead artist. What would be the harm in that?

I looked at the phone. I looked at the piece of paper on the desk in front of me. For a moment I thought about deciding the way we used to resolve things when I was eight: one potato, two potato, three potato, four.

I exhaled slowly and then I reached for the phone.

35

Peter showed up at the library at exactly quarter after eight. Right on time. I unlocked the front door and let him in, locking it behind him again because I didn't want anyone wandering in and interrupting us.

My heart was pounding and my palms were sweaty. I wasn't so sure this was a good idea anymore. I could hear my mother's voice in my head telling me to act confident even if I didn't feel it, although she probably would have rescinded the advice if she'd known how I was using it.

Peter faced me, hands in his pockets, his back to the checkout desk. "Okay, Kathleen," he said. "You said on the phone that you have proof that Christian—Jaeger's death wasn't an accident."

I nodded.

"And you said you didn't want to go to the police."

"I don't," I said.

He shifted restlessly from one foot to the other. "Are we going to keep playing games or are you going to tell me why you called me? I assume you want legal advice."

I tucked my hair back behind one ear with a gesture that I hope looked smooth and unconcerned. "Actually what I want is two hundred and fifty thousand dollars," I said.

His mouth twisted in something that looked like a smile but wasn't. "Excuse me?"

"Two hundred and fifty thousand dollars," I repeated and my voice didn't quaver at all.

He shook his head and pulled his keys out of his pocket. "I don't know what kind of game you're playing Kathleen, but I don't have time for this."

I held up a crumpled corner of paper. "You probably can't read this because the writing is so small and it's not really that easy to read even if you're up close to it, so I'll just tell you that it says Carroll Stennett."

I made a show of looking at the writing and then I turned the paper so it faced him again. "Actually it says Carroll Stennett, Carroll Stennett, Carroll Stennett, Carroll Stennett and Carroll Stennett to be exact."

He was unfazed. Nothing changed in his demeanor or expression or even his voice. "So?" he said.

"So Carroll Stennett was your great-uncle. He left you a lot of land in his will." I crossed my free arm over my chest.

"Yes, he did."

I smiled, hoping it didn't look as fake as it felt. "A handwritten will that Jaeger Merrill—or Christian Ellis if you prefer—forged."

Peter smiled back at me. It wasn't warm and it wasn't real. "Really? Was this will an oil painting or did he make it out of old gears and broken spoons?"

"Funny," I said. I let the hand holding the scrap of paper drop. "Jaeger created the provenance—all the various documents—that proved the authenticity of the artwork he forged. You knew that. You were his lawyer. Creating a handwritten will was a challenge, but one he was up to, especially since you could provide him with writing samples."

He looked around the empty library and then focused his attention back on me. "And you figured all this out from a scrap of paper with my uncle's name on it?"

I checked the bit of paper again and then put it in my pocket. "Pretty much. That and the fact that Jaeger put his portfolio and the puzzle box he made in with some of Maggie's things. You must have been furious when Maggie called Marcus Gordon instead of you when she found them. They were his insurance policy."

Peter crossed his arms casually over his chest. "An insurance policy? Because . . . ?"

I felt like I'd swallowed the metal kettle ball Maggie liked to work out with. "Because Jaeger was blackmailing you. He didn't trust you. He knew it didn't matter what their differences were, if something happened to him, Maggie would take those things to the police."

"If that were true, wouldn't the police have come to talk to me by now?" he asked. He seemed so at ease standing there and I couldn't help noticing how much bigger he was than me.

"They're missing the most important piece," I said, reaching into my other pocket and pulling out the cap to a fountain pen. "This is part of the pen Jaeger used to make that will for you. The other part was in the puzzle box. The police will be able to compare it and the ink inside to the handwriting of the will. Once they know they should look at the will."

Peter's jaw tightened. "What do you want?"

"I told you," I said. "Two hundred and fifty thousand dollars."

"I don't have two hundred and fifty thousand dollars."

I put my hand back in my pocket. "You can get it."

"I could," he said.

Something had changed in his voice and his body language. He took a step toward me and I automatically took a step backward, glancing over my shoulder as I did.

"Detective Gordon's not coming," he said.

My mouth went dry. "I uh, I don't know what you're talking about," I stammered.

"Now that's a lie," Peter said, shaking his head. "You tried to set me up, Kathleen. You thought I was stupid enough to fall for this little Miss Marple subterfuge."

"Where's Marcus?" I said. My voice shook and so did my hands still jammed in my pockets.

Peter looked at his watch. "Larry Taylor's pretty good with his hands. He got that old pump working over at the co-op. The thing about that gas powered motor is it needs lots of ventilation."

Both my hands were squeezed into tight fists. I needed to stay focused and keep him talking. "You did something to that . . . that pump. Is Marcus there? Is Maggie?"

"Maggie is in her studio. I just talked to her. As for Detective Gordon, I'll stipulate that we're not going to see him." He took another step toward me.

I knew if I tried to bolt for the door he'd grab me. "Why did you kill Jaeger?" I asked. "Was he blackmailing you?"

Peter held out both hands. "Classic mystery moment," he said. "The detective gathers all the usual suspects in the library and then unmasks the killer. I'll give you points for the setting, but the detective isn't coming. And I'm not answering any of your questions."

He came at me then, but I was ready for him. I'd been watching his feet out of the corner of my eye. I darted left.

"You're wasting your time, Kathleen," he said. "You're wasting mine."

The computer area was more or less behind me and the stacks were to the right. Peter probably figured he had me trapped but this was my library. I knew what I was doing and I was mad.

"You ran me off the road the other night," I said.

"Did I?" he said. One eyebrow went up. He took a step toward me.

I took a step back. "Stop playing lawyer," I said. "You killed Jaeger. You pushed him down the stairs, he hit his head and you left him there to drown. What did you do? Swipe Ruby's keys to the store?"

He gave a snort of laughter. "Speculation."

"Fact. You didn't hurt your hand in the parking lot at your office. You did that on the railing of the basement steps at the co-op." I held up my hand. "Same as I did. Same as Jaeger did when he grabbed for the railing to save himself. Except my cut got cleaned out twice. I bet there's little bits of wood still in yours. Evidence."

"Shut up," he said.

I took a step sideways and back. "Jaeger was black-mailing you. I think you found out he was forging more than just that will for you. You knew he'd get caught again and you weren't going down with him." I laughed. "You showed up. He put the evidence against you in one of Maggie's boxes. Pretty smart."

"Christian was an idiot," Peter said. "A spoiled little

pissant who'd never done a decent day's work in his life. He couldn't swim, you know. And for the record, I didn't push him. I just didn't pull him out."

He lunged at me, and this time I wasn't fast enough. He grabbed me, turning me around with his arm tight against my neck, slowly cutting off my air supply. I struggled to catch my breath.

Marcus came out from behind the new shelving unit. "Let her go," he ordered.

Little pinpricks of light were swirling around the edge of my vision but I knew I had to take advantage of Peter's surprise. I drove the heel of my right hand up and back with as much force as I could. It made very satisfying contact with Peter's nose. He sucked in a wet breath and I twisted free from his grasp. Marcus grabbed my arm and pulled me back against him as Derek Craig came around the other side of the shelves.

I smiled up at Marcus and felt for the tiny, wireless transmitter under the V-neck of my sweater. "What took you so long?" I wheezed.

36

Marcus drove me over to Eric's Place where Maggie was waiting. "Is your throat all right?" he asked.

I pulled down the visor and looked in the little mirror on the backside. There was a wide red mark on my neck, even though Peter had had hold of me for only a few seconds.

My throat felt a little raw, as if I'd been talking too much. "I'm okay," I said. "It's nothing that a cup of Eric's coffee won't fix."

"I can't believe I agreed to that," Marcus said as we pulled up to the café.

"Neither can I," I said, unfastening my seat belt.

"I'm glad you're not hurt."

"Do you think I broke Peter's nose?" I asked. It had been bleeding heavily onto an old but clean towel I'd found in the staff room.

"Don't worry about it. I don't think you did." He gave me a knowing look. "Unless, you wanted to."

"No comment."

He laughed. "You're a pretty good actor."

"I liked working with you," I said, smiling up at him.

"So did I," he said.

We stood there on the sidewalk, having a little moment. I don't know how long it would have lasted except I started to cough. My throat was dry, probably more from fear and all the talking I'd been doing than from anything Peter had done to me.

"You need to sit down and have something hot to drink," Marcus said.

He led the way inside. Maggie was at the counter talking to Eric. She came right over to us.

"You all right?" she asked.

I nodded.

"Go sit down," Marcus said. "I'll get you some coffee."

Maggie led the way to a table by the end wall where her tea was waiting. "What happened to your neck?" she asked, squinting at me across the table.

I touched my throat. "Peter grabbed me," I said. "I bloodied his nose."

"Is it broken?" she asked.

I shook my head. "Marcus doesn't think so. Am I a bad person because part of me hopes it is?"

"After what he did and what he tried to do? No."

Marcus came over to the table then with a mug for me, and a take-out cup for himself. "I have to get to the station. I'll call you later."

"All right," I said, taking the cup from him and wrapping my hands around it. "Is it all right to go back to the library?"

He shook his head. "No. Not tonight. Have your coffee. Go home." He looked at Maggie. "Keep her out of trouble," he said.

She rolled her eyes. "Of course," she said. "That always goes so well."

He laid a hand on my shoulder. "I'm glad you're okay."

"I'm glad you're okay too," I said. I watched him walk out and cross the sidewalk to his SUV.

When I looked at Maggie her head was tipped to one side and she had an aw-shucks grin on her face. "You two are just so cute," she said.

I set my cup on the table and reached for the sugar. "I'm ignoring you," I said.

She laughed and leaned back in her chair. Then her face turned serious. "I can't believe Peter killed Jaeger."

"I'm not defending him. But I think he acted in the heat of the moment."

"Peter never struck me as someone who did anything in the heat of the moment," Maggie said.

"Getting Jaeger to forge that will was stupid," I said, adding cream and stirring my coffee.

"So why did he do it?"

"I don't know. Maybe he got tired of being the good guy and getting nothing for it, kind of like Ray." I leaned my forearms on the table. "Peter took care of that great-uncle for years, but the only other will Marcus could track down left everything to some distant cousin's kids. Peter was only related by marriage and for some people 'blood' is everything."

"So you don't think he planned to kill Jaeger?" Maggie lifted the lid of her little teapot and then looked around for Claire who nodded and held up one finger.

"No. But it's clear Jaeger didn't trust him. I think that's why he put his things in your box."

"Just in case."

Claire came over with the hot water and refilled Maggie's tea. "Could I get you anything else?" she asked. "Eric has a great beef stew."

"Yes!" Maggie and I answered at the same time.

Claire smiled. "Just give me a couple of minutes."

Maggie poked the tea bag with her spoon and then poured another cup. "So you figured you asking Peter to meet you at the library was going to raise his suspicions?"

I took a sip of my coffee and nodded. "I did. Plus Marcus didn't think my getting forced off the road was an accident. If Peter was Jaeger's killer, then it made sense he might be trying to scare me, considering I was asking questions about Jaeger and what he'd been doing."

I took another drink. "Marcus made sure I was fitted with the wireless transmitter well in advance. Then he played along when Peter asked to meet him at the co-op before Peter was supposed to meet me at the library." I ran my fingers over the side of my neck. "I don't know if Peter underestimated Marcus, or if he'd gotten arrogant and careless because he'd already gotten away with so much. Anyway, Derek Craig hid in the storage closet. Peter did something to the pump. Then he locked Marcus in the basement. As soon as he left, Derek let Marcus out."

"I told you Peter was a mechanic before he went to law school." Maggie leaned forward. "Your neck looks better."

"He probably had me for less than a minute. As soon as he grabbed me, Marcus stepped out and it was over."

"How did you get Marcus to agree to this whole thing?"

I set my mug on the table. "I don't exactly know."

Maggie looked at me and a huge smile spread over her face. "He likes you," she said in a singsong voice.

I made a face at her, stuck a finger in each ear, and started to hum softly. That didn't stop Mags. She just leaned in a little closer and repeated the words.

I pretended I couldn't hear her, but I could, and it didn't really sound so awful.

EPILOGUE

The sun was warm, the sky was an endless, deep blue overhead and the faintest breeze blew through the open windows of the library on the afternoon of the building's one-hundredth birthday celebration. Everett and I cut the ceremonial red ribbon at the front door as most of the town gathered below. Then everyone streamed into the building.

Two of Oren's father's sculptures commanded the computer area. Oren stood by the windows overlooking the garden—with the new gazebo he'd finished the week earlier—his face glowing with pride. I walked over to join him.

"My father would have loved this, Kathleen," he said. "Thank you."

I smiled back at him. "Thank you for letting me bring these pieces down here." I looked up at the beautiful metal eagle that seemed to be poised in midflight in the room. "I'm glad he's getting the recognition he deserves."

Harry Junior had found a way to suspend Maggie's

collage panels from the ceiling and they followed the curve of the windows. Rebecca and Mary were standing by the panel that told the story of The Ladies Knitting Circle, smiling and answering questions. Rebecca had insisted the women's story be told when Everett had wavered and she'd worked closely with Abigail and Maggie. When the centennial celebrations were over, the panels would be moved over to the reading area where they were staying on permanent display.

Rebecca caught sight of me, smiled and waved. The light caught the sparkling diamond on her left hand. Everett had proposed a couple of days ago and they were both as giddy as a couple of teenagers.

Roma tapped me on the shoulder. "Hi," she said. She looked around. "This is wonderful. I don't know where to look first."

"Where's Eddie?" I asked.

"In the parking lot discussing the best way to plank a salmon with Eric."

"Oh, don't tell me he cooks too?" I said.

She nodded and grinned.

Roma had had a very simple graveside service for her father. Putting his remains to rest seemed to have put the past to rest for her as well. Today she had the cat that swallowed the funky chicken air about her.

"What's up with you?" I asked.

"Later," she said. "This is your day."

"This is the library's day," I said, pulling her aside. "What is it?"

"I bought Wisteria Hill." The words came out in a rush.

I stared at her and I think my mouth fell open. "What?"

"I bought Wisteria Hill." She said it a little more slowly this time.

"That's . . . that's wonderful!" I didn't know what else to say so I hugged her.

I studied her face for a moment when I let go and I could see how happy she was. "How did this happen?" I asked.

"I've been thinking about it for weeks. I love the place. And Everett doesn't want to live out there. So I asked him." She grinned. "He said yes." She twisted the heavy silver ring she wore around her finger. "The place needs work, but it's livable for now and what Eddie can't fix I'll get Oren to do."

I shook my head. "He fixes things too? That boy is practically perfect."

She nodded. "Yes he is." She looked around. "Have you seen Maggie?"

"She's around somewhere with a cute, stubbled bartender who is in reality only a part-time bartender and a full time PhD candidate in psychology."

"Which she found where?"

"Remember me telling you about Maggie and me doing a little bar crawl last winter when we were trying to figure out what happened to Agatha Shepherd?"

She nodded.

"He was the bartender at Barry's Hat. He took one look at Maggie and pretty much forgot how to tie his shoes. I guess I'm the only one still uncoupled now."

Roma was already starting to grin. I shook a finger at her. "Don't you start! Maggie is bad enough. I don't need another matchmaker."

She held up her hands as though she were surrendering. "Okay, but there's someone tall, dark and handsome watching you from across the room."

I could see Marcus out of the corner of my eye. "Go away," I said. "I'm quite happy with Owen and Hercules."

She laughed and went off to look for Maggie.

I walked around for a while myself, answering a few questions and hearing a lot of congratulations. I was proud of the library. The building was beautiful and usage was up and staying there. I saw Everett coming from the reading area where Abigail and Susan had set up a display of banned books. I walked over to him.

"Kathleen, this is a wonderful celebration," he said. Like Roma, he seemed to be at peace now with the past.

"Thank you," I said. "It wouldn't be happening without you."

"Or you," he said.

Susan was trying to get my attention, standing by one of the magazine carrels, holding a twin by each hand. "Excuse me," I said to Everett. "I think Susan needs me."

He touched my arm. "Come see me tomorrow. We should talk about the future."

"I will," I promised.

"Can you keep an eye on things here?" Susan asked, as I walked up to her. She blew a loose strand of hair out of her face. It looked like she had a piece of bamboo in her topknot. "I need to take these two monkeys out to my mother."

"Hi Kathleen," the boys said in unison. They were the pictures of blue-eyed innocence.

"Hi guys," I said, crossing my eyes, which always sent them into a fit of giggles. I made a shooing gesture at Susan. "Go," I said.

She was back in a couple of minutes. "The boys are barbecuing," she said.

"Is that bamboo in your hair?" I asked.

She nodded. "Yeah. It's good luck." She headed across the room to join Abigail.

I wandered back out into the main part of the library in time to see Harrison Taylor, aka Old Harry, come through the library entrance with his sons . . . and his daughter. I blinked away the prickle of tears. Harry's daughter, the result of a relationship he'd had while his wife was dying, had been placed for adoption at birth. I'd been lucky enough to have found some papers that had helped the old man find her. It had been worth almost getting blown up.

I walked over to them. Harry smiled when he caught sight of me. I took the hand he held out and leaned in to kiss his cheek. "I'm so glad you're here," I told him.

"Wouldn't miss it for the world," he said. He turned to the young woman beside him. "Kathleen, this is my daughter, Elizabeth."

"Elizabeth, I'm so happy to finally meet you," I said. She had her father's smile.

"I'm happy to meet you too," she said. "Harrison told me that without your help we might never have found each other. Thank you." She looked up at him and I could see affection in her gaze.

I had to swallow away a lump in my throat before I could speak. "I did very little," I said. "But you're welcome."

Harry Senior looked around. "Where did you put Karl Kenyon's sculptures? I'd like to show them to Elizabeth."

"Over in the computer room," I said.

"Go ahead," Harry Junior said. "I'll be right there."

Larry Taylor leaned sideways as he passed me. "It looks great, Kathleen," he whispered.

"Thanks for helping with the extra lights," I said.

"Anytime," he said with a smile.

His big brother stood beside me and we watched the three of them make their way across the floor. "How's it going?" I asked.

"Better than I hoped," Harry said.

"What's she like?"

"Stubborn, opinionated, like Boris with a bone when she thinks she's right."

"In other words she fits right in," I said.

He laughed. "Yes, she does."

I patted his shoulder and walked outside. There was a tent set up in the parking lot and Eric was working at a large grill. Eddie was beside him with one of the twins on his shoulders. I couldn't see the other, which I hoped wasn't a bad thing.

I made my way around the side of the building to the new gazebo in the reading garden. It was a little larger than the one in Rebecca's backyard; Oren had built it using Harrison Taylor's original design. Like everything both men were involved with, it was beautiful.

"Oren does nice work."

I turned to smile at Marcus standing behind me. "Yes, he does. Have you seen his father's sculptures?"

"I'd swear that eagle had feathers."

I nodded. "I had the same reaction the first time I saw it."

Marcus looked back at the building. "You've probably been wondering why I don't have a library card."

"It's not really any of my business," I said, but I could feel my cheeks getting pink.

His eyebrows went up.

"All right, yes, I'm curious," I admitted. "Why don't you have a library card?"

We walked across the grass to the retaining wall overlooking the water. "I couldn't read until I was almost ten," he said.

"Dyslexia?" I asked.

"Yes." He looked out across the lake. "For a long time the library was just about my least favorite place in the world. School was right up there too."

I thought about all the times I'd complained to Maggie about Marcus not having a library card and I was ashamed of my narrow-minded attitude. "I can see why," I said quietly.

"I started building my own library, that way no one would know how long it took me to read a book." He turned to face me. "I'd love to show you my books sometime."

"I'd like that," I said. He was so close I could smell the unique warmth of his skin.

He hesitated, took a deep breath and exhaled slowly. "Could I make you dinner Saturday night?"

"I'd like that too," I said.

For a moment I thought he was going to kiss me, but he didn't. He just smiled that gorgeous smile at me.

My heart started doing the cha-cha in my chest because I knew that if—when Marcus Gordon kissed me, I was definitely going to kiss him back.

ABOUT THE AUTHOR

Sofie Kelly is an author and mixed-media artist who lives on the East Coast with her husband and daughter. In her spare time she practices Wu-style tai chi and likes to prowl around thrift stores. And she admits to having a small crush on Matt Lauer.

Sofie Kelly

Curiosity Thrilled the Cat
A Magical Cats Mystery

When librarian Kathleen Paulson moved to Mayville Heights, Minnesota, she had no idea that two strays would nuzzle their way into her life. Owen is a tabby with a catnip addiction and Hercules is a stocky tuxedo cat who shares Kathleen's fondness for Barry Manilow. But beyond all the fur and purrs, there's something more to these felines.

When murder interrupts Mayville's Music Festival, Kathleen finds herself the prime suspect. More stunning is her realization that Owen and Hercules are magical—and she's relying on their skills to solve a purr-fect murder.

Available wherever books are sold or at
penguin.com

OM0043

Sofie Kelly

Sleight of Paw
A Magical Cats Mystery

Small-town librarian Kathleen Paulson never wanted to be the crazy cat lady. But after Owen and Hercules followed her home, she realized her mind wasn't playing tricks on her—her cats have magical abilities.

When the body of elderly do-gooder Agatha Shepherd is found near Kath's favorite local café, she knows Owen's talent for turning invisible and Hercules's ability to walk through walls will give the felines access to clues Kath couldn't get without arousing suspicion. Someone is hiding some dark secrets—and it will take a bit of *fur*tive investigating to catch the cold-hearted killer.

Available wherever books are sold or at
penguin.com

Leann Sweeney

The Cat, the Quilt and the Corpse
A Cats in Trouble Mystery

Jill's quiet life is shattered when her house is broken into and her Abyssinian, Syrah, goes missing. Jill's convinced her kitty's been catnapped. But when her cat-crime-solving leads her to a dead body, suddenly all paws are pointing to Jill.

Soon, Jill discovers that Syrah isn't the only purebred who's been stolen. Now she has to find these furry felines before they all become the prey of a cold-blooded killer—and she gets nabbed for a crime she didn't commit.

"A welcome new voice in mystery fiction." —Jeff Abbott, bestselling author of *Collision*

Available wherever books are sold or at penguin.com

Melissa Bourbon

Pleating for Mercy
A Magical Dressmaking Mystery

When her great-grandmother passes away, Harlow leaves her job as a Manhattan fashion designer and moves back to Bliss, Texas. But soon after she opens Buttons & Bows, a custom dressmaking boutique in the old farmhouse she inherited, Harlow begins to feel an inexplicable presence...

One of her first clients is her old friend Josie, who needs a gown for her upcoming wedding. But when Josie's boss turns up dead, it starts to look as if the bride-to-be may be wearing handcuffs instead of a veil. Suddenly, Josie needs a lot more from Harlow than the perfect dress. Can Harlow find the real killer—with a little help from beyond?

Available wherever books are sold or at penguin.com